The Lion's Den

Many a young lady might feel herself at risk if she found herself alone late on a stormy night with the Earl of Dunraven in his isolated manor house.

Many a young lady would have felt endangered when his eyes ran over her in the nightgown he had provided, and his gaze lingered on her partially exposed breasts.

Any young lady would have fought like a tiger when he drew her to him and covered her lips with his in a passionate kiss that seemed to go on forever.

But instead Georgiana found herself returning that kiss with matching fervor, until she came to her senses and gasped, "You forget yourself, my lord!"

"Yes, but I don't think I was the only one to do so," Dunraven replied, with a smile that promised Georgiana a night to remember. . . .

D0684873

SIGNET REGENCY ROMANCE
Coming in February 1997

Elisabeth Fairchild
The Rakehell's Reform

Barbara Hazard
Lady at Risk

Karen Harbaugh
Cupid's Mistake

1-800-253-6476
ORDER DIRECTLY
WITH VISA OR MASTERCARD

The Infamous Earl

Margaret Summerville

A SIGNET BOOK

SIGNET
Published by the Penguin Group
Penguin Books USA Inc., 375 Hudson Street,
New York, New York 10014, U.S.A.
Penguin Books Ltd, 27 Wrights Lane,
London W8 5TZ, England
Penguin Books Australia Ltd,
Ringwood, Victoria, Australia
Penguin Books Canada Ltd, 10 Alcorn Avenue,
Toronto, Ontario, Canada M4V 3B2
Penguin Books (N.Z.) Ltd, 182–190 Wairau Road,
Auckland 10, New Zealand

Penguin Books Ltd, Registered Offices:
Harmondsworth, Middlesex, England

First published by Signet, an imprint of Dutton Signet,
a division of Penguin Books USA Inc.

First Printing, January, 1997
10 9 8 7 6 5 4 3 2 1

Copyright © Margaret Summerville, 1997
All rights reserved

 REGISTERED TRADEMARK—MARCA REGISTRADA

Printed in the United States of America

Without limiting the rights under copyright reserved above, no part of this
publication may be reproduced, stored in or introduced into a retrieval system, or
transmitted, in any form, or by any means (electronic, mechanical, photocopying,
recording, or otherwise), without the prior written permission of both the copyright
owner and the above publisher of this book.

BOOKS ARE AVAILABLE AT QUANTITY DISCOUNTS WHEN USED TO PROMOTE PRODUCTS OR
SERVICES. FOR INFORMATION PLEASE WRITE TO PREMIUM MARKETING DIVISION, PENGUIN BOOKS
USA INC., 375 HUDSON STREET, NEW YORK, NEW YORK 10014.

If you purchased this book without a cover you should be aware that this book is
stolen property. It was reported as "unsold and destroyed" to the publisher and
neither the author nor the publisher has received any payment for this "stripped
book."

Chapter 1

Entering her sister's darkened bedchamber, Kitty Morley peered at the recumbent form in the canopied bed. "Georgie, are you awake?" When there was no response to her inquiry, she spoke again in a louder voice. "Georgiana! You cannot be sleeping!"

"What?" replied a groggy voice as Georgiana opened her eyes to stare at her sister.

"Good, you are awake," said Kitty. "I daresay it is time you were up. It's nearly eleven o'clock." Going over to the window, she pulled open the draperies, allowing bright sunlight to flood the room.

"Oh, Kitty," moaned Georgiana, placing a pillow over her face to block out the offending light. "Do go away."

"I shan't go away," said Kitty, coming over to her sister's bed and sitting down upon it. "I've been up for hours waiting for you. Have you forgotten that you promised to tell me all about the ball?"

"I shall tell you about it later, Kitty," said Georgiana, her voice rather muffled by the pillow. "I'm so very tired. Do be a darling and leave me."

"But Agnes will be here in a moment," replied her sister. "Mama has given her orders to rouse you. I thought I should save her the trouble, since one can never be sure if you will be in a foul temper."

"I'm never in a foul temper," said Georgiana.

"Indeed?" said her sister with a smile. "That would surprise, Agnes, I daresay. You must get up, Georgie. You know Papa does not approve of slugabeds." She pulled the pillow off Georgiana's head. "Now do tell me about the ball."

"Oh, I suppose you will not cease plaguing me until I do,"

said Georgiana, sitting up in bed and regarding her sister with a long-suffering look.

Kitty grinned. "Well, it is not my fault that I am fourteen and am not out yet. I would have rather gone to the ball myself. But since I am confined to the schoolroom, I must rely on you to tell me everything. Did you have a splendid time?"

"Oh, I did have a wonderful evening, Kit," said Georgiana, her vexation vanishing at the thought of the previous evening. Reaching her arms over her head, she stretched. "It was truly splendid. Indeed, I don't believe I have had a more marvelous time all Season."

"Tell me about the ball."

"Oh, there is so much to tell. It was a great crush of people. Everyone was there, of course. The ballroom was magnificent."

"Was the Prince there?"

Georgiana nodded. "Yes, he was. And he looked very handsome, although rather stout."

"And were you besieged by gentlemen asking for a dance?" asked Kitty eagerly.

"I will admit that I did not lack for partners," said Georgiana. "I believe I danced every dance even though my feet were starting to hurt dreadfully. Of course, I didn't notice my feet when I was dancing with Thomas." A rather dreamy look came to Georgiana's face. "If only I might have danced every dance with him."

"I don't think Mama and Papa would have approved of that," said Kitty.

"You're right," said Georgiana, frowning. It was a distressing fact that she had lost her heart to a young man who was, according to her parents, entirely unsuitable.

"Did you dance with Lord Belrose?"

Georgiana nodded. "I did, for I could scarcely refuse him. It is such a bore that our parents wish me to marry him. What a dull, dreary fellow he is, Kit. Why, he scarcely said two words to me all the time we were dancing. And then he trod upon my foot."

"Oh, dear," said Kitty.

"The poor man is as graceful as an ox. He apologized so profusely and grew very red in the face. It was so very hard not to burst into laughter. Fortunately, my foot hurt enough that I could maintain a somber expression."

Kitty laughed. "How perfectly frightful."

"Yes, but Belrose was so unnerved by his nearly laming me that he did not ask me for another dance. I was most grateful for that. Oh, I suppose that he has his good qualities, but when I compare him to Thomas, he falls very short indeed. Of course, all gentlemen fall short when compared to Thomas. It is monstrous that our parents detest Thomas simply because he has no fortune."

Kitty nodded sympathetically. Throughout the Season she had eagerly followed her sister's romance with Lord Thomas Jeffreys. Georgiana had had a fondness for him even before coming to London. She had met him when he was staying with his uncle at Pelham Manor, an estate near their own country house in Suffolk. In London, Georgiana had had many occasions to see him and her feelings had grown stronger with each meeting.

Kitty could well understand why her sister had lost her heart. Lord Thomas was terribly handsome and quite dashing. Since her father had been railing against him for weeks, Kitty was also aware that her parents would never consider him as a husband for her sister. It was a most unfortunate situation. "It is such a pity that he is not the eldest son," said Kitty reflectively.

"If only he were heir to his father's estate." She sighed. "For him to be the youngest child in a family of five brothers and four sisters is unaccountable bad luck."

Kitty nodded. "Do you think he will offer for you?"

"My dear Kitty, he asked me to marry him last night."

Kitty's eyes grew wide. "At the ball? I daresay that is a very public way to propose marriage."

"Oh, it was so marvelously romantic. I had gone out for a breath of air with Margaret Chadwyck. Thomas followed and Margaret took her leave. She is such a dear girl. Thomas and I had only a few minutes, of course, but he asked for my hand."

"But what did you say?" said Kitty.

"That I would marry him in a trice if I could," said Georgiana. Her face took a look of theatrical melancholy. "Oh, Kitty, I do not know if I can bear it. It is so like *Romeo and Juliet*, is it not?"

"I suppose a little," said Kitty.

"It is intolerable that Papa and Mama should disapprove of him. How could they care so little for my happiness?"

"Yes," returned Kitty. "Lord Thomas is such a fine gentleman. And he is so handsome."

"I must convince our parents to reconsider. How shall I be able to live if I cannot marry Thomas?"

Kitty was about to make a sympathetic reply to this declaration, but she was prevented by the appearance of their maid, Agnes, who strode into the room in a businesslike fashion. "So there you are, Miss Kitty. Her ladyship is looking for you. And Miss Georgiana, 'tis time you were dressed. The day is nearly gone. Come along with you, miss."

"Tyrant," said Georgiana, reluctantly tossing her covers aside and rising from her bed.

Agnes seemed pleased that her young mistress needed no further persuasion. She then turned to Kitty. "Lady Morley is in the morning room, miss. You must go to her."

"But Georgiana was just starting to tell me about the ball, Aggie."

"She will tell you about it at breakfast. Your mother wants you."

"Oh, very well," said Kitty. She knew better than to argue with Agnes. Having been with the family for twenty years, Agnes Taylor was a person of authority in the household. A tall, large-boned woman of forty with carroty-red hair, she had a commanding presence that belied her servant's position. Kitty promptly left the room.

Going to the finely crafted cherry wardrobe that stood against the wall, Agnes opened it and studied Georgiana's dresses. "I should think the blue sprigged muslin would do nicely this morning, miss."

Georgiana, who had sat down at her dressing table, stared forlornly at her reflection in the mirror. "Whatever you think, Agnes. I cannot be concerned with such trivial things when my heart is breaking."

Agnes turned from the wardrobe and raised an eyebrow in the direction of her young mistress. "Come, come, Miss Georgie, it cannot be as bad as that."

"But it can," said Georgiana, picking up her hairbrush and

starting to run it over her disheveled light blond curls. "My parents are determined to ruin my happiness."

"They only want what is right for you, miss," said Agnes, coming away from the wardrobe and taking the brush from Georgiana's hand. "You'd best allow me to do that."

As Agnes brushed her hair, Georgiana continued to gaze into the mirror. She was a very pretty girl with a pert, heart-shaped face and dainty, doll-like features. Georgiana's fair countenance had a pixieish quality with its short, turned-up nose and large blue eyes that were fringed with long lashes. She had a tiny cleft in her chin and charming dimples that appeared in her cheeks when she smiled. Small in stature, Georgiana had an excellent figure with curves designed to please masculine admirers. In short, many gentlemen thought Georgiana Morley utterly adorable.

Indeed, both the Morley girls were exceedingly attractive young ladies. Georgiana's sister Kitty, who, despite being the younger by five years, was taller than her petite sister. Kitty had lovely brunette hair, sparkling hazel eyes and a slim, elegant figure.

At that moment, however, Georgiana was completely indifferent to her appearance. She frowned at her reflection in the mirror, thinking that fate was indeed miserable. Although she would have liked to bemoan her situation with Agnes, Georgiana knew that it was better to remain silent. After all, Agnes would only tell her that her parents knew best where Lord Thomas was concerned.

When she had dressed, Georgiana went downstairs. She found Kitty and her mother in the morning room seated upon the sofa. "Good morning, Mama," said Georgiana, going over to her mother and kissing her on the cheek.

"Good morning, my dear," said Lady Morley, smiling fondly at her daughter. Her ladyship was a good-looking woman of nine-and-thirty. She had flaxen hair like Georgiana's and classical features that more closely resembled Kitty's. One of society's great beauties in her day, Lady Morley had maintained her attractive appearance even though her figure had, of late, grown decidedly more matronly. "Did you sleep well?"

"I did indeed," said Georgiana, sitting down in a delicate

armchair near her mother and sister. "I should have been sleeping still if Kitty had not come in to wake me up."

"One cannot sleep the day away," said Lady Morley. "You know that your father detests slugabeds."

"I know that well enough," said Georgiana with a trace of a smile. Her father was accustomed to keeping country hours even in town. By nature he was an early riser and he could never grow accustomed to sleeping the morning away. Unfortunately, his wife and elder daughter much preferred staying up until the wee hours and staying in bed for most of the morning. Since Sir Arthur Morley was a gentleman of forceful character, the other members of his family had to conform to his ways. "But where is Papa?"

"He has gone to see someone about a horse," said Kitty.

"A horse?" said Georgiana.

Lady Morley nodded. "He rose very early to be off. I cannot imagine why he wants another horse. But you know how he is about the creatures."

Georgiana nodded. Her father was so mad about horses that he scarcely could talk of anything else. While Georgiana was fond of horses and riding, she could not equal her father's enthusiasm for all things equestrian. "We were discussing the ball," said Kitty. "Mama says it was utterly wonderful. I can't wait until I am old enough to go to balls."

"It won't be long, my dear," said Lady Morley. "And I daresay you will be a great success like your sister. Georgiana was the most sought after girl there."

"What nonsense, Mama," said Georgiana with becoming modesty. "Lady Anne Neville was the most sought after. The gentlemen simply swarmed about her."

"That is only because she is a duke's daughter," said Lady Morley. "And she isn't as pretty as you by half."

"I suspect you are a trifle prejudiced, Mama," said Georgiana with a smile.

"Not in the least," protested her mother. "Indeed, I shouldn't doubt if our Georgiana receives some offers very soon. Lord Belrose was most attentive."

"But he trod on Georgie's foot," said Kitty. "He is not a good dancer. Surely you could not wish her to marry him, Mama."

"I never considered dancing to be a very important accomplishment for a gentleman," said Lady Morley. "Lord Belrose is a fine young man. I warrant he is neither witty nor clever, but he is a marquess and very rich. Nearly every girl in society has set her cap for him."

"Mama, I pray you do not talk on about Lord Belrose. I should be miserable married to him." Georgiana almost expressed the opinion that she would be miserable married to anyone but Thomas Jeffreys, but she stopped herself. There was no point discussing the subject at such a time. "Lord Belrose and I aren't at all suited."

"And why not?"

Georgiana was rather taken aback by the question. How could her mother think that she and Lord Belrose were in the least compatible? The idea was ludicrous. "He is such an old stick, Mama."

"I believe you are blinded to his virtues," said Lady Morley. "Indeed, you seem to be blind to the virtues of any gentleman except Lord Thomas Jeffreys."

"I have not mentioned Lord Thomas, Mama," said Georgiana guardedly.

"I am heartily glad of that. You know very well your father's opinion of him."

"But what is your opinion of him, Mama?" said Kitty, entering the conversation.

Lady Morley frowned. "I know he can be perfectly charming, my dears, but I never liked him very much. And, of course, he scarcely has a penny to his name. And the fact that he is Sir Francis Pelham's nephew does not commend him to your father. You know that he detests Sir Francis."

"I know," said Georgiana glumly.

"Well, there are many other gentlemen who would make perfectly good husbands, Georgiana. If you will not have Lord Belrose, you must consider one of the others."

"Perhaps I shan't marry at all," said Georgiana.

"That is ridiculous," replied Lady Morley, eyeing her daughter as if she were a wayward child. "You really must act more sensibly, Georgiana. Yes, you must begin to think seriously about the acceptable young gentlemen with whom you have become acquainted."

Georgiana did not reply, for at that moment, her father, Sir Arthur Morley, walked into the room. Nearly fifty years of age, the baronet was a handsome, distinguished-looking man with graying hair and blue eyes. Although he was not very tall, he had an aristocratic bearing that marked him as a gentleman of substance. He was in a particularly good mood as he greeted them. "Good morning, my dears," he said, smiling cheerfully. "What a splendid morning it is."

Kitty jumped up from the sofa and hurried to kiss her father. "Good morning, Papa. I daresay you must have found a very good horse."

"Indeed, I did, my girl. What a fine bit of blood and bone he is. And a beauty. Black as coal and more than seventeen hands, with fire in his eye. He has the heart of a lion. By God, I've never seen a finer horse in all my life."

Georgiana's interest in horses caused her to forget about her miserable condition for a moment. Her father was a fine judge of horseflesh. If he was this enthusiastic, the horse must be splendid. "Did you bring him?" said Georgiana. "Can we see him?"

"They're bringing him round tomorrow. You'll see him then. But I am famished. Come, let us go in to breakfast. I must tell you all about Demon Dancer."

"Demon Dancer?" said Lady Morley.

"Yes, that is his name," replied her husband. "He is by Orpheus out of Fairy Queen. You'll find no better pedigree than that."

Georgiana, who had heard of the horse's sire and dam, was impressed. Pleased to see her father in such a good mood, she resolved that she would try to keep him so. When the time was right, she might bring up the matter of Lord Thomas, but for now she would talk horses and steer clear of controversy. As her father talked excitedly about his new horse, they proceeded toward the dining room.

Chapter 2

Breakfast went very well, since conversation centered on Sir Arthur's new horse. While the baronet was not a talkative man most of the time, he found a great deal to say about his new acquisition. The horse's many marvelous attributes were discussed at great length.

Since Lady Morley found horses exceedingly dull, she attempted to change the subject to last night's ball. Georgiana, however, did not think it wise to discuss the ball since the topic of her dancing with Lord Thomas Jeffreys might arise.

Georgiana, therefore, steered the conversation back to horses every time her mother began talking about the ball. This kept Sir Arthur in a very good humor.

A short time after breakfast, Georgiana and Kitty went out for their morning walk to the park. This excursion was a daily ritual conducted while in town. Since Lady Morley always had some excuse for avoiding exercise, the girls were usually accompanied by Agnes.

While Georgiana always looked forward to her morning stroll, she was particularly impatient to be off to the park that day. The reason for her eagerness was the fact that last night at the ball, she had arranged to meet Lord Thomas there.

Agnes, who was unaware of this, was happy to go with the young ladies. A country woman born and bred, Agnes found the park was the only thing she liked about London, for its greenery reminded her of her beloved Suffolk. The daily walk with Kitty and Georgiana always perked Agnes up, especially when the weather was particularly fine as it was that day.

Starting off from the house, Agnes walked several paces behind her young charges. Georgiana looked very fetching in a close-fitting pelisse of lilac silk. Atop her head was a stylish hat festooned with silk flowers that matched her pelisse. Kitty was

no less grandly attired. Her peacock-blue pelisse was trimmed
with silver braid and her bonnet adorned with feathers.

Agnes eyed the young ladies with an almost maternal pride.
She was very fond of them both. Having been employed by
the Morley family for many years, her first position in the
household had been that of nursery maid when Georgiana was
born. Georgiana had been such a dear baby and an affectionate
little girl, that Agnes had adored her. By the time Kitty was
born, Agnes had progressed to parlor maid. Now Agnes was
lady's maid to Georgiana and Kitty, and both of the young
ladies relied on her very much.

As they walked briskly toward the park, Kitty looked over
at her sister. "I am so glad you didn't say anything to vex Papa
at breakfast, Georgie."

"I'm not so birdwitted as to do that when he was in such a
fine mood. No, I shall bide my time."

"Do you believe you can bring him round, Georgie?"

Georgiana frowned. "I cannot say, Kit. I shall certainly try. I
only hope that if he comes to know Thomas better, he will
change his mind. I am not worried about Mama. She would accept Thomas, if only Papa were not so adamantly opposed to
him."

"It is really very much like the novel I am reading, *The Unwilling Princess*."

"Is it?" said Georgiana, regarding her sister with interest.

Kitty nodded. "You must read it, Georgie. In the book the
heroine—Lady Rosamond is her name—is wildly in love with
a handsome army officer. Her father forbids her from seeing
him because he wishes her to marry Prince Rupert. The prince
is very rich, you see, and the nephew of the emperor. Poor
Lady Rosamond has no choice but to marry him.

"But Prince Rupert is such an evil man. He is very cruel to
her and she suffers so at his hands. Oh, Georgie, it is so tragic.
When she can endure it no longer, Rosamond runs away. Her
husband pursues her. It is very exciting. Oh, I shouldn't tell
you any more, for you will want to read it for yourself. I will
only say that her father soon regrets forcing her into such a
horrible marriage. In the end, he wishes he had allowed her to
marry her true love who is a noble, wonderful young man."

"Perhaps Papa should read this book," said Georgiana with
a smile.

Kitty laughed. "That is a good idea. What a pity that Papa does not read novels. Indeed, the only thing I have seen him reading is *The Sporting News*. But I do think that your situation is not unlike Lady Rosamond's. Of course, there is no Prince Rupert, which is very fortunate."

"There is Lord Belrose," suggested Georgiana.

Both young ladies erupted into gales of laughter, causing Agnes to address them. "Girls, what is so amusing?"

"It is only that Georgie thinks Lord Belrose is like Prince Rupert."

Agnes, who thought her charges were exhibiting a bit more high spirits than proper for young persons on the public sidewalk, frowned. "Who is Prince Rupert?"

"He is a character in a novel, Aggie," said Georgiana.

"A very wicked one," said Kitty.

"By all accounts Lord Belrose is a most kindly and distinguished young gentleman," said Agnes.

"He is indeed," said Georgiana. "I daresay he isn't like Prince Rupert in the least."

"No, he isn't," said Kitty. "I don't know if anyone is truly as wicked as Prince Rupert. Novels do tend to exaggerate."

"I don't know, Kit," replied Georgiana. "I daresay there are a good many wicked gentlemen in London." She smiled back at Agnes. "Don't you agree, Aggie?"

"Indeed I do, miss," said Agnes. "Far too many, I'll be bound."

Georgiana suppressed a smile. Agnes was known for her strict moral rectitude. She had often made it clear that she considered London a modern-day Sodom and Gomorrah. They continued on toward the park, with the sisters chattering about a good many things. Agnes followed closely behind them.

Arriving at their destination, Georgiana tried to hide her eagerness. She scanned the green and wooded park for a glimpse of Lord Thomas. It did not take her long to spot him. He was standing near the belvedere that commanded a view of the park entrance. Catching sight of Georgiana, Thomas strode forward.

Agnes frowned as she spied a gentleman coming eagerly toward them. Since Georgiana was one of the most sought after young ladies of society, it was not unusual that she would command masculine attention in the park. Indeed, fending off the admiring males was one of Agnes's duties.

"Why, it is Lord Thomas," said Georgiana, hoping she sounded convincingly surprised.

Agnes frowned again at the name. She was well aware of her young mistress's infatuation with this gentleman. She also knew that Sir Arthur would be very displeased at his daughter meeting him in the park. A perceptive woman, Agnes had little doubt that Lord Thomas's appearance there was no coincidence.

Coming up before them, Thomas doffed his tall beaver hat and bowed slightly. "How do you do, Miss Morley and Miss Kitty? What great good fortune finding you here."

Georgiana smiled at him, her pretty face lighting up at the sight of him. He was a very handsome man, who paid a good deal of attention to his appearance. One of the dandy set, Lord Thomas Jeffreys considered fashion a very serious matter, indeed. He stood there before them, a credit to the renowned tailor Weston.

Of medium height, Thomas was favored with a fine masculine figure. His close-fitting coat of dove-gray superfine fit his broad shoulders to perfection, and his pale ivory pantaloons hugged his muscular legs in such a way as to raise the pulse of feminine observers. Thomas's snowy-white neckcloth was skillfully tied and his dark blond curls were arranged in the fashionable Corinthian style.

Thomas was also blessed with a face that reminded more than one feminine admirer of classical Greek statuary. His pale blue eyes, high cheekbones, finely chiseled nose, and square chin were much appreciated by the ladies of society.

As she met his gaze, Georgiana reflected that Thomas was the most handsome man in London. "Lord Thomas, I did not expect to find you here," she said, wondering if Agnes would believe her. "You haven't met my Agnes. She takes very good care of Kitty and me."

"M'lord," said Agnes, dropping a respectful curtsy.

Since Thomas was not accustomed to paying much notice to servants, he nodded rather curtly and returned his attention to Georgiana. "How beautiful you look, Miss Morley."

"You are too kind, sir," replied Georgiana.

"You always look utterly enchanting," said Thomas. "I

daresay it must be tedious for the other ladies to compete with you. Last night at the ball you nearly took my breath away. When you entered the ballroom, it was as if Venus herself had arrived."

While Agnes raised her eyes heavenward at this flummery, Georgiana appeared delighted. "Oh, Lord Thomas, you need not flatter me so outrageously," said Georgiana, smiling coquettishly.

"I only speak the truth," said Thomas, gazing at her with a devoted expression.

Kitty could only stare at the dashing gentleman standing before them and think her sister a very fortunate creature.

"Might I walk with you for a time, Miss Morley?"

Agnes cleared her throat at this suggestion. "I beg your pardon, miss, but you mustn't stay long in the park."

"We have only just arrived, Aggie," said Georgiana, directing a warning look at the servant. She then smiled at Thomas. "I should enjoy a walk, Lord Thomas."

Thomas extended his arm, which Georgiana accepted eagerly. To Kitty's great delight, Thomas offered her his other arm. They started walking with a disapproving Agnes following behind them. Very displeased with her young mistress, Agnes frowned. At least, she reflected, there were few people of quality about to observe Georgiana and the young lord. Indeed, it would not do at all for the girls to be seen in the park with him.

"Did you speak to your father?" said Thomas, addressing Georgiana in a low voice.

"I did not dare to do so," said Georgiana, whispering to him. Then in a louder voice, she added, "Yes, the park is lovely today, Lord Thomas."

"Shall I go to see your father?" said Thomas.

"No," said Georgiana. "I fear that wouldn't do at all." Looking back at Agnes, she noted the older woman's frown. She continued in a low voice, "I had an idea. I believe I should try it."

"What do you mean?" said Thomas.

"I cannot tell you now, but I believe it may work."

Thomas regarded her curiously, but Georgiana felt it prudent to say nothing more.

"Miss Georgiana," said Agnes, who was increasingly feeling that she was neglecting her duty. "'Tis time we were returning home."

"Nonsense, Aggie," said Georgiana.

"Indeed, miss, it grows late." Agnes directed a stern look at Georgiana. "Lady Morley did not wish us to be gone long, miss."

Georgiana could tell by Agnes's tone that she was quite vexed with her. "I suppose it is," said Georgiana, deciding it was best not to irritate her any further. "It was very nice talking with you, Lord Thomas."

He smiled fondly at her. "Good day, Miss Morley." Then tipping his beaver hat once more, he set off.

Kitty sighed as she watched him go. "What a handsome man," she said. "I would be in love with him, too, if you weren't already, Georgie."

"One silly mooncalf is enough for one family, Kitty," said Agnes severely.

"Aggie!" said Georgiana. "I do not like being called a silly mooncalf."

"Then you shouldn't act like one. Don't think you've hoodwinked old Agnes, miss. I know very well you'd arranged to meet that young gentleman. And I daresay you expect I won't say a word to her ladyship."

"Oh, Aggie, you wouldn't!" cried Georgiana.

Agnes folded her arms and regarded her with a stern expression. "Very well. I'll not say a word this time, but I'll warn you, Miss Georgie, you're not to meet his lordship like this. Not when Aggie Taylor is responsible for you. Why, your father would have my head."

"I promise I'll not do it again, Aggie. I am sorry."

Thinking the young lady looked properly contrite, Agnes was only too happy to forgive her. "Come along then, miss. I think it best that we go home now."

This suggestion brought protests from both Kitty and Georgiana. When Kitty pleaded that they be allowed to walk a little farther since the weather was good and they hadn't been gone so awfully long, Agnes relented.

They continued their stroll through the park. After seeing Thomas, Georgiana was in the best of moods. Although she was eager to talk more about him to her sister, Georgiana wisely refrained from doing so. Kitty was only too happy to discuss other subjects, and she chattered on about a variety of topics.

After a time, they stopped near a bench to admire the view of a pond and flowers. "It is a lovely day," said Kitty.

"It is rather too windy for my liking," observed Agnes. "And I shouldn't be surprised if it doesn't rain."

"What an old stick you are, Aggie," said Georgiana, smiling at the maid. "It is quite beautiful! Too windy, indeed!" But scarcely had she said these words when a gust of wind blew her stylish hat from her head, sending it flying through the air to land some twenty feet away.

Kitty laughed as her sister hastened after her hat. Just as she was about to retrieve it, a small dog appeared from behind some shrubbery, pounced upon the hat, and ran off with it.

Georgiana stared at the dog in some astonishment. "Why, you wretched thing! Come back with my hat!" She started off after the dog, breaking into a most unladylike run.

Kitty erupted into gales of laughter at the sight of her sister chasing the canine miscreant. Agnes, however, viewed the development with horror. It was bad enough that some ill-bred cur had stolen her young mistress's hat, but it would not do at all for Georgiana to be seen dashing across the park.

"Miss Georgiana!" cried Agnes, following in pursuit. "Do stop!" Kitty, still laughing, hurried after the maid.

Ignoring Agnes's cries, Georgiana raced ahead in the direction the dog had gone. A swift little creature, it had vanished behind some trees. When Georgiana caught sight of it again, she saw that the dog was running toward a tall gentleman who stood a short distance away. When the animal arrived in front of the man, it dropped the hat and looked up expectantly at him.

Seeing the man looking in her direction, Georgiana stopped running and proceeded in a more sedate fashion.

"What the devil have you done, Macduff?" she heard the man say to the dog. He reached down, picked up the hat, and came toward her.

Georgiana observed that he was a handsome man, who was perhaps in his late twenties. His well-cut clothes pronounced him to be a gentleman of some means, but he dressed in an understated way and was obviously not one of the dandy set.

He was tall and lean, with an aristocratic countenance that

featured a prominent brow, strong chin, and a pair of arresting brown eyes framed by dark eyebrows. He wore a hat, which he raised in deference to her, revealing a head of unruly dark brown hair. "I suspect this is your hat, madam," he said, holding it out to her.

"Yes, your dog stole it."

"Macduff, you scoundrel," he said, a faint smile appearing on his face. "The lady has called you a thief. What do you have to say for yourself?"

The dog, a small grayish-brown terrier, only cocked his head in reply and appeared delighted with the attention.

"You are a very naughty dog, Macduff," said Georgiana, who couldn't help but smile at the mischievous canine.

"I am sorry that he has damaged your hat. I shall gladly pay for it," said the gentleman.

Georgiana looked down at the hat and then up at him. When her blue eyes met his brown ones, she felt oddly discomfitted. Her discomposure rather surprised her. After all, she was well accustomed to meeting gentlemen and she wasn't in the least shy. Yet something about this tall stranger's gaze was different.

"Oh, I don't think it's really damaged," she said.

"No, I shall give you money to buy another," he said, reaching inside his coat to extract some money.

"No, truly, sir, that isn't necessary," said Georgiana, gazing up at him once again.

By this time Agnes and Kitty had come up behind her. Panting a bit from her exertion, Agnes wasn't too pleased to see Georgiana conversing with a total stranger. She eyed him with disapproval. "Come, miss," she said, taking Georgiana's arm, "we must be going home."

"Yes, I should be going," said Georgiana, putting her hat on.

The stranger, who had taken out a bank note, unfolded it, and extended it to her. "Take this for a new hat."

"Why, I couldn't," said Georgiana. "But I do thank you, sir."

"Come along, miss," said Agnes, speaking more forcefully this time.

Casting one last look into the stranger's eyes, Georgiana allowed herself to be led away. Kitty walked alongside her. "Oh, you looked so awfully silly, Georgie, running after that dog. What an adorable little fellow he was. And his master was so very handsome. Did he introduce himself?"

"He didn't have that opportunity," said Georgiana, clearly disappointed. "Aggie was so eager to have me come away."

"Indeed I was, miss," said Agnes sternly. "It will not do to speak to strangers in the park."

"Well, under the circumstances, I can't see the harm," said Georgiana. "And it was good of him to offer to pay for a new hat."

"Imagine the idea of accepting money from a stranger," said Agnes, frowning.

"I do wonder who he was," said Kitty. "You don't remember seeing him anywhere, do you, Georgie?"

Georgiana shook her head, knowing that she would have certainly remembered meeting him. When they had gone a short way, she glanced back to see that he was walking off with the mischievous little dog now safely on a lead.

Turning her attention in the other direction, Georgiana noticed that a phaeton had pulled to a halt and its inhabitant, a well-dressed lady, was waving to them. "Who is that?" said Kitty.

"I believe it is Mrs. Kendall," said Georgiana. "Yes, it is. We must go and say hello to her." Mrs. Kendall was well known to them, for she often called on Lady Morley.

Although her ladyship didn't really approve of Mrs. Kendall, thinking she spent too much time gossiping, Georgiana liked her very much and enjoyed listening to her stories. Mrs. Kendall knew everyone in town and she was always eager to spread the latest news about those in society's upper circles.

The girls and Agnes made their way to Mrs. Kendall's carriage. "How do you do, Mrs. Kendall?" said Georgiana when they had come alongside the phaeton.

"Very well, my dears," said Mrs. Kendall. Forty years of age, Mrs. Kendall was a wealthy woman who had devoted her life to being a grand lady of fashion. An attractive woman, she was splendidly dressed in a modish pea-green silk dress and spencer. Atop her head was a matching bonnet trimmed with ostrich plumes. "I do hope you will join me in the carriage." She continued in a more serious tone. "Indeed, I insist that you do. I must speak with you, Miss Morley, and I shall be happy to drive you home."

Surprised at Mrs. Kendall's somber tone, Georgiana nodded. "Very well, ma'am."

Mrs. Kendall addressed a groom who was riding beside her driver. "James, assist the ladies into the carriage."

The servant hopped down to hand Georgiana, Kitty, and Agnes up into the vehicle. "It is very kind of you, Mrs. Kendall," said Georgiana, seating herself next to that lady.

Mrs. Kendall gave the driver orders to proceed to the Morley house and the phaeton set off, its bay horses trotting smartly. "Did you see the dog with Georgiana's hat, Mrs. Kendall?" said Kitty. "It was so very funny."

"I did, indeed," returned the older lady. "And I hope that I was the only person to see what happened."

"Oh, I know I must have looked quite foolish," said Georgiana rather sheepishly. "But, you see, the dog made off with my hat."

"I am not speaking of that, my dear. I refer to your talking with that gentleman. I'm sure you have no idea who he was or you wouldn't have spoken with him."

Georgiana regarded her in surprise. "But who was he?"

"That was the Earl of Dunraven," said Mrs. Kendall, casting a significant look at Georgiana.

"The Earl of Dunraven?" repeated Georgiana, looking blankly at Mrs. Kendall. "I fear I have never heard of him."

Mrs. Kendall regarded her incredulously. "Never heard of Dunraven? My dear, you have led a sheltered life. Why, Dunraven is notorious. No respectable young lady would ever be seen talking with him. Fortunately, I was the only witness. And I shall keep mum on the subject."

Although Georgiana thought it remarkable that Mrs. Kendall would keep mum on any subject, she smiled and thanked her.

"You must tell us about Lord Dunraven, ma'am," said Kitty eagerly.

"I don't know if he is a suitable subject for such young ears as yours, Kitty," said Mrs. Kendall.

"But I am not so young, ma'am," said Kitty. "I am fourteen."

Mrs. Kendall smiled. "Well, I suppose I might tell you about him. After all, it is my duty to warn young girls about such a man. I do believe Dunraven is one of the most disreputable men in all of England. No one will receive him. Indeed, the Prince Regent has declared him persona non grata."

"But why?" said Georgiana, thinking of the handsome stranger and how she had been so affected by his intense brown eyes.

"It was that dreadful scandal with Lady Coningsby. Of course, you are very young and this happened some time ago. Why it must be nearly ten years now. Good heavens, time passes so swiftly.

"Dunraven was very young at the time. He had scarcely turned twenty. He had been so wild as a boy, always drinking and fighting and getting into trouble at school." She hesitated as if wondering if she should say more. "And he became involved with low women at a very young age. His father quite despaired of him. Of course, his poor father died when Dunraven was only nineteen, and he became his own master.

"But the worst thing was his affair with Lady Coningsby. What a great scandal it was! We scarcely talked of anything else for months. Yes, it was a dreadful business, my dear. She was older than him by five or six years and married to Colonel Sir William Coningsby. He had been a very distinguished officer. Sir William was and continues to be a good friend of His Royal Highness's.

"While Sir William was away with his regiment, Dunraven began an illicit affair with his wife. Everyone knew of it, for they weren't in the least discreet. And if that wouldn't have been bad enough, Dunraven ran off with Lady Coningsby. She quite abandoned her husband. Everyone was quite shocked as you might imagine. Poor Sir William was devastated and the Prince himself was furious."

"But where did they go?" said Georgiana. "What happened to them?"

"Oh, they went to the Continent, taking a villa in Italy where they lived together quite openly. Yet in six months we heard that Dunraven had nearly killed some Italian gentleman in a duel and Lady Coningsby had left him."

"Good heavens!" cried Georgiana.

"Dunraven returned to England, but he was completely ostracized. To this day, he is considered quite unacceptable in society. The Prince Regent will never forgive him."

"And what happened to Lady Coningsby?" said Kitty, very much interested in the story.

"I last heard of her several years ago. It was said that she was the mistress of a Bavarian count. No one knows what became of her. She is still living on the Continent I suppose."

"And no one receives Lord Dunraven?" said Georgiana, a thoughtful expression on her face.

"Indeed not. He continues to live in town for much of the year. One often sees him riding about in a curricle with a light-skirt beside him. It is clear that he has not mended his ways and I daresay his sins will see him to an early grave."

"But he didn't look so very wicked," said Kitty. "You didn't think he looked wicked, did you, Georgiana?"

Georgiana shook her head.

"Appearances are often deceiving, my dear girls," said Mrs. Kendall.

"Yes, I suppose they may be," said Georgiana. She paused a moment before continuing. "Does Lord Dunraven have a wife?"

"A wife?" said Mrs. Kendall. "No, thank God. I pity any woman who would marry him. It's said that he is addicted to gaming and drink and that he is shamelessly extravagant. He is hardly a prize in the marriage mart. Indeed, I shouldn't think that the Countess of Dunraven would ever be welcomed in society. If he wishes to marry, he will doubtless pick some tradesman's daughter eager for a title.

"In future, my dear Miss Morley, if you happen upon Dunraven, you must hurry in the opposite direction."

"I assure you I shall," said Georgiana. "I daresay my mother will be quite distressed to hear that I spoke with him. I should appreciate it if you don't mention it to her, Mrs. Kendall. I prefer to tell her myself."

"Of course, my dear. I shan't breathe a word of it. After all, you had no idea who he was. That is why a lady doesn't speak with gentlemen unless she has been properly introduced."

Georgiana nodded gravely. To think that she had been talking to such an infamous character as Lord Dunraven, she told herself. Her sister began talking with Mrs. Kendall, but Georgiana was so engrossed in her own thoughts that she scarcely listened. Kitty's earlier words about the novel she had read had given her an idea. As they continued on, Georgiana maintained a thoughtful silence.

Chapter 3

It would not have surprised Richard Augustus Fitzmaurice, seventh Earl of Dunraven, that he was the subject of gossip. His lordship knew very well that his name was often mentioned in society. That was apparent by the icy looks he received from gentlemen and ladies of fashion as he drove about town.

Dunraven, however, was completely indifferent to the opinions of others. He had always scorned the approval of society, which was fortunate in light of the fact that his reputation was so tarnished that he could never restore it.

That evening the earl sat in the drawing room of his London town house, drinking a glass of wine and staring into the fireplace. At his feet lay Macduff.

Those acquainted with the earl's reputation might have expected his drawing room to be decorated in an opulent, Oriental style. They would have been surprised to find the room appointed with the spare elegance preferred by his lordship, who favored French furniture and Italian paintings.

Dunraven continued to stare into the flames, a pensive look on his face. Since arriving home that afternoon, he had found himself spending an unusual amount of time thinking about his meeting with the petite young lady who had lost her hat. He was frankly surprised that she had stayed in his thoughts.

While he hadn't yet attained his thirtieth year, the earl was a very world-weary man. As his reputation would attest, he was hardly immune to feminine charms. Yet he had for some years become convinced that he had no fear of losing his head over any woman. That was why it was a bit troubling to find himself remembering the afternoon's encounter with the blond-haired girl. There was something about her large blue eyes and bright smile that affected him.

The earl frowned. He didn't want to be affected by a pretty face, especially one belonging to a well-bred young lady undoubtedly intending to make a respectable marriage.

Dunraven took another sip of wine. He was not in a particularly good humor. He was oftentimes so, for he was not a happy man. In fact, of late, he had found himself reflecting quite often that he had made a terrible muddle of his life. He was interrupted from his somber thoughts by the appearance of a liveried servant.

"Begging your pardon, m'lord."

"Yes?" said the earl, regarding the servant with a frown.

"Mr. Buckthorne is here, m'lord."

"Show him in, Rogers."

"Aye, m'lord," replied the servant, who bowed slightly and then left. He reappeared in a few moments with a gentleman following behind him. "Mr. Buckthorne, m'lord," Rogers intoned solemnly.

The earl rose from his chair to greet his visitor. "Good evening, Buck."

"Dunraven, my dear fellow," returned the visitor, smiling broadly at the earl. "And Macduff. Good evening to you, sir." The last remark was directed to the dog, who hurried to the newcomer, wagging his stubby tail excitedly. Buckthorne reached down to give the dog a clumsy pat.

"I know I'm early, Dunraven, but I thought we'd get an early start. I feel lucky. Indeed, I've felt lucky all day."

Dunraven motioned Buckthorne to be seated. A stout, good-natured man, Buckthorne was the earl's best and perhaps only friend. Dunraven had known him since they were boys together at Eton. "I hate it when you feel lucky," said the earl dryly. "You always lose a damnable sum and I have to loan you money."

"That isn't true in the least," protested Buckthorne. He grinned. "And in any case, you can well afford to loan me a few pounds."

A slight smile appeared on Dunraven's face. He was very fond of Buckthorne, who was the only one of his friends who had stuck by him. Buckthorne was a lovable character, big-hearted and quick with a joke.

He was a rather unprepossessing man whose round face was dominated by a large bulbous nose. Of average height, Buckthorne had pale blue eyes and thinning sandy-colored hair. Something of a dandy, he wore a tight-fitting coat of olive superfine, a mustard-colored waistcoat, pale ivory pantaloons, and gleaming Hessian boots.

"Will you have a glass of wine, Buck?"

"I shall not refuse," returned Buckthorne.

Dunraven poured his friend a glass and handed it to him. "I don't know if I shall go to Mrs. Trotter's tonight."

"What?" cried Buckthorne in some surprise. Mrs. Trotter's was a gambling establishment known for the high stakes of its wagers and the elegance of the ladies of the evening who plied their trade there. "Not go to Mrs. Trotter's? That will not do at all. Don't forget I am feeling monstrous lucky, Dunraven."

"And I am feeling monstrous unlucky," returned the earl. "And I grow tired of Mrs. Trotter's. It is a damned bore."

"Mrs. Trotter's a damned bore?" said Buckthorne, eyeing his friend in astonishment. "I fear you are unwell, Dunraven."

Dunraven laughed. "I have never been better. You must go without me, Buck."

Buckthorne shook his head and reached down to pet the dog, who was sitting behind him. "If you aren't going, neither shall I. I'll stay and keep you company."

"That is good of you, Buck, but it isn't necessary. Don't forget that you are feeling lucky tonight."

Buckthorne shrugged. "Well, if the truth be told, I suppose I feel lucky every night. Tomorrow will do as well. Let us speak no more of Mrs. Trotter's. I shall stay here and rouse you from your blue devils. Of course, I had planned to dine there. Perhaps you might provide me with sustenance?"

"I imagine something can be arranged," said Dunraven, smiling at his friend. He rose from his chair to ring for a servant. When the footman arrived, the earl ordered supper.

"You're too good, Dunraven," said Buckthorne as the footman left the room. "As you have one of the finest cooks in town, I daresay I shall not regret missing one night at Mrs. Trotter's. And I did wish to speak to you about that Suffolk property. Do say you have decided to buy Longmeadow."

"I am sorry to disappoint you, Buck, but my solicitor advises me against it."

"Oh, Armstrong advises against everything. You are too imprudent a man to have such a prudent solicitor."

Dunraven smiled. "That is why I must have such a man. As I seem determined to ruin myself, I must have him to bring me to my senses."

Buckthorne grinned, but he knew very well that his friend, for all his fabled extravagance, had become a shrewd manager of his many assets. While Mrs. Kendall and most of society thought that Dunraven had lost most of his money, they were entirely wrong.

Although he had squandered a fortune in his time, he was still a man of considerable wealth. In recent years, he had taken a keen interest in the management of his estates. This, combined with a number of wise investments, had greatly increased his fortune.

"I should think you would wish to keep the property in the family, Dunraven," said Buckthorne.

"Good God, Buck, the place was owned by my second cousin twice removed. I visited there once. I believe I was nine years old. I still remember it vividly. The house was damnably uncomfortable. The chimneys smoked. It was damp and cold and the food was abominable."

"Oh, that is to be expected in a country house," said Buckthorne. "But the hunting, Dunraven! There is none finer in all of England. I hunted with Harry Montjoy near there many years ago. What sport we had! Old Harry's pack was legendary. What hounds they were! If you would buy Longmeadow, I could bring my hounds."

"Hounds? What hounds?"

"The pack I shall buy. I heard that Sir Charles Gilroy is selling his dogs."

"God in heaven, Buck, you have no money to buy and keep a pack of hounds."

"True enough, my lad, but you have the money for it."

"So I am to buy these hounds for you and house and feed them?" said the earl, frowning at his friend.

"Exactly," returned Buckthorne. "Come, come, Dunraven, it would be a great lark. And you are evidently in need of diversion since you find Mrs. Trotter's so dull."

"You are a knave, Buck," said the earl, trying to maintain a stern expression. In truth, he had been considering purchasing Longmeadow. While he would never have admitted it, he had not been indifferent to the plight of one of his distant kinswomen, the elderly widow of the last master of Longmeadow. She had written to him in desperation, explaining that the estate was heavily mortgaged and that she was forced to sell the property. Dunraven was in the position to help her by purchasing the house and land outright.

"Really, Dunraven, this place Longmeadow would be a capital investment for you," said Buckthorne. "You could spend the winter there. You know how you detest Dunraven Castle. And Longmeadow is far better situated than Westings. It is beautiful country, my dear fellow. I am sure there are no finer views anywhere."

"Good God," said the earl, "one might think you were selling the place. Oh, very well, I shall buy Longmeadow, if only to have you keep quiet on the subject."

"You will?" cried Buckthorne. "That is marvelous, my dear fellow! I am sure you will not regret it."

"And I am sure that I will," returned Dunraven, directing a sardonic smile at his friend before taking another drink of wine.

Chapter 4

While Dunraven conversed with his friend, Georgiana had dinner at home with her parents and Kitty. Although Kitty hadn't seen any reason not to tell Sir Arthur and Lady Morley about their encounter with the notorious earl in the park, Georgiana had persuaded her to say nothing about it.

After a quiet evening of cards, Georgiana and Kitty retired to their rooms. Once attired for bed, Georgiana went to her sister's bedchamber. "Kitty, I must talk to you about something."

Kitty put down her book. "What is it?"

"You gave me a very good idea this morning."

"I did?"

Georgiana nodded. "Yes, when you told me about *The Unwilling Princess.*"

"I cannot imagine what idea I could have given you," replied Kitty.

"About evil Prince Rupert. Since returning home, I've scarcely thought of anything else. You have given me the idea for a plan that will make Papa agree to my marrying Thomas."

"I did? I daresay I don't remember doing so. Pray, tell me of this plan!"

"It is rather simple. What if I told Papa that I do not wish to marry Thomas? What if I told him that I had met someone else and that I wished to marry him?"

Kitty regarded her sister with a perplexed expression. "I don't understand, Georgie."

"My dear mutton head, it is very simple. I shall tell Papa I have fallen in love with some other gentleman, a gentleman who is far more undesirable than Thomas. I shall say I am in love with Lord Dunraven and wish to marry him."

"Georgiana!" cried Kitty.

Georgiana laughed. "By comparison, Thomas will appear in

a far more favorable light. Don't you think Papa would rather have me marry Thomas than Dunraven?"

Kitty regarded her sister skeptically. "I believe he would prefer you would marry Lord Belrose."

"Lord Belrose isn't one of the choices, Kit," said Georgiana. "Don't you see? If I can convince Papa that I want to marry Dunraven, he may come to realize that Thomas would not be a bad choice for son-in-law."

"That would be splendid if he did," said Kitty.

"It is certainly worth trying," said Georgiana. "Oh, I do believe it might work."

"But what will Mama and Papa say when you tell them about Lord Dunraven? Oh, Georgie!"

Both of the sisters burst into laughter, and then Georgiana continued to talk about her scheme.

In the morning, Georgiana awakened eager to put her plan into action. However, when she joined her family for breakfast, she was disappointed to find that Sir Arthur was not there.

"Where is Papa?" asked Georgiana, sitting down at the dining room table beside her sister.

"He has gone out," said Lady Morley. "He was so excited about that new horse of his that he couldn't wait for the creature to be brought round. He thought he and Shaw should go fetch him, so off they went. They'll return soon."

"I can scarcely wait to see him," said Georgiana. "Demon Dancer must be a very fine horse indeed for Papa to go to such bother."

"Yes, yes, I should not doubt that he is a veritable Pegasus," said Lady Morley, "but I do wish your father was not so mad for horses. He can scarcely talk of anything else."

"At least he can talk of something," said Georgiana. "Unlike Lord Belrose."

"Georgiana," said her mother, frowning disapprovingly, "I do wish you liked Belrose a little."

"I don't dislike him, Mama, said Georgiana. "It is only that I don't like him well enough to consider marrying him."

"I do wish you would like a suitable young man for a change," said her mother. "You know that young Jeffreys will not do at all."

Georgiana tried hard to feign indifference. "I must admit

that my feelings regarding Lord Thomas are undergoing some changes."

"Changes?" replied Lady Morley.

"I suppose I must be a fickle creature, but I confess I have come to realize there are other gentlemen in the world than Lord Thomas Jeffreys."

Georgiana's mother regarded her in some surprise, causing Kitty to nearly burst into laughter. "I am very glad to hear it," said Lady Morley.

Kitty grinned. "Georgie has found another gentleman she fancies," she said.

Lady Morley looked from her younger daughter to Georgiana. "What does Kitty mean, Georgiana?"

"Oh, Kitty is speaking nonsense," said Georgiana.

"Indeed, I am not," said Kitty. "You should tell Mama that you have a *tendre* for a new beau."

"Come, come, my dear," said Lady Morley eagerly, "if your affections have been diverted from Thomas Jeffreys, I shall be very glad to hear it. Whom does Kitty mean? Have you formed an attachment for someone else?"

Georgiana glanced over at her sister, who was regarding her with an expectant look. But before she could speak, they were interrupted by the appearance of one of the footmen. "The master is back with the new horse, my lady," he said. "He says you must come and see him."

"We are eating our breakfast, Edward," returned her ladyship.

"Oh, Mama, I haven't even started," said Georgiana. "Do let's go and see Demon Dancer."

"I do detest that name," said Lady Morley, placing her napkin on the table. "Oh, very well, girls."

They all rose from the table to hurry out to the stables, where they found Sir Arthur looking very pleased with himself. "There he is, Demon Dancer!" said the baronet, motioning to one of the stalls.

"Oh, Papa!" cried Georgiana, catching sight of the gleaming black stallion. Demon Dancer was a tall, powerfully built animal. A spirited creature, he snorted and pawed the ground. The girls hurried over for a better look. Shaw, the head groom, was standing there admiring his master's latest acquisition.

"I've never seen a finer animal, Miss Georgiana," said

Shaw. He was a small, wiry man of forty-five with a ruddy complexion and dark hair. "But do not get too close, miss. He's a bit nervous. All is new and strange to him."

"Shaw, he is a beauty!" cried Georgiana.

"Indeed!" said Kitty. "What a lovely creature." She looked back at her father. "Oh, Papa, he is wonderful!"

"That he is," said Sir Arthur. "And he is fast as the wind."

The girls stood there for what seemed to Lady Morley a considerable time, praising the stallion and declaring that their father had undoubtedly bought the finest horse in England. Her ladyship allowed her husband to bask in the glow of his daughters' compliments for a time before insisting that they have their breakfast.

It was with great reluctance that Sir Arthur left the stables to escort his wife back to the house and into the dining room. When they were finally seated at the table with their breakfast, Sir Arthur and his daughters continued to talk excitedly about Demon Dancer.

After listening to this conversation for half an hour, Lady Morley's patience was exhausted. "It is clear that your horse is a very fine one, my dear, but could we not speak of something else? I must confess I am eager to return to the conversation I was having with Georgiana and Kitty before you arrived. I daresay you will wish to hear it, Arthur. It seems our dear girl has become interested in another gentleman. Someone other than young Jeffreys."

"What?" said the baronet, looking at Georgiana. "Now this is excellent news. Is this true, my dear?"

Georgiana nodded with seeming reluctance. "I do wish Kitty had said nothing. You will think me utterly foolish. I scarcely know the gentleman and yet he has put the thought of all others out of my mind."

"If he has put the thought of Thomas Jeffreys from your mind, I am heartily grateful to him. But who is he? I hope you will not tell me he is a penniless nobody."

"He is a peer, Papa."

"A peer?" said Sir Arthur. "Now this does sound promising. Who is he? When did you meet him?"

"Only yesterday, Papa. I met him in the park."

"Yesterday?" said Lady Morley with a frown. "You spoke with a strange gentleman in the park?"

"I know it is irregular," said Georgiana, "but we met by accident. It was very windy and my hat flew from my head. A little dog ran away with it."

"A dog ran away with your hat?" said the baronet in a tone that implied he thought the idea quite ridiculous.

Georgiana nodded. "He was a mischievous terrier named Macduff. I followed after him and he returned to his master. He was a very kind, handsome gentleman. I was very much taken with him. He had such beautiful eyes." She adopted an appropriately dewy-eyed look. "He picked up my hat and gave it to me. Then he introduced himself."

"I don't believe I like this very much," said Sir Arthur. "Wasn't Agnes with you? She should not allow you to converse with strangers in the park."

"Oh, Agnes was with us, of course," said Georgiana, proceeding cautiously with her tale. "But I had run ahead chasing the dog. Agnes and Kitty followed behind."

"I certainly don't like the idea of your chasing some mongrel in the park," said Lady Morley. "Really, Georgiana, you must be more sensible."

"Your daughter is hardly sensible if she fell in love with a complete stranger who handed her her hat in the park," said the baronet.

"You mean to say that a few minutes were enough for you to meet a strange gentleman and lose your heart to him?" said Lady Morley.

Georgiana sighed in a melodramatic fashion. "Yes, my meeting with the gentleman was very short, but it was as if Cupid's arrow reached my heart the moment I saw him."

"What?" said Sir Arthur, regarding her skeptically. "What nonsense is this? You are doing it a bit too brown, my girl." He looked at his wife. "I fear Georgiana is gammoning us."

"I am very serious, Papa," returned Georgiana.

Sir Arthur turned to his younger daughter. "Kitty, is this true? Did your sister indeed meet someone in the park?"

Hoping she looked convincing, Kitty nodded gravely. "It was a very brief meeting, Papa, but Georgiana was strangely affected by it. It was as if she were bewitched."

"Indeed?" said Sir Arthur. "This is a very strange story, my girl."

"So do tell us the name of this man, Georgiana," said Lady Morley.

"His name is Lord Dunraven," replied Georgiana. "The Earl of Dunraven."

If Georgiana had pulled a pistol from beneath the dining room table and fired it into the ceiling, she could have scarcely provoked a more stunned response from her parents. Sir Arthur gaped at her in astonishment. Lady Morley was utterly dumbfounded. She stared at Georgiana with a pained expression.

"What is the matter?" said Georgiana, directing a look of wide-eyed innocence from one parent to another. "Do you know Lord Dunraven?"

"Know him!" cried Sir Arthur. "I know of him. Everyone knows of him. He is notorious!"

"What can you mean?" said Georgiana. "He was very kind and utterly charming. I gave him my card and asked him to call."

"Good God!" exclaimed the baronet. "You asked Dunraven to call?"

"Surely, he wouldn't dare, Arthur," said Lady Morley. "He'd know that we wouldn't receive him."

"This must be some sort of prank," said Sir. Arthur. "I do not find it in the least amusing, my girl."

"I assure you it is no prank," insisted Georgiana, trying hard to sound convincing. "And do tell me why Lord Dunraven's name so upsets you. I thought you would be pleased. He is an earl after all. Do tell me what is the matter."

"Georgiana, your father has said the man is notorious," said Lady Morley. "He has been involved in a great scandal. And don't ask me what scandal because I certainly won't discuss it in front of Kitty."

"Oh, Mama," cried Kitty, "I'm not a baby!"

Ignoring Kitty, Sir Arthur frowned at his elder daughter. "I do not believe a word of your story, Georgiana."

"But, Papa, Georgie did meet Lord Dunraven," said Kitty. "Aggie will tell you so. She was there, Papa."

"Perhaps you did meet him," said Sir Arthur, pointing a finger at Georgiana, "but the very idea that you have fallen in love with him! I know what you are trying to do, my girl. You think that you can make me tolerate Thomas Jeffreys better with the prospect of Dunraven looming about."

"Oh, Papa!" cried Georgiana, directing a hurt look at her father before bursting into tears.

Sir Arthur's face grew red with anger. "I thought that having a London Season would make you forget Jeffreys. I did not know that he would come to town and somehow arrange to turn up at virtually every affair we attended. We might have stayed in Suffolk and saved the expense, for all the good it did.

"Indeed, I think it is time to go back to the country. Yes, there is no point in remaining here."

"Arthur!" cried Lady Morley. "Return to the country now? Why, the Season hasn't yet ended."

"It has ended for Georgiana," said Sir Arthur. "We will return to Highcroft as soon as possible. You may as well start packing your things today."

"My dear, I pray you reconsider," said her ladyship.

"You must, Papa," said Kitty. "I do love London. It is so dull in the country."

"I will hear no further arguments from any of you," said the baronet. "I've made my decision and you will abide by it."

Lady Morley sighed. When her husband adopted this dictatorial air, as he did occasionally, there was no point in arguing. "Very well, my dear," she said.

"Now go to your room, Georgiana," commanded Sir Arthur.

Rising to her feet, Georgiana tearfully exited the room. "And you are to remain here and finish your breakfast, Kitty," said the baronet. Nodding, Kitty meekly obeyed.

Chapter 5

Georgiana sat quietly in the carriage as the vehicle made its way along the country road, passing through the rich agricultural land of Suffolk. There were fields of wheat and barley and pastures dotted with sheep and cows.

Far too preoccupied with her own problems, Georgiana seemed unaware of the lovely bucolic landscape. Glancing at her father, who was seated across from her, Georgiana frowned. Sir Arthur had been exceedingly vexed with her ever since she had related her tale about the Earl of Dunraven. He sat there gazing out the window, saying little.

Lady Morley and Kitty carried on what little conversation there was, and the journey from London was an unhappy one. Georgiana's mother had not wished to return to Suffolk so soon. Although her ladyship had pleaded with Sir Arthur to reconsider, the baronet had remained adamant. London, he had said, was exerting a bad influence on Georgiana and it was time to return to Highcroft.

Noting her father's sour expression, Georgiana sighed. She had certainly made a mess of things with her ridiculous tale about being in love with Dunraven. No wonder her father had so easily figured out her plan. Now they were far from London and far from Thomas. She had no idea when she might see him again.

Georgiana thought wistfully of Thomas. She was sure that he would be devastated when he heard they had left town. Perhaps, considered Georgiana, he might come to Suffolk and stay with his uncle, Sir Francis Pelham. Yet even if he did so, how would she contrive to see him? Georgiana grew more gloomy as she pondered the matter.

Kitty, who was seated beside her sister, was gazing out the carriage window. "Why, we are almost home. There is the lane to Longmeadow. And there it is!"

Lady Morley craned her head out the window to take a look at the stately country home that was the nearest neighbor to Highcroft. "Yes, we'll soon be home and I must say that I am glad of it." As the carriage continued on, its inhabitants were afforded a good look at the impressive mansion. It was situated far from the road on a hill surrounded by woods. "Longmeadow does look very imposing from this vantage point."

Georgiana did not bother to look. Knowing that she was almost at Highcroft filled her with gloom.

"Do look, Arthur," said her ladyship. "Don't you think Longmeadow looks very grand?"

The baronet leaned across the carriage seat to peer out his wife's window. "If one did not know of the condition of the place, one might think so," said Sir Arthur. "Why, it is nearly in ruin."

"It is such a pity that poor Mrs. Bainbridge has had so many misfortunes," said Lady Morley.

"Her misfortune was to marry Bainbridge," said the baronet. "The man was a blackguard and a wastrel."

Lady Morley nodded. "I fear you are right, my dear. But Mrs. Bainbridge is such a dear lady. We will have to call on her very soon."

"I shall be happy to see Charlotte," said Kitty, referring to her best friend and cousin who lived in the nearby village of Richton. "She will be very surprised that we are returned. Why, I do believe I'm glad that we'll be back at Highcroft."

Georgiana glanced over at her sister, thinking that at least someone was happy to be back in Suffolk. She herself was completely miserable.

They arrived at Highcroft soon afterward. The servants greeted their employer and his family with sincere enthusiasm, for life had been a good deal duller with the Morleys in London. They were especially glad to see Agnes and the other servants who had accompanied the family to town. Certainly there would be many stories about the great metropolis that would be told in the servants' hall.

Georgiana retired to her room to change her clothes and rest after the journey. Entering the familiar chamber, she went to the window and looked out. There was a splendid view of the garden, which now in midsummer was a riot of color. Highcroft was justly famous for its extensive flower gardens. Resting her elbows on the windowsill, Georgiana gazed thoughtfully out at the view. She had to admit that the gardens were some consolation. She dearly loved the vast array of flowers, and she would be able to occupy herself there assisting the gardeners.

"There you are, miss."

Georgiana turned from the window to see Agnes. "I daresay you are happy to be home."

"I am indeed, miss," returned the servant.

"I wish I could say the same, Aggie," sighed Georgiana.

"But aren't you the least bit glad to be back at Highcroft, miss?"

Georgiana shook her head. "Why should I be? I will die of boredom here. In town I would have gone to Lady Braxton's ball this evening. And I would have seen Lord Thomas there."

"Now, miss, you know that I share your father's view where his lordship is concerned. The master is only thinking of what is best for you."

"What is best for me?" A scornful laugh escaped Georgiana. "I cannot see how it does me good to be back in Suffolk where I shall see no one."

"May I remind you, miss, that 'twas you who told the tale about falling in love with that other gentleman. You should be very glad that I didn't tell the master about your speaking with Mrs. Kendall and her telling you all about Lord Dunraven."

"I am grateful to you for that, Aggie," said Georgiana.

"In future, miss," said Agnes severely, "if you wish to deceive your father, I suggest you come up with a better plan than that one. To suggest you were in love with such a man as that only to make Sir Arthur think better of Lord Thomas." Agnes made a tisking noise.

"But I had to do something," muttered Georgiana. "You cannot believe that I would sit idly by while my father conspires to ruin my life."

"Nonsense," said Agnes. "You must make the best of things, Miss Georgiana. 'Twill not do to mope about when you're here at Highcroft."

"I can hardly be cheerful," said Georgiana glumly.

"Well, let us speak no more of it, miss. Come, you must put on a new frock."

Georgiana nodded, glad that Agnes had changed the subject.

*   *   *

By dinnertime that evening, Sir Arthur was in far better spirits. Since he disliked the city, the baronet was very pleased to be back at his beloved home. His new horse had been brought from town and Sir Arthur looked forward to showing him off to his neighbors. The stallion had pranced about the paddock, snorting and kicking up his heels while the grooms and stablemen had eyed him with admiration.

Lady Morley was also in a far better humor. Since she loved the gardens as much as Georgiana, she was pleased to see them looking so splendid. This had lessened the disappointment of missing Lady Braxton's ball. As her ladyship thought about seeing some of the friends and relations she had missed in London, being back in the country had not seemed so bad.

Georgiana remained glum, however. After changing her clothes, she had written to Thomas. Since her parents had forbidden her from communicating with him, she had secretly given the letter to one of the footmen to post for her. The servant, being very young and a bit smitten with Georgiana himself, had been happy to be of service.

At dinner, Georgiana was lost in her thoughts about Thomas. Wondering how he was spending the evening, she imagined him at Lady Braxton's ballroom, dancing with any number of eager young ladies. It was maddening to think of it.

Despite Georgiana's unhappiness and inattention, dinner passed without incident. Afterward, the family played cards for a time in the drawing room before retiring early.

The next two days passed uneventfully, since word was only beginning to get out that the Morleys had returned to Highcroft. On the third day, Lady Morley's cousin, Elizabeth Fanshawe and her daughter, Charlotte, appeared. They were quickly ushered into the drawing room where Lady Morley and her daughters greeted them warmly.

Since Charlotte was her best friend, Kitty was especially thrilled to see them. She greeted Charlotte with a happy embrace.

"Charlotte! How good it is to see you!"

"And we are so very glad to see all of you." Mrs. Fanshawe smiled at Lady Morley and her daughters. She was a stout woman with a loud voice and a cheerful countenance.

"Do come in, dear Elizabeth," said Lady Morley, guiding

them to chairs. "How well you both look. And I do believe you have grown taller, Charlotte, and a good deal prettier."

Charlotte, who was a rather plain but pleasant-looking girl with a bright smile and attractive brown curls, said, "Thank you, Cousin Isabelle."

Once they had all seated themselves, Elizabeth smiled. "It seems London agreed with all of you. But we were so surprised that you had returned."

"I would have preferred to stay in town for a while longer, Eliza, but my husband wished to return to Highcroft. You know how he detests London."

Elizabeth nodded. "Nearly as much as Mr. Fanshawe, I daresay. I am always pleading that he take us to London, but he refuses to even discuss the matter."

"I do wish we could go to London," said Charlotte wistfully.

"It is rather exciting," said Kitty, "but it is very dirty. Sometimes one can scarcely believe the soot from all the chimneys. And it is terribly noisy."

"But it is London," said Charlotte, who would happily put up with such inconveniences to be in the thick of things.

"I am so glad that you are returned," said Elizabeth with a smile. She turned to Georgiana. "Were you happy to leave London, my dear?"

"Indeed not, Cousin Elizabeth," returned Georgiana. "I adored London."

"I should think you would," said Elizabeth. "Your mother wrote that you were such a great success." She winked at Georgiana. "I was told you had a good many suitors. And your mother mentioned a certain young gentleman, Lord Belrose."

Georgiana directed a long-suffering look at her mother before replying. "I fear Mama was fonder of Lord Belrose than I."

"Yes," said Lady Morley, "Georgiana was simply odious about young Belrose. He was very fond of her. Had she given him the least encouragement, I am sure that he would have made an offer for her."

"And he didn't?" said Elizabeth, clearly disappointed.

"No, he did not," said Georgiana. "And I am glad of it, for I should not have liked to have refused him."

"You wouldn't have refused Lord Belrose?" cried Elizabeth.

"Indeed, I should have done so, even though Mama and Papa would have been furious."

"Oh dear," said Elizabeth, directing an understanding look at Lady Morley. "Well, perhaps things will work out better next Season. Truly, my dears, I had expected that we would call today and learn that Georgiana had made a brilliant match. But you are young, Georgiana, and I know that you will find a suitable young man."

"I do hope so," replied Lady Morley. "But, Eliza, let us talk about you. I do hope Mr. Fanshawe is well and the boys."

"Oh, exceedingly well," said her cousin. "But I must tell you the news. I do hope you haven't yet heard."

"Heard what?" said Lady Morley.

"About Longmeadow."

"Longmeadow?" said Lady Morley.

Elizabeth nodded. "It has been sold."

"Sold!" cried Lady Morley.

"Yes," replied Elizabeth, delighted that she had been the one to relay this astonishing information. "And Mrs. Bainbridge has gone to Brighton to live with her sister."

"I can scarcely believe it," said Lady Morley, shaking her head.

"Longmeadow sold?" said Georgiana, who was as surprised as her mother at the news. Having lived her entire life at Highcroft, Georgiana had always known Mrs. Bainbridge. She knew that there had been Bainbridges at Longmeadow for nearly as long as there had been Morleys at Highcroft. It had never occurred to her that Longmeadow would leave the Bainbridge family. The news was disturbing.

"Yes," said Mrs. Fanshawe, "I admit that I was quite shocked to hear it. Oh, we all knew that Mrs. Bainbridge had no money and Longmeadow was quite going to ruin. A very sad affair indeed. But no one knew that she was trying to sell it. It seems she appealed to a distant kinsman, a man of considerable wealth. He agreed to buy it. And you will never guess who this man is. Indeed, we were all quite amazed to hear it. I daresay Mrs. Bainbridge never spoke of the connection, not that I blame her."

"What can you mean, Eliza?" demanded Lady Morley. "Who has bought Longmeadow?"

Elizabeth paused, relishing the task of imparting another amazing bit of news. "The Earl of Dunraven," she said.

"The Earl of Dunraven!" cried Lady Morley, placing her hand on her breast.

Georgiana and Kitty exchanged startled glances. "Dunraven!" said Georgiana, scarcely believing that she had heard correctly.

"Oh, I see that you are acquainted with his lordship's reputations," said Elizabeth. "I didn't know a thing about him, but Mrs. Radcliffe knew of him. It seems he is quite infamous."

"Are you certain that it is the Earl of Dunraven, Eliza?"

"My dear Isabelle, I am quite certain of it. Of course, no one knows if he will reside there. He has many other residences, of course. His principal seat is Dunraven Castle in Norfolk. It is highly unlikely that he will spend any time here. I shouldn't doubt that he will find a tenant for Longmeadow. I do hope it doesn't remain empty for long. A house should be lived in, don't you think?"

Lady Morley was so astonished by her cousin's revelation that she could hardly reply. The Earl of Dunraven had bought Longmeadow? She looked closely at Georgiana, wondering if her daughter might have known of this, but Georgiana seemed genuinely surprised at the news.

Georgiana could only regard her mother with a bewildered look. How could such an amazing coincidence have occurred? she wondered.

It took a moment for Lady Morley to regain her composure and reply to her cousin. After a time, the conversation switched to other matters. Elizabeth and Charlotte stayed for tea and then took their leave.

When they had gone, Lady Morley rose from her chair in some agitation. "Lord Dunraven has bought Longmeadow? What do you know about this, Georgiana?" said Lady Morley. "I find this monstrous strange indeed."

Before Georgiana could reply, her father walked into the room. Not overly fond of his wife's cousin, Sir Arthur had waited until Elizabeth and her daughter had left before entering the drawing room. "It didn't take your cousin long to call. I expect she has informed you of all the current gossip."

"She has informed me of something very odd, my dear."

"Indeed?" said Sir Arthur, regarding his wife with interest as he sat down beside her on the sofa.

Lady Morley nodded gravely. "Longmeadow has been sold."

"Longmeadow sold? Whatever can you mean?"

"It appears that Mrs. Bainbridge found it necessary to sell the estate. But what is even more remarkable is the identity of the buyer."

"Come, come, my dear, do tell me whom you mean," said the baronet.

"Longmeadow has been purchased by the Earl of Dunraven," said Lady Morley.

It took a moment for this remarkable information to sink in. "The Earl of Dunraven? Good God!"

Both of her parents turned their expectant gazes upon the elder of their daughters. "If you know anything about this, Georgiana, I do think you should tell us," said Lady Morley.

Ever since hearing the news, Georgiana could only think of the astonishing coincidence. To think that the Earl of Dunraven had bought Longmeadow! She stared at her parents, wondering how to reply.

"It is so romantic, isn't it?" said Kitty, breaking the silence. "Lord Dunraven is so in love with Georgiana that he bought Longmeadow to be near her!"

"What!" cried Sir Arthur.

"It is the only explanation," said Kitty.

"You see?" said Georgiana, happy to take her sister's cue. "Lord Dunraven felt the same way as I did. And you thought I was making it up that I had fallen in love with him."

Both of her parents stared at her dumbfounded. Finally Sir Arthur spoke. "Then you knew about this?"

"Not precisely," said Georgiana, her mind turning rapidly. "When I met Lord Dunraven, I did mention where we lived in Suffolk. I do now recollect that he said that he knew of a nearby estate for sale. Of course, since it was mentioned in passing and our acquaintance was so very brief, I didn't think anything of it."

"By my honor!" exclaimed Sir Arthur. "This is incredible!"

Georgiana adopted the look of one who had been very much

wronged. "How it has pained me to know you both thought me a liar."

Lady Morley shook her head. "It was only that it was so difficult to believe that you could have fallen in love with him after just meeting him once and so briefly at that."

"The villain," said Sir Arthur, growing rather red in the face. "That he had the impertinence to fall in love with my daughter! If ever I shall meet him, he will rue the day!"

"Do calm yourself, my dear," cried his wife, worried at her husband's expression.

Sir Arthur shook his head. "I see I have wronged you, Georgiana. You must forgive me. You aren't at fault. You had no idea what sort of man he is. He is completely unsuitable. You are never to think of seeing him again."

"Oh, Papa, but I do love him!" cried Georgiana, feeling a tinge of guilt for once again deceiving her parents.

"Do you believe Dunraven will come to Longmeadow, Arthur?" said Lady Morley, directing a worried look at her husband.

"I'm sure of it. The man must be a lunatic. To meet Georgiana only once and fall in love with her is bad enough, but to buy an estate so that he might be near her is insane!"

"I think it wonderful" said Kitty.

"Wonderful?" snapped Sir Arthur. "It isn't in the least wonderful. Dunraven is not fit company for anyone, least of all a young lady such as Georgiana. The very idea that he would speak to her. He is not received in any respectable drawing room. And if he thinks he will see Georgiana again, he is very much mistaken. If he dares to call at Highcroft, I'll have him tossed out."

"Good heavens, my dear," said Lady Morley, "you cannot have an earl tossed out, even if he is as disreputable as Dunraven."

Georgiana tried hard to keep from laughing at this remark. Maintaining as solemn a face as possible, she reflected that things had certainly changed for the better due to the Earl of Dunraven's unexpected and fortuitous choice of property.

Chapter 6

The Earl of Dunraven climbed out of his carriage. Tucked under his arm was the terrier Macduff, whom he placed on the ground. "Here we are, Macduff, your new domain." The dog pricked up his ears and sniffed the air. "I daresay there will be rabbits enough for you," said Dunraven, pausing to survey the area around his most recent acquisition.

Longmeadow stood before him, an imposing edifice despite signs of neglect. The house had been built more than two hundred years earlier during the reign of King James I. It was typical of the buildings of the time with its gray stone and turreted corners.

Dunraven's brown eyes took in the ivy-covered walls, noting that repairs would doubtless be necessary. Yet in general, his lordship's first view of Longmeadow was favorable. The house had a certain stately charm that pleased him.

The earl walked about the grounds, studying the various aspects of the home. It was well situated on high ground that afforded pleasant views from all sides. As he looked out at the placid countryside that surrounded Longmeadow, he had an unusual feeling of satisfaction.

"Lord Dunraven?"

The earl turned around to face a thin elderly woman in a plain gray dress and lace cap. Standing beside her was a short, solemn-looking, middle-aged man dressed in the black coat of a butler. "Yes?" said his lordship.

"I am Mrs. Hastings, the housekeeper, my lord. And this is Mr. Canfield, the butler."

Canfield bowed gravely. "My lord," he said.

"Canfield," said Dunraven, nodding at the man.

Mrs. Hastings, who loved dogs, eyed Macduff with a smile. "What a lovely wee terrier, my lord."

"That is Macduff," said the earl.

Macduff, who seemed happy at the attention, wagged his tail furiously, causing Mrs. Hastings to stoop down to pet him. Rising, she returned her attention to her new employer. "Your lordship did not say whether you were bringing any servants," she said.

"I have brought only my valet. Until I find a necessity for making changes, I shall continue with the present staff."

The announcement pleased both Mrs. Hastings and Canfield, who had been rather concerned that they would have to leave posts they had occupied for many years. Canfield eyed his new master with keen interest. He was glad to see that the earl was a handsome, dignified gentleman. From all the gossip he had heard about him, he had half expected that Dunraven would have horns and a tail.

"Would you like to see the house, my lord?" asked Mrs. Hastings.

Dunraven nodded and then accompanied the servants inside, with Macduff following behind them. The earl's first glimpse of the interior gave him a less sanguine view of Longmeadow. The octagonal-shaped entry hall was dimly lit and sparsely furnished. As Mrs. Hastings led him around each of the rooms, Dunraven realized that the place was in need of major restoration. There was dampness in some of the walls and plaster coming down from several of the ceilings. The furniture, which had been purchased with the house, was, for the most part, worn and hideous. Since the Bainbridges had sold off most of their valuables long ago, all that decorated the walls were a few moth-eaten tapestries and family portraits.

The housekeeper kept glancing over at the earl to see his reaction to the various rooms. However, Dunraven viewed all he saw with seeming indifference, making few comments and appearing unconcerned with the sorry state of things. Mrs. Hastings was rather surprised at his equanimity, for she had not expected to find him in the least good-natured. When the tour was concluded, he thanked her in a civil manner and retired to his room, leaving Mrs. Hastings to feel that her new employer may not be nearly so bad as she had thought.

While Dunraven settled himself into his new Suffolk property, Georgiana sat in the drawing room at Highcroft, absently adding a few stitches to her needlework. Nearly a week had passed since the startling revelation that Dunraven had bought Longmeadow. Since hearing the news, Georgiana had been thinking a good deal about her meeting in the park with him.

Of course, her thoughts had most often been directed toward Lord Thomas Jeffreys. She hadn't heard from him and was beginning to worry. After all, Thomas should have written by now.

"Georgie!" Kitty entered the room, taking off her stylish straw bonnet as she did so. "Here you are indoors when it is one of the most beautiful days one will ever see."

"Have you returned from the village, Kit?"

Tossing her bonnet onto the sofa, her sister nodded before taking a seat. "Mama and I had such a pleasant meeting with Cousin Elizabeth and Charlotte. You should have come, Georgie."

"I wasn't in the mood," said Georgiana, sticking her needle into the canvas.

"Well, you were a goose to miss it. We had such fun. Charlotte and I took a lovely walk." Kitty's face broke into a delighted grin. "And I've heard the most exciting news. You'll be so very happy to hear it."

"What is it? I can't think of anything to make me happy unless you are going to tell me that Thomas has come to stay with his uncle at Hatfield. Good heavens, has he, Kit?"

"Oh, no. It's not that, but it is nearly as good. Indeed, perhaps it's better." She paused for effect. "Lord Dunraven has arrived at Longmeadow."

"What!" cried Georgiana.

"Yes, isn't it famous! I daresay it is fate that he has come here. I shouldn't be surprised if you do marry him."

"What a ninnyhammer you are, Kitty," said Georgiana with a frown.

"I do think it is all so amusing. I'll not soon forget the day Cousin Elizabeth told us that Dunraven had bought Longmeadow. I was certain that I should burst out laughing and ruin everything. I daresay it was rather clever of me to give Mama and Papa the idea that he had bought Longmeadow to be near you. Of course, had he never come, it would have been for naught. But he has come! His carriage was seen passing through the village. It was a very grand carriage pulled by four perfectly matched grays. Mr. Weeks got a very good look at it. He told Cousin Elizabeth that he had never seen a more splendid equipage."

"I can scarcely believe he has come," said Georgiana.

"Nor can I. Oh, Georgie, isn't it the most wonderful thing? And I thought him very handsome. Why he is very like Prince Rupert. Wicked gentlemen are often handsome, don't you think?"

"I'm sure I don't know," said Georgiana rather impatiently. "I am not acquainted with any other wicked gentlemen."

Kitty smiled. "Do you think he will call on us? Of course, Papa would not receive him in any case. But if he is to stay at Longmeadow, I am sure we will have a glimpse of him sometime."

"Oh dear," said Georgiana, suddenly having a thought. "What if Papa should meet him and say something about me?"

"Oh, I shouldn't worry about that. Papa would certainly snub him. And I doubt that Lord Dunraven will stay here for very long."

"I do hope so," said Georgiana. "Mama didn't tell Cousin Elizabeth about our story that the earl is in love with me, did she? It would be very bad if she did."

"Oh, no," said Kitty. "Mama did not say a word." However, Georgiana's sister neglected to mention that she had told Charlotte the tale. Her friend had been very much impressed at the idea of wicked Lord Dunraven being in love with Georgiana. Charlotte had been sworn to secrecy, of course, so Kitty was confident she would not tell a soul.

As Kitty continued to talk about Dunraven's appearance, Georgiana shook her head. She could only wonder at this new and surprising development.

Thomas Jeffreys rolled over in bed. Opening his eyes, he glanced at the clock sitting on the mantel in the bedchamber. "Damn and blast," he muttered as he noticed the lateness of the hour.

"What is it, Tom?" said a sleepy feminine voice from the other side of the bed.

Thomas leaned over and kissed a bare white shoulder. "Time for me to get up, my love," he said. "I've got to meet Sheffield at the club. I'm late already."

"Don't go," she said. She was a very pretty woman with disheveled black curls and bright green eyes. Rising up on one elbow, she pulled aside the covers to reveal her plump, voluptuous form.

"You can't think I'd wish to," replied Thomas, eyeing the lady's ample breasts with admiration.

Reaching over, his companion caught one of his hands and pulled it to her chest. "You must stay, m'lord."

"You are a beauty, Claire," said Thomas, his hands caressing her breasts and then wandering down her body. Suddenly he pulled away. "You'll not distract me, wench. I can't tarry in bed all day." He rose from the bed and grabbed his clothes from the chair. "I must return home and make myself presentable before I go to the club."

Claire gazed appreciatively at his muscular body as he dressed. "Will you come to the theater tonight?" she said.

"Yes, of course. I don't wish to miss seeing you. You look so beautiful on the stage. But I must say I always enjoy myself more afterward when we're here."

Claire smiled in reply. "I am glad that I please you, m'lord."

"That you do, my girl," said Thomas, turning to the mirror to tie his cravat.

Claire rose from the bed and slipped on her dressing gown. Coming up behind him, she encircled his waist with her arms and buried her face against his back. "Oh, Tom, I do love you."

"Claire, I have to finish," he said, disentangling himself from her embrace.

"I do wish you might stay."

"You know I can't."

Claire's face took on what she hoped as a charming pouting expression. "If I were that lady of yours, that Miss Morley, you'd stay."

"Don't be absurd. Miss Morley can't hold a candle to you, Claire."

"And still you wish to marry her."

"My God, wench. You know I've got to marry money. I've none of my own. And when I'm wed to Miss Morley, I'll have enough to buy you all the pretty things you like."

"You won't throw me off then, when you're married?"

"Do you take me for a fool?" he said, smiling at her. He

looked back at the mirror. "But you may have no cause to
worry about Miss Morley. Her father is adamantly opposed to
me marrying her. Of course, the silly little goose is still mad
about me. She has written me every day since she left.

"I am considering going to Suffolk to stay with my uncle. I
can do nothing to further my cause with her if I remain in
town."

"Oh, Tom you'd not leave me!" cried Claire.

"It wouldn't be for long."

Claire threw her arms around his neck. "I'll not bear to be
parted from you. I shall go to Suffolk with you. I shall leave
the theater company."

"Don't be absurd," he said a trifle impatiently. At times he
found Claire Stevenson's clinging manner rather tiresome.
She so adored him, he thought, looking down at her. Indeed,
he seemed to inspire such devotion in females. Glancing once
more at his handsome face in the mirror, he told himself that
being irresistible to women was sometimes a mixed blessing.
Then, disengaging himself from Claire's arms, he took his
leave.

Dunraven awoke after his first night at Longmeadow feeling
strangely refreshed. He had slept very well, far better than he
had in months. It seemed particularly odd, especially since he
had gone to bed far earlier than was his habit. Of course,
thought the earl, it had been a tiring journey.

Hearing his master stir, Macduff rose to his feet from his
place on the floor near the earl's bed and hurried to greet him.
"Good morning, you wretched little beggar," said Dunraven,
rising from his bed. The dog wagged his tail happily at his
master's words.

Walking to the window, the earl pulled open the draperies
and looked out. There was a morning mist in the air, giving the
park surrounding the house a dreamy quality. It was so very
green and undeniably beautiful. While Dunraven was not the
sort of man to care much for scenery and country views, he
was not unaffected by the picturesque landscape.

He was joined shortly by his valet, who assisted him to
dress. When the earl went downstairs, he found that breakfast
was ready in the dining room. Pleased to find the food exceptionally good, he ate heartily. Macduff, who was seated on the

floor beside his master's chair, was fortunate to receive a plump sausage.

Dunraven then spent the morning walking around the property. Macduff ran happily ahead of him, chasing rabbits. As he walked, the earl reflected that he was enjoying himself. The fact struck him as odd, for he had not expected that he would find a country walk so entertaining. Indeed, his lordship had always been one to scoff at simple country pleasures.

In the afternoon, the earl sat at a desk in the drawing room writing a letter to his solicitor. He was interrupted by the appearance of the butler. "There is a gentleman to see you, m'lord," He said, extending a silver salver that contained a calling card.

Dunraven's dark eyebrows arched slightly. A caller already? He might have known that some busybody would show up. He took the calling card and looked down to see the name, "George Buckthorne, Esq."

"Do show him in, Canfield."

The butler bowed and left, returning a few minutes later with the earl's friend. "Dunraven, old fellow."

"Buck," said the earl, rising from his chair to extend his hand to his visitor.

Buckthorne shook it warmly. "Well, old chap, it appears Longmeadow is a bang-up place. I knew you'd like it."

"I have not said that I like it," said the earl.

"Of course, you do," said Buckthorne. "And there is Macduff. Good day to you, sir." Macduff wagged his tail in greeting as Buckthorne sat down in a well-worn armchair.

"What are you doing here, Buck? I didn't expect you for a week."

"I thought I should come at once," replied Buckthorne. "Town seemed too dull without you. And besides, Mrs. Buckthorne announced that her mother was arriving from Bath. It seemed best that I clear out."

A slight smile appeared on the earl's face. "The life of a married man is not easy."

"'Pon my honor it isn't," said Buckthorne. "But not every woman is Mrs. Buckthorne. I'm told there are a few tolerable ones about." He grinned. "I must say, Dunraven, they are talking about you already."

"Who is talking about me?"

"The natives," replied Buckthorne, grinning again. "Yes, indeed, my driver had to stop in the village about some problem with one of the wheels. I stopped at an inn to have a quick pint. Imagine my surprise to find you are the subject of gossip."

"That is indeed surprising," said the earl with an ironical smile.

"But it was not the usual gossip, Dunraven. When I mentioned to a local fellow that I was going to Longmeadow, he became exceedingly friendly. He asked me if it were true that you had bought the house to be near a certain lady who resides nearby."

"What?" said Dunraven, regarding him in some surprise.

"The man was told that you are in love with a lady named Georgiana Morley, who lives on an adjoining estate. By his account, she is a damned pretty girl and rich besides. I daresay I thought you might have confided to me about her."

"I don't know what the devil you are talking about. I don't know any Georgiana Morley."

"It seems she knows you" said Buckthorne. "The fellow said that she was quite taken with you when you met in town."

"I hope that you told this rumormonger that his information was nonsense."

"How could I know that it was nonsense, my dear fellow? For all I knew, perhaps you had met this Georgiana and become enamored of her. Oh, I realize it seemed absurd, but one never knows. I am relieved to find out it is false. You were never the sort of man who would lose his head over a woman. And imagine a fellow buying an estate to be near a girl. What an idea! Now, to buy it for the hunting is understandable."

"Yes, most sensible," returned Dunraven, smiling again.

"Well, it is dashed odd that false stories about you are being bandied about. I wonder who this Georgiana Morley might be. You're certain you have never met her?"

"Never," said the earl.

"I don't believe I have made her acquaintance," said Buckthorne, looking thoughtful. "I do remember my wife mentioning a Miss Morley. Something about young Belrose being besotted with her. Of course, I could be wrong. I don't really listen to Mrs. Buckthorne. But, in any case, Dunraven, how do you like Longmeadow? It seems a capital place to me."

"It's scarcely better than a ruin, Buck," said the earl. "I daresay it will cost a fortune to make it livable."

"So what is that to you?" said his friend. "You've need of ways to spend your blunt now that you've given up Mrs. Trotter's. Of course, I'm sure you've only given it up for a time." Buckthorne rose from his chair and strode about the drawing room, surveying the furniture and checking the views from the windows. "Good views, what?" he said. "A fine wood and a dashed pretty stream. They say the fishing is good hereabouts. The fellow from the inn told me so."

"I do think you were spending too much time with this 'fellow,'" said the earl. "But I must warn you, Buck, you may not find the accommodations here to your liking. The rooms upstairs are sorry indeed. Mine is the only decent bedchamber."

"Oh, I'm not staying at Longmeadow tonight," said Buckthorne.

"You're not staying here? Whatever do you mean?"

"Oh, I must be off to Gilroy's. I am to see the pack of hounds."

"Surely that can wait."

"It can't wait. I have heard there is some other chap interested in them. He who hesitates is lost, as they say. I'll not be gone long."

"I am not convinced that I want a pack of hounds here at Longmeadow," said Dunraven. "I daresay Macduff will not want anything to do with them."

Macduff, who had been lying on the floor, lifted his head at the mention of his name.

"You must tell your master that is stuff and nonsense, my lad," said Buckthorne, smiling at the dog. "You'd love having a pack of hounds in the kennel, wouldn't you, Macduff? You see, Dunraven? He looks very pleased at the idea. I say, Dunraven, we will have the most marvelous hunts here. If only it were hunting season."

The earl made no reply. While he hunted occasionally, he was not hunting mad like his friend, nor was he particularly ecstatic over the idea of a pack of howling hounds about the place.

"Do not think you are bringing these hounds of yours back here for me to kennel."

"No, no, of course not," said Buckthorne, knowing full well

that he intended to do so. "Now do tell me about this place. For example, how is the cook?"

"Quite adequate, it appears." He smiled indulgently at his friend. "I expect you are eager to test the caliber of the cook for yourself."

"What a discerning fellow you are, Dunraven. I am famished."

Ringing for a servant, the earl genially ordered food for his guest and himself.

Chapter 7

After returning from an afternoon ride with her father, Georgiana went to her room to change her clothes. She was met by Agnes, who eyed her plum-colored riding habit in horror. "Miss Georgiana, you've got mud all over your skirt!"

"Oh, how could I help it, Aggie?" said Georgiana, removing the pins from her high-crowned hat. "One cannot go for a gallop on a rainy day without getting a bit muddy."

Agnes sighed, but made no reply as she started to assist her young mistress to take off the jacket of her riding habit. "Did you enjoy your ride, miss?" she said finally.

"I did indeed, but I do wish Papa had allowed me to ride Demon Dancer. He is so wonderful."

"He is hardly a horse for a lady," said Agnes.

"What nonsense," said Georgiana. She took her hat from her head and handed it to her maid. "I could certainly ride him."

"Aye, you could, miss," said Agnes. "But it does give the master so much pleasure to ride such a horse. Shaw said he quite dotes on him already."

"Yes, he does," said Georgiana. "I must say I'm glad, for he is in a wonderfully good mood."

"The country agrees with him," said Agnes.

Georgiana nodded. "I fear it does. He'll never wish to return to London. It seems we are doomed to stay at Highcroft forever."

"Doomed, miss? What a thing to say. Highcroft is the pleasantest place in the world."

"Oh, it is pleasant, Aggie," said Georgiana, stepping out of her skirt. "But what I mean is that it is rather dull compared to town."

Agnes could not disagree, for she was sure that a young lady like Georgiana would certainly find the country dull.

After all, her mistress had been attending so many social functions in town. Agnes did not doubt that Highcroft would seem dreary after all the parties and balls and theater engagements.

When Georgiana was finished dressing, she joined her mother and Kitty in the library. After tea, Kitty complained of a sore throat. Fearing that her daughter was coming down with a cold, Lady Morley commanded her to retire to bed.

"I do hope Kitty will feel better," said Georgiana.

"If she rests, I daresay she will," said her mother. "I do fear we will have more rain. I do think you should stay indoors for the rest of the day."

"But, Mama, the sky has cleared. I did so wish to take a walk. I won't go far. Will you not come with me?"

"No, indeed. I must see Cook about the menus." She glanced out the window. "It does look better. I fancy it will do no harm for you to take a short walk about the grounds, but do not go far."

"Papa was going to see Mr. Baxter, was he not?" said Georgiana.

Lady Morley nodded. "He had to speak to him about a cow or perhaps it was a bull." Her ladyship looked perplexed. "He did have to see Baxter about something."

"Then I shall walk toward the Baxters' cottage. Perhaps I shall meet Papa coming back."

"That is a good idea," said her ladyship.

Georgiana left the library to return to her room. There she changed her clothes once again and put on her walking boots. Agnes insisted she wear a cloak and take an umbrella before sending her on her way.

Walking briskly away from the house, Georgiana grew pensive. Since arriving at Highcroft she had scarcely had a moment to herself. It felt good to be alone with her thoughts.

As she walked along, she wondered what Thomas was doing. Did he miss her as much as she missed him, she asked herself. She imagined him sitting in his lodgings, pining for her. She was certain he could not bear to go to any parties or balls now that she was away. The idea that he might be miserable pleased her.

That morning she had written to him about the strange coincidence of Dunraven buying Longmeadow. She knew he would find it very amusing.

As Georgiana continued along, she thought about the earl, wondering whether he could be as bad as she had been led to believe. She thought again of their brief meeting and how his dark eyes had been fixed upon her blue ones with unsettling effect.

Continuing to think about Dunraven, Georgiana walked on until she came to an intersection of two paths. One led toward the Baxter cottage and the other in the direction of Longmeadow. Georgiana stopped. Longmeadow was scarcely two miles distant, an easy walk for her.

The idea occurred to Georgiana that she could walk to Longmeadow and perhaps catch a glimpse of the earl. She knew that there were woods and several good vantage points on the path to the house.

After hesitating for a few moments, Georgiana turned toward the path going to the Baxters' cottage. When she had taken only a few steps, she stopped abruptly. Then turning around, she strode off toward Longmeadow.

Buckthorne had not lingered long at the home of his friend. After eating a delicious meal, he had taken his leave, saying he would return in a day or two. After watching Buckthorne's carriage drive off, the earl returned to the library.

Late that afternoon, Dunraven decided to take a ride. He had brought one of his best saddle horses from town, a fine bay mare, and he was eager to give the animal some exercise. As he walked to the stables, Dunraven noted that the sky was gray and the air turning cooler.

Arriving at the stables, his lordship called for his horse. It was quickly saddled and brought to him. Climbing agilely into the saddle, Dunraven set off, with an enthusiastic Macduff running alongside him.

Dunraven turned his horse onto a wooded path and cantered along, enjoying the ride immensely. It rather surprised him that he could find pleasure in a quiet ride in a placid rural setting.

He knew that his London acquaintances would have been amused at the idea. The earl reflected that he was a cynical, jaded fellow, who seldom found pleasure in anything. Yet there he was delighting in the fine scenery and brisk air.

After riding some distance away from Longmeadow, the

sky began to grow darker. Suddenly, it began to rain. "Damn
and blast," said Dunraven, pulling his horse to a stop. "We'd
best get back. Come along, Macduff," he shouted to the dog as
the rain started to come down harder. Turning the mare
around, he headed back toward the manor house.

The earl was very glad that he had started to head back, for
within minutes, the rain turned into a downpour. The sky was
now very black and the wind cold and gusty.

Coming out of the wooded path into the open road, Dunraven could see Longmeadow in the distance. He patted his
horse's neck. "You'll soon be warm and dry, my girl," he said,
urging the mare forward.

He had only gone several yards when he spied a lone figure
on another path that intersected the road. A woman was attempting to walk away, but the wind was hampering her
progress. Dunraven watched her struggle with her umbrella,
which kept flying up and nearly out of her hands. The rain was
pouring down, drenching her.

Catching sight of a stranger in his newfound territory, Macduff raced ahead. Nearing her, he barked furiously.

While Dunraven was not accustomed to coming to the aid
of strangers, he could not be indifferent to the plight of this
woman, especially since his dog was doubtlessly scaring her to
death. Tapping the mare with his riding crop, he rode up the
path to where she continued to grapple with her umbrella.

"Quiet, Macduff!" shouted the earl. The terrier instantly
obeyed.

Looking down at the unfortunate woman, Dunraven got a
glimpse of her face for the first time. Recognizing her immediately as the young lady he had met in the park, he regarded her
in considerable amazement.

The rain began to come down even harder and there was a
loud clash of thunder that caused Dunraven's mare to skitter
nervously. An expert horseman, the earl controlled his mount
easily. "Where are you going?" he said, shouting down at her.

"To Highcroft," cried Georgiana Morley, eyeing him war-
ily. Her walk to Longmeadow had turned into a disaster.
Scarcely had she come in sight of the house when the torren-
tial downpour had started, completely soaking her in minutes.
Now she stood there in the most embarrassing predicament of
her life.

Assuming that Highcroft was a neighboring house, Dunraven thought that it must be some distance away. "You had best come to Longmeadow. You can be taken there in a carriage."

"Oh, no," she shouted, regarding him with alarm. "There is no need of that. Highcroft isn't far."

The earl eyed Georgiana with some impatience. She stood there, refusing assistance while they both were getting soaked. He jumped down from his horse and took her umbrella, which the wind had turned inside out. "Your umbrella is ruined. You are drenched to the bone. You must go to the house."

Before she could protest, Dunraven picked her up and placed her atop the mare. Georgiana was so astonished that she could not reply for a moment. The earl jumped up behind her and started briskly toward the house.

Georgiana didn't know what to do. There she was with Dunraven's arms around her, heading for Longmeadow. She tried to say something, but her words were blotted out by another deafening crack of thunder. The earl's arm tightened around Georgiana who, for all her dismay, found it not an unpleasant sensation.

It was not long before Dunraven arrived back at the house. Seeing his employer ride up, the butler hurried out of the house, accompanied by a footman. Seeing the servants, the earl lifted Georgiana down. "Take care of the lady, Canfield," commanded the earl. "I shall see to my horse." He then rode off toward the stables with Macduff racing after him.

Canfield and the other servant ushered Georgiana inside. They were met in the entry hall by Mrs. Hastings. "Miss Morley!" she cried. "Why, you are soaked! Do come by the fire before you catch your death of cold."

Soon Georgiana was standing before a roaring fire in one of the small parlors that lined the entry hall. Mrs. Hastings took her bonnet. "My poor young lady," she said, "you are so wet. Do give me your cloak."

Georgiana unfastened the clasp of the cloak and handed the garment to the housekeeper. "It is soaked, miss. And look at your dress. You must have dry clothes at once. I fear you'll have to wear something of mine." She frowned. "Of course, you are so much smaller than I." She called to a footman, who was lingering near the doorway. "Jim, take Miss Morley's cloak to the kitchen and dry it by the fire." The servant, a gangly young man, hastened to do as he was told.

"I assure you, Mrs. Hastings, there is no need to make a fuss. I shall be fine now that I am here. I will soon be dry. But I do have to return to Highcroft at once."

"But were you out walking, miss? Did his lordship find you?"

"I wasn't far from Longmeadow when Lord Dunraven found me. You see, Mrs. Hastings, the rain came up so suddenly. I had promised my mother that I wouldn't go far and I know that she will be worrying about me. Lord Dunraven said that I might use his carriage to go home."

Glancing out the window, Mrs. Hastings took in the black sky and the rain pelting hard against the windowpanes. "That is kind of his lordship," said the housekeeper, "but you may wish to wait a bit until the rain subsides. Oh, here is the master now."

Georgiana looked over to see Dunraven enter the room. She regarded him with keen interest. The earl looked tall and imposing as he strode toward her. Noting his unruly dark hair, handsome chiseled features, and dark eyes, Georgiana thought he looked exactly as she had remembered him.

Although he had adopted his usual pose of indifference, the young lady before him had provoked a more than usual amount of interest. As impossible as it seemed, she was most certainly the girl he had met in the park.

Dunraven's critical gaze fell upon her as she stood beside the housekeeper near the fire. As before, her enormous pale blue eyes had a rather disquieting effect upon him. He found the wet curls that framed her face charming, and he also did not fail to note the way her damp frock clung to her body, revealing an excellent figure.

"My lord, your coat is very wet," said Mrs. Hastings, eying him like a disapproving mother hen. "You must go and change at once. And I shall find Miss Morley some dry things."

"Miss Morley?" The earl frowned slightly, remembering at once that this was the name Buckthorne had mentioned. They were saying in the village that he had bought Longmeadow to be near Miss Georgiana Morley.

"Why, yes, of course, my lord," said the elderly housekeeper. "I shall introduce you. Miss Morley, may I present

Lord Dunraven? My lord, this is Miss Georgiana Morley. She is your neighbor from Highcroft."

"How do you do, my lord?" said Georgiana, dropping a polite curtsy.

"Your servant, Miss Morley," replied the earl with a bow. "I believe you were recently in London."

Georgiana found herself blushing. It was obvious that he remembered their meeting.

"Oh, have you met Miss Morley already, my lord?" said Mrs. Hastings.

"We have not been formally introduced until now, but we did meet briefly in town."

"Yes, his lordship returned my hat to me in the park," said Georgiana, hoping she was hiding her discomfiture. "I should be most obliged to you, Lord Dunraven, if I might borrow your carriage to return to Highcroft. It is not very far."

Dunraven did not reply at first, but continued to stare at her, causing Georgiana to feel very uncomfortable under his gaze. "I feel it inadvisable to send my horses out in such weather, Miss Morley," he said. "I shall have a servant take word to Highcroft that you are here. When the rain is over, I shall escort you back to your home."

"Oh, really, Lord Dunraven, I don't believe that is necessary," said Georgiana, feeling very ill at ease. "Indeed, I could not impose upon you in such a way. I assure you I can walk home if you might loan me the use of an umbrella."

Dunraven could not help but smile at this remark. At that moment there was one more thunder clap and the wind blew against the window with such force that it flew open and Mrs. Hastings had to rush to close it. "You see, Miss Morley, the storm is at its worst. You'll have to stay at Longmeadow for a while. I shall be happy to have your company." He walked to the bell pull and rang, causing Canfield to appear in the room. "Canfield, have someone go to Miss Morley's home so that her family will know that she is safe. Tell them that I shall see she is returned to them as soon as possible."

"Certainly, my lord," said Canfield, bowing and retreating.

"I do think Miss Morley should have some dry clothes," said Mrs. Hastings. "And so should you, my lord."

"Of course, you are right, Mrs. Hastings," said the earl. "Do see to Miss Morley."

"Very good, my lord," said Mrs. Hastings. "Do come along, my dear miss. I shall find you something and we will dry your own things."

Mrs. Hastings escorted Georgiana from the room. She then led her slowly up the stairs and down the long corridor to the housekeeper's quarters. Mrs. Hastings's accommodations were very modest, but her small sitting room and bedchamber seemed cozier than the rest of the house.

Georgiana was no stranger to either Longmeadow or Mrs. Hastings. She had called there numerous times over the years. As she entered the housekeeper's rooms, Georgiana found herself thinking it seemed very odd that Mrs. Bainbridge was no longer there and that Longmeadow had a new master.

"I do have something that might do, Miss Morley," said the housekeeper, going to a vast oaken wardrobe and rummaging through her clothes. "It is rather old, for I wore it when I was young. I was far more slender in those days, miss. It's rather silly to save such an old dress, but I had such fond memories from the time I wore it. Yes, here it is." She pulled out a pale green dress and held it out to Georgiana. "I know it is very old and out of fashion."

Georgiana nearly laughed as she beheld the old dress. A modest creation, it had been fashioned in her grandmother's time. Taking the dress, Georgiana noted the faint scent of lavender from sachets that were pinned inside. She could not imagine wearing such a garment, but did not know how to refuse without hurting Mrs. Hastings's feelings. Therefore, she suppressed a sigh and allowed the housekeeper to assist her out of her wet things and into the dress.

Once he had changed his clothes, Dunraven went to the drawing room where he sat down upon the sofa to await his guest. Macduff, having been thoroughly dried by one of the servants, now joined his master. "Well, you little ruffian," said the earl, "you're to sit and mind your manners."

Cocking his head to regard his master with a serious look, Macduff went obediently to a place by the earl's feet and sat down. Dunraven picked up a newspaper that sat on the table by the sofa. After reading it for a short time, he tossed it aside. The news did not interest him as much as Miss Georgiana Morley.

According to Buckthorne, she had put it about that he was in love with her. The earl frowned at the thought. While he was well aware of his appeal to the opposite sex, it seemed remarkable that the young lady could have lost her head over him upon so brief an acquaintance. Indeed, he had assumed she hadn't known who he was. Frowning again, he resolved to get to the bottom of the matter.

After what seemed a very long time, Mrs. Hastings and Georgiana entered the room. Dunraven stood up. Seeing Georgiana's attire, he raised his eyebrows, thinking that it had been at least twenty-five years since he had seen such a dress.

The earl had to admit that as peculiar as it was to see a lady attired in such a manner, Miss Morley looked singularly attractive. The dress featured a tight-fitting bodice and very low neckline that revealed Georgiana's admirable figure to good advantage. Unlike the high-waisted creations favored by modern fashion, the dress Georgiana wore had a waist just above the hips and a wide skirt.

"Miss Morley looks quite wonderful, doesn't she, my lord?" said Mrs. Hastings. "But she is such a beautiful young lady that she looks well in everything."

Georgiana could tell by the way Dunraven was regarding her that he thought she looked ridiculous. She could only pretend that she didn't care what he thought. Walking into the room, she seated herself in an armchair. "I do believe the storm is lessening," she said. "I shall be able to return to Highcroft soon."

"It seems to me that it is growing worse," said Dunraven.

"In any case, you mustn't worry about it, Miss Morley," said Mrs. Hastings, sitting down in a chair next to Georgiana. "You can always stay to dinner."

"Oh, I couldn't possibly," said Georgiana, alarmed at the prospect. What would her father say if she had dinner with the Earl of Dunraven? "I could not impose on his lordship's hospitality."

"It is no imposition, I assure you," said Dunraven.

Looking toward the window, Mrs. Hastings found that it was still raining very hard. "I daresay I can scarcely remember a worse storm," she said. "It reminds me of the time so many years ago when we had the terrible flood. You would have been a little girl, Miss Morley. Perhaps you don't remember it." When Georgiana replied that she did not, the housekeeper was only too happy to tell them all about it.

Dunraven only half listened as Mrs. Hastings talked on and on. He found himself watching Georgiana. She took great care not to look in his direction, a fact that amused him.

After Mrs. Hastings had nearly exhausted her recollections of the flood, Canfield appeared at the door. "I beg your pardon, my lord."

"What is it, Canfield?"

"One of Martin Parsons's lads has come with a message. Mr. Parsons is one of your lordship's tenants, m'lord. He has a cottage along the path to Highcroft near the bridge over the stream. You see, m'lord, I sent Jim to Highcroft about Miss Morley being here, and Parsons saw him about to cross the bridge. Parsons warned him there was danger as the water was coming up onto the bridge, but Jim crossed anyway."

"Oh, don't tell me something has happened to Jim!" cried Mrs. Hastings, clasping her hands together.

"No, Mrs. Hastings, the lad be fine. He got over well enough, but no sooner had he gone across than the water rose even higher and 'twas clear the bridge would soon be impassable. Jim asked Parsons to get word back to Longmeadow that no one else will be able to get to Highcroft until the water goes down."

Dunraven looked at Georgiana. "It seems you'll have to stay the night at Longmeadow, Miss Morley."

"Oh, I couldn't!" cried Georgiana, horrified at the prospect.

"Oh, dear," said Mrs. Hastings, shaking her head. "'Tis very bad indeed. But you need not be alarmed, Miss Georgiana. Jim will tell your parents that you're here safe and sound so they won't worry."

Georgiana nearly laughed. She could imagine what her parents would think when they heard that she was staying the night at Longmeadow. She had no doubt that her mother would have an attack of the vapors and that her father would have a fit of apoplexy. "There must be some way that I could get back to Highcroft," said Georgiana.

"I fear not, miss," said Canfield. "There is nowhere else one might cross over with a carriage, not for many miles. And the weather is still very bad, miss."

"I fear you'll have to stay, Miss Morley," said Mrs. Hastings, "but we'll take good care of you."

"I shall be happy for your company, Miss Morley," said the earl. "And Mrs. Hastings will join us for dinner."

"I should be honored," said the housekeeper, realizing that she would have the important role of chaperone.

Very disturbed at the knowledge that she would be forced to stay at Longmeadow, Georgiana rose from her chair. "I do hope you will excuse me. I am rather tired. Perhaps Mrs. Hastings will show me where I might rest until dinnertime."

"Of course," said the housekeeper, rising to her feet. The two women left the room, leaving Dunraven to reflect that it might be a very interesting evening.

Chapter 8

Fortunately, it did not take long for Georgiana's clothing to dry and she was soon able to change out of Mrs. Hastings's absurdly old-fashioned dress. Attired once again in her own clothes, she felt considerably better.

Seated beside Mrs. Hastings in that lady's sitting room, she engaged in conversation with the housekeeper while Mrs. Hastings knitted. "So you saw his lordship in town, Miss Morley?" said Mrs. Hastings, highly interested.

"I only spoke a few words to him," said Georgiana. "It was really rather funny. My hat blew off and Macduff ran off with it."

"Oh, the little rascal!" cried Mrs. Hastings, laughing.

Georgiana smiled. "I suppose I looked very silly dashing after him. He went right to his master and dropped my hat at Lord Dunraven's feet. Of course, I didn't know who the earl was. We only exchanged a few words and didn't introduce ourselves."

"And now you find him again here at Longmeadow," said Mrs. Hastings.

"Yes, it was rather a surprise," said Georgiana, making a considerable understatement.

"Well, it was a surprise to me to find he was such an amiable gentleman," said Mrs. Hastings. "I had feared he would be difficult, being an earl and with what I'd heard . . ." She stopped abruptly, realizing that she was being indiscreet. It wouldn't do to mention his lordship's reputation to Miss Morley. "I believe we are very fortunate that the earl has taken Longmeadow."

Thinking that her parents would hardly agree, Georgiana suppressed a smile. She looked gratefully at Mrs. Hastings, thanking Providence for her presence. The housekeeper was a well-known and well-respected member of the community. Certainly, she would lend countenance to Georgiana's situation. And besides, everyone would certainly understand that it had been the storm that had forced her to stay here. Surely she could not be condemned for something that was beyond her control.

Buoyed by these thoughts, Georgiana felt more cheerful. She would look at this evening as an adventure, she told herself. Indeed, Kitty would be green with envy at the idea of her having dinner with "Prince Rupert." A smile came to Georgiana's lips at the thought.

"I see it is time for us to go down," said Mrs. Hastings, glancing at the clock and then putting down her knitting. "I should not doubt that you are very hungry, Miss Morley."

"I must admit that I am," replied Georgiana. She accompanied Mrs. Hastings to the drawing room where Dunraven stood with his back to them, staring into the fireplace. Hearing the ladies enter, he turned to greet them.

Having dressed for dinner, the earl was now attired in black. Georgiana thought he looked very handsome in his splendidly cut coat and knee breeches. He had the elegant understated look made fashionable by that arbiter of fashion, George Brummell.

"Miss Morley," he said, nodding at her.

"My lord," said Georgiana, feeling rather underdressed in her dress of striped jaconet muslin. It was of simple cut with close-fitting sleeves, a high waist and high collar. The earl, who did not pay much attention to female fashions, thought she looked very charming.

Georgiana had scarcely seated herself when Canfield arrived to say that dinner was ready. Since she was quite famished, Georgiana was very happy to go at once to the dining room.

A footman pulled out a chair for Georgiana and she sat down at the long cherry table. Mrs. Hastings took a seat across from her, while the earl sat at the head of the table between the ladies.

The room was lit by candles that burned in candelabras sitting on the table. It was rather dark and Georgiana could hear the storm continuing to rage outside.

Mrs. Hastings was very pleased at finding herself seated

with the earl and Georgiana. Since it was not a housekeeper's place to join her master at the dinner table, Mrs. Hastings was well aware of the honor being bestowed upon her. She smiled brightly as the footman served the soup.

"What a dreadful storm," said Mrs. Hastings. "What a blessing it is to have a roof over our heads." The housekeeper prudently refrained from mentioning that Longmeadow's roof was leaky. At that very moment, servants were scurrying around to several of the rooms in the upper story trying to catch the water in buckets and other containers. "I should not like to be out on such a night. I am glad that Miss Morley is safe with us."

"Indeed," said the earl, dipping his spoon into the soup.

"Miss Morley, perhaps you will tell us about your stay in London," said the housekeeper, eager to make conversation. "I know that you must have had a very exciting time. Some weeks ago Mrs. Bainbridge told me that she heard from Miss Charlotte Fanshawe that you saw the Prince Regent at a ball."

"I do hope you were not overwhelmed by the experience, said Dunraven, casting an ironical glance at Georgiana.

"I fortunately managed to refrain from swooning, my lord," replied Georgiana.

"I can scarcely imagine such glittering company," said the housekeeper. "It must be very grand to attend such affairs."

"It is rather splendid," said Georgiana. "And there is always such a great crush of people. But it is not always so very wonderful, for one is usually hot or hungry or else one's feet hurt."

This remark amused his lordship, who smiled slightly. "I fear you are disillusioning Mrs. Hastings, Miss Morley," he said.

"Oh, I don't mean to do so," said Georgiana. "On the whole, one has a marvelous time."

Mrs. Hastings seemed pleased to hear it. She continued to ask Georgiana about London. This topic occupied much of the dinner conversation. At the conclusion of the meal, Mrs. Hastings and Georgiana left the earl so that he could drink his port.

When they were alone in the drawing room, Mrs. Hastings appeared very pleased with the meal. "That was so very enjoyable, Miss Morley," she said.

"Yes," replied Georgiana. "The food was excellent. You must tell Mrs. Grayson how much I enjoyed everything. I must say she is probably the best cook in the county, although I should not like it if our own cook heard that I said it."

Mrs. Hastings smiled. "The earl seems very pleased with Cook. I am so very relieved that his lordship is keeping the staff on."

"That is good," said Georgiana, "but does he intend to spend much time at Longmeadow?"

"I cannot say, miss. He has several other residences and gentlemen do like to spend a good deal of time in London. Perhaps he will not stay long, but I shall be grateful for whatever time he spends here."

After a short time, Dunraven joined them in the drawing room. They conversed for a time before the earl suggested a game of cribbage. Mrs. Hastings begged to be excused, but Georgiana agreed.

When Georgiana joined his lordship at the card table, the housekeeper sent a servant for her knitting. Once she had it, she sat down near the card table and began to work industriously.

"I shall doubtless make a cake of myself," said Georgiana as Dunraven dealt the cards. "I am hopeless at games. Gentlemen are always so good at them."

"That is because we scarcely do anything else," said his lordship.

Georgiana smiled at him and then, picking up her cards, perused her hand. As they began to play, the earl soon found that his guest was not in the least hopeless at cards. She played cleverly and won several hands.

"You have misled me, Miss Morley. You are obviously a practiced cribbage player."

"I confess that my sister, Kitty, and I play a good deal," said Georgiana, "but I never thought I was very good. It is Kitty who always wins."

"Then I take care to avoid playing cribbage with your sister," replied the earl.

Georgiana smiled at Dunraven, who found himself thinking that she had a remarkably radiant smile. His lordship also noted that the dimples appearing on her cheeks when she smiled were particularly charming.

As they continued to play, it rather surprised Georgiana to find that she was enjoying herself. She was far more relaxed now, having decided that the earl was not so very threatening. Realizing suddenly that it had been some time since Mrs. Hastings had made any comments, she glanced over at the housekeeper. To her surprise, Mrs. Hastings was fast asleep with her head slumped forward and her hands motionless on her knitting.

"Oh, dear, it seems Mrs. Hastings has fallen asleep. I should rouse her and then we should retire."

"Allow her to sleep for a moment, Miss Morley. This is a good opportunity for you to explain some things to me."

At the words Georgiana had an uneasy feeling. "Explain some things, my lord?"

Dunraven nodded. "Earlier today I was visited by a friend, who heard a peculiar story when pausing in the village. A man informed my friend, Mr. Buckthorne, who for all his faults is a reliable fellow, that it was being said that I bought Long-meadow so that I might be near you. And furthermore, the story was that you were quite taken with me. I must say that I had no idea when I handed you your hat that I had made such a conquest."

"Don't be absurd," said Georgiana indignantly. "This is Kitty's fault. I shall box her ears! She must have told Charlotte and Charlotte told her mother who told everyone in the entire village! Oh, what will I do now? What will Papa say? What must you think of me?"

The earl, who was thinking she was an adorable-looking featherhead, raised his eyebrows. "I should be obliged if you would explain what this is about."

"Oh, I suppose I must tell you, Lord Dunraven. You will be very vexed with me, but it is only right that I confess the matter to you."

"Yes?" said the earl, eagerly awaiting the confession.

She nodded. "First I must tell you that I am very much in love with someone."

"But not me?" said his lordship.

"Oh, no!" cried Georgiana. "I am in love with Lord Thomas Jeffreys."

"I see," said the earl, although, in truth, he did not see at all.

"I love Thomas and he is in love with me. He has asked me to marry him, but my father will not allow it. He dislikes Thomas. Oh, I know Thomas has no fortune, but what does

that signify when I shall have a very large marriage settle-
ment? Papa is very rich, you see. But my father is quite unreasonable where Thomas is concerned."

"I fail to see how my name is connected to this tragic story,"
said the earl.

"It is because I told my father that I had met another
gentleman. That I had met you and you had made me forget
Thomas."

"Indeed?" said his lordship, regarding her with an amused
look.

"Yes," said Georgiana. "I shouldn't have invented such a
story. You see, I thought that if I told Papa that I was interested in . . . in another gentleman, he might view Thomas in a
more favorable light."

The earl, who was a very clever man, paused for a moment
to mull over this curious conversation. It did not take long for
a flash of enlightenment to come to him. "I think I see. Because my reputation is . . . less than sterling, you thought that
your father would much prefer this Thomas over me. So you
knew who I was when we met in the park?"

Georgiana shook her head. "No, I didn't, but then Mrs.
Kendall told me about you."

"And what she said was less than flattering, I presume."

Georgiana paused awkwardly. "Perhaps a little," she said finally. This caused the earl to burst into laughter. "I hope I did
not offend you, Lord Dunraven."

"Offend me? Why, not in the least," said Dunraven, laughing again.

Mrs. Hastings was roused by the noise. She looked about in
a disoriented way. "Oh, was there a joke?" she said.

"Not really," said the earl, taking on a more serious expression. "Cribbage can be an amusing card game."

"Indeed, my lord?" said Mrs. Hastings. "I shall have to learn
to play. Perhaps Miss Morley will teach me."

"Oh, I should be happy to do so, Mrs. Hastings," said Georgiana, who felt very uncomfortable now that she had told Dunraven the truth. What must he think of her, she wondered. "But
we'll have to play another time, Mrs. Hastings. I am very tired.
I should like to retire."

"Yes," said the housekeeper. "I am beginning to grow a bit

weary myself. If his lordship will excuse us, I shall escort Miss Morley to her room."

"I shall do so reluctantly," said the earl, rising from his chair at the card table as Georgiana and the older woman took their leave.

Taking up a candle, the housekeeper led Georgiana up the great staircase. "I do hope you'll be comfortable. Unfortunately, many of the rooms aren't liveable on such a night as this. The roof, you know." Arriving at the top of the staircase, Mrs. Hastings continued on down the corridor until they arrived at the door of the room that had been prepared for Georgiana. "You'll find this room nice and dry, miss," she said, opening the door. "I do hope you will sleep well."

"I know I shall. Thank you so much, Mrs. Hastings, and good night."

When the housekeeper had gone, Georgiana looked around the room that had been prepared for her. Lit only by one candle and a dwindling fire, the room seemed dark and uninviting. The storm continued unabated and Georgiana could hear the rain pelting against the windows, which were cloaked with heavy draperies.

Then eager to get to bed, she undressed and changed into the cotton nightgown that had been laid out for her. A voluminous garment belonging to Mrs. Hastings, the nightgown was much too large for the diminutive Georgiana. Glancing into the mirror, Georgiana could perceive her reflection rather dimly. She could not help but laugh at the ludicrous picture she presented attired in the oversize garment.

Georgiana climbed into the high four-poster bed and lay there thinking. While the object of her nightly reflections was usually Thomas Jeffreys, that night it was Dunraven who occupied her thoughts. She pictured him sitting there at the card table, regarding her with those dark eyes of his. He undoubtedly thought her a complete ninny, she concluded. She wasn't quite sure what she thought of him.

Leaning over from the bed to blow out the candle, Georgiana stopped herself. Although tired, she felt wide awake and she doubted that she would be able to sleep. There was a book on the night table and she picked it up. Finding it to be a novel entitled *The Curse of Don Ernesto*, Georgiana eagerly began to read.

After the first chapter, she wasn't sure that it was a good idea to go on. The book was a gothic tale that featured a sinister castle, a mad villain, and a host of fiendish ghosts. It was, Georgiana realized, not the sort of book one should be reading in a strange bedchamber on a stormy night. Besides, the light was quite inadequate, and Aggie would have warned her that she would ruin her eyes.

Still, Georgiana found the story irresistible so she continued reading. Completely engrossed in the book, she shivered as Don Ernesto slowly ascended his marble staircase to the room that was always mysteriously locked. Taking the key from his waistcoat pocket, he put it into the lock. The heavy door creaked open slowly. . . .

At this point, Georgiana's reading was cut short by a loud crash of thunder that made her jump. Startled, she looked up from the book to see the draperies begin to billow wildly. There was a creaking sound and then a thump.

The candle flickered and nearly went out, causing Georgiana to gasp. Was someone at the window? Straining to see in the near darkness, she thought she saw something move beneath the drapes. Terrified, Georgiana screamed.

Dunraven, who had just retired to his bed in the room across the hall, heard the cry just as he was about to put out his candle. "What the devil!" he said, jumping up from the bed and hastily pulling on his dressing gown. He took up his candle while Macduff raced to the door, barking furiously. When Dunraven opened it, Macduff rushed out, arriving at Georgiana's door where he stood barking.

"Miss Morley!" said the earl, flinging open the door to her room. "What is wrong?"

By this time Georgiana had risen from her bed and was hurrying to the door. Tripping on a loose floorboard, she fell into his arms.

"You are trembling! What has happened?"

Georgiana, very much embarrassed, pulled away from him. "I believe someone has come in my room through the window!"

"I shall take a look."

"Oh, no! It could be dangerous!"

"Don't worry," said Dunraven in a calm voice, "I'm sure it is nothing. There are many odd noises in rooms like these." He smiled and cast an amused look down at the small terrier at his feet. "And I have nothing to fear with Macduff at my side. Come, my lad, let us see what is the matter. Now you stay here, Miss Morley."

"But shouldn't you call some of the servants, my lord?"

"I don't think that is necessary," returned his lordship, "Wait here, Miss Morley." He walked into the room. Macduff ran ahead to the window where he dashed about as if looking for an intruder. When none could be found, he returned to his master.

Dunraven went to the open window where the draperies were fluttering wildly. Rain poured into the room and the earl hurried to secure the window. "It was only the wind," he said, turning to her.

Georgiana stood in the doorway. "Are you certain?"

"I shall look everywhere," he said, holding his candle in front of him, and searching about the room. Cocking his head, Macduff regarded his master curiously as if wondering what he was doing.

Georgiana, her fear vanishing, felt exceedingly foolish. She was suddenly aware that she was standing there in an oversize nightdress while one of the most notorious gentlemen in the kingdom, in his dressing gown, looked about her room.

When he had finished, he joined her at the doorway. "You can be assured that there is no one here, Miss Morley," he said finally. "If there were, Macduff would have ferreted him out. It was only the wind pushing open the window. It is securely latched now."

"Oh, I feel like such a goose," said Georgiana, looking up at him with her blue eyes. "You must think me the greatest ninnyhammer."

Dunraven stared down at her, noting her ridiculously large nightgown and her blond curls that were in wild disarray. The garment's oversize neckline, now slightly askew, afforded his lordship an enticing display of Georgiana's lovely breasts. "I don't think so at all," he said.

Georgiana continued to gaze up at Dunraven, her lips slightly parted and a questioning look upon her face. Dunraven was suddenly aware of an overpowering urge to take her into his arms. Unable to resist, he drew her to him and covered her lips with his own. Kissing her passionately, he nearly crushed her against him.

While Georgiana was vaguely aware that she should protest, she had no desire to free herself. His lips upon hers had awakened sensations within her that she had never felt before. She returned the earl's kisses hesitantly at first and then with surprising fervor.

Then suddenly Georgiana came to her senses. What was she doing? she thought, pushing him away. "You forget yourself, my lord!" she cried indignantly.

"Yes, but I don't think I was the only one to do so," said the earl.

Georgiana's cheeks burned with mortification. Had she really allowed him to kiss her like that? And to make it even worse was the fact that she was in love with Thomas. What would he think if he had seen her in Dunraven's arms. "How dare you?" she said.

A slight smile appeared on his face. "Forgive me," he said.

She regarded him in confusion. "Do go, I pray you."

"Shall I call Mrs. Hastings?"

"No, I am fine. Good night, my lord."

The earl nodded and retreated, calling to Macduff to follow him. When they were gone, Georgiana closed the door and bolted it. She then returned to her bed. Georgiana lay there listening to the rain and wind and thinking of the passionate kiss she had shared with Dunraven. What sort of girl was she, she asked herself, to allow a notorious rake to kiss her in such a manner. She pondered this troubling matter for a long time before finally falling into a fitful sleep.

Chapter 9

When Dunraven awakened in the morning, he rose from his bed and went to the window. The rain had finally stopped and the park surrounding Longmeadow looked green and inviting. The early morning sky was blue and there was the promise of fine weather.

Turning away from the window, the earl looked down at Macduff, who was regarding him with a solemn expression. "So you think I acted like a blackguard kissing Miss Morley, do you, old lad?" The dog cocked his head and studied his lordship with the intense look canines often fix upon their masters.

"Well, perhaps I did," continued Dunraven, "but one is only human. By God, what could I do with the way she was standing there?" Macduff regarded him solemnly, and the earl smiled. "She is a lovely creature, isn't she, Macduff? There is something about her." He paused. Yes, he had felt something the first time he saw her in the park. And this initial attraction was intensified by last night's adventure.

When he had dressed, Dunraven went downstairs and entered the morning room. In a short time Mrs. Hastings appeared at the door, looking exceedingly cheerful. "Good morning, my lord. I trust you slept well."

"Tolerably well," he replied, although, in truth, he had not slept very much at all.

"I am so glad, my lord," replied the housekeeper. "The rain is over and it looks as if it will be a lovely day. What a blessed relief after such a terrible storm. I do hope Miss Morley slept well enough. I rather worried with the rain and the wind and thunder to keep her awake."

"Miss Morley has not yet risen, Mrs. Hastings?"

"No, but I have sent Molly to see to her. I'm sure she will

be down soon. Would you wish to have breakfast now, my lord, or do you prefer to wait for Miss Morley?"

"Oh, I shall wait for my guest. And you must join us as well, Mrs. Hastings."

"I should be very honored," returned the elderly woman, clearly delighted. She curtsied and departed, leaving the earl to peruse the newspaper.

It was nearly an hour before the butler appeared in the morning room to inform his lordship that Miss Morley and Mrs. Hastings awaited him in the dining room. Putting down the paper, Dunraven rose and proceeded to join them.

He found Georgiana seated at the table. Attired in the muslin dress she had worn yesterday, she looked quite lovely. Thanks to the attentions of one of the maids, her hair was now carefully coifed and she appeared the soul of decorum. He could not help but think of her as she looked the night before in her disheveled nightdress, with her hair falling down around her shoulders. As if sensing his thoughts, Georgiana blushed.

"Good morning, Miss Morley," he said.

"Good morning, my lord," she replied, careful to avoid looking directly at him. Mrs. Hastings, who had risen at the entrance of her noble employer, smiled brightly. "Breakfast is ready on the sideboard, my lord. Miss Morley, do have some food."

Georgiana rose from her chair and went to the sideboard, where she stood rather awkwardly beside the earl, who was examining the contents of one of the silver chafing dishes.

"Miss Morley said she slept very well, Lord Dunraven," said Mrs. Hastings. "I was so happy to hear it."

"I am very happy as well, Miss Morley," said his lordship, glancing down at Georgiana.

Again avoiding his gaze, Georgiana spooned some food onto her plate, and then she returned to her seat. The earl and Mrs. Hastings joined her.

As she sat there trying to eat her breakfast, Georgiana was finding it exceedingly uncomfortable sitting so near to Dunraven. She was very glad that Mrs. Hastings was there beside her. The housekeeper chattered on about a number of subjects while Georgiana silently tried to concentrate on her breakfast.

After a time, one of the footman approached Mrs. Hastings. Leaning down, he whispered something into her ear. "Oh dear," said the housekeeper. "We have a small problem in the kitchen, my lord. If you will excuse me, I shall see to it. I'll not be gone long." Rising from her chair, she hastened out of the dining room.

Although Georgiana was not at all happy to find herself alone with Dunraven, she tried hard to maintain her composure.

"I imagine you would prefer we said nothing more about last night, Miss Morley," said the earl.

"I should very much prefer that, my lord," returned Georgiana, looking down at her plate.

"I must apologize for my behavior."

"It is best forgotten, Lord Dunraven," she replied, finally looking at him. "I should appreciate it if you would forget about it."

"I fear you ask a good deal of me, Miss Morley. But I shall do my best to oblige you. After all, I mustn't forget that you do fancy yourself in love with that fellow Thomas Jeffreys."

"I do not *fancy* I am in love with him," said Georgiana, rather offended. "I am most certainly in love with him."

"Are you?" said Dunraven with a smile. "From the way you kissed me, I suspect you might have mistaken me for him last night."

"The way *I* kissed you?" said Georgiana. "Indeed, my lord, it is *you* who kissed me!"

Dunraven nodded. "Yes, that is most certainly true. Well, I must say that Jeffreys is a dashed lucky man."

Georgiana's cheeks reddened. She was spared the necessity of a reply by the appearance of another footman. "Sir Arthur Morley is here, my lord. He is in the morning room."

"My father here!" cried Georgiana, alarmed at the prospect.

The earl rose as well. Tossing his napkin on the table, he smiled again. "I shall be very glad to meet your father, Miss Morley." He addressed the footman. "Tell Sir Arthur we will be there directly." The servant nodded and retreated.

"But he won't be at all happy to meet you, my lord," said Georgiana.

"Yes, I know that he disapproves of your infatuation for me." The earl smiled and Georgiana realized that he was enjoying himself at her expense.

"I must warn you, Lord Dunraven, that my father is a hot-tempered man."

"That may be," said the earl, smiling again, "but I cannot keep him cooling his heels. I don't doubt he is very eager to see you."

Filled with trepidation, Georgiana rose from the chair. Somewhat reluctantly, she allowed the earl to escort her to the morning room where they found the baronet standing there alone looking rather impatient. "Georgiana," he said, frowning at her.

"Oh, Papa!" she cried, hurrying over to him and throwing her arms about him. "I am so glad to see you."

Sir Arthur, who despite his anger at her being there, was relieved to see his wayward offspring. He hugged her in return. However, his expression was rather stern when he extricated himself from her embrace. "Georgiana, we were nearly sick with worry. I am very vexed with you for going off as you did."

"I am so sorry, Papa," said Georgiana looking very contrite.

The earl, who had followed her into the morning room, stood regarding them with interest. Looking over at him, the baronet frowned.

"Oh, Papa, I must introduce Lord Dunraven to you. My lord, may I present my father, Sir Arthur Morley?"

"Your servant, sir," said his lordship, nodding at Sir Arthur.

"Dunraven," said the baronet, bowing slightly, and then regarding the earl with a distinctly unfriendly look.

"Will you join us for breakfast, Sir Arthur?"

"I have eaten, sir," returned the baronet coolly.

"Then do have a seat," said Dunraven, motioning to an armchair.

"No, thank you," said Georgiana's father. "We cannot stay. But, before we go, I have a few words to say to you, sir."

Georgiana did not like the sound of this. Taking her father's arm, she regarded the baronet in some alarm. "Come, Papa, I do think we should be going."

"Not before I say a few words to this . . . gentleman. I must tell you, Dunraven, that I know very well what you are about."

"Indeed?" said the earl, raising his dark eyebrows slightly.

"We know about your meeting Georgiana in town."

"Papa!" said Georgiana, pressing his arm. "Do let us take our leave of Lord Dunraven."

"I shall be happy to do so as soon as I say what I must say." He frowned at the younger man. "When Georgiana told us that you had paid addresses to her, I must say that I scarcely believed it. I thought that even a man like you would not dare speak to a respectable young lady without her parents' knowledge. But when I heard that you had taken Longmeadow, it became clear that what Georgiana had told us was true. You had designs upon her.

"I do not doubt that her coming here last night is your doing," continued Sir Arthur. "Your reputation is well known, sir, and it is despicable that you would seek to take advantage of an innocent child. I must make it perfectly clear, Dunraven, that I will not tolerate your further attentions to my daughter. She is an honorable young lady of good family, sir." Sir Arthur's face had grown very red while giving this speech and Georgiana feared he might have a fit of apoplexy.

"My dear Sir Arthur," said the earl, appearing not in the least disconcerted by the baronet's impassioned words. "I fear you are under some unfortunate misapprehension." Georgiana looked nervously at Dunraven as he continued. "I have only the greatest respect for Miss Morley. If you suspect I plotted to have her come here last night, you are mistaken. I was, however, so very pleased to see her.

"You reproach me for speaking with her in London, sir, but we met quite by accident. I couldn't help exchanging a few words with her. And am I to be faulted if Miss Morley's beauty simply blinded me? And then her wit and charm completely devastated me. I quite lost my heart."

At these words Georgiana's eyes opened wide in surprise. The earl, who was now enjoying himself very much, thumped his hand against his chest. "Yes, I lost my heart. I know you think me a dissolute fellow, Sir Arthur and, indeed, perhaps my reputation is deserved. But sometimes a man meets a sweet, innocent lady and he finds he can change. I know I should have come to you at once, but considering how I am regarded in society, I suspected you would not consider me as a suitor for your daughter. And until now . . ." He directed a meaningful look at Georgiana. "Until now I hadn't been sure that Miss Morley felt as I do.

"You believe my intentions toward Miss Morley are dishonorable, sir, but you are mistaken. You see, Sir Arthur, I wish to marry your daughter."

Both Sir Arthur and Georgiana regarded his lordship in considerable astonishment. "You wish to marry Georgiana?" said the baronet. "Why, you hardly know her."

"That may be true, but I assure you I am in earnest."

"This is altogether too sudden," said Sir Arthur.

Georgiana looked up into Dunraven's face. She could tell he found the entire business an excellent joke. Her astonishment quickly turning into irritation, she frowned at him. Dunraven only smiled. "I know I am not considered respectable and I do not deny that in the past I have committed follies. But meeting Miss Morley has quite reformed me. Do think on the matter, Sir Arthur. I am a wealthy man and can well support her. And we would spend much time at Longmeadow, so she would be near you. No, there is no need for you to answer. Give it some thought."

The baronet was quite unsure how to respond. "I must say you have surprised me, sir," he said. "I shall think on the matter, but you must not take this to mean that I will approve of such a match."

"All I ask is that you do not dismiss my offer out of hand."

"Indeed, I shan't do so," said the baronet, rather taken aback by the whole thing. "But we must take our leave, Dunraven. Georgiana's mother and sister are very worried about her. Good day to you."

Sir Arthur then led his daughter from the room. As she walked by the earl, she cast a look of such confusion at him that he nearly burst into laughter.

When they had gone, Dunraven returned to the dining room, where he found Mrs. Hastings had just returned herself. "But where is Miss Morley, my lord?"

"I fear her father has come for her. She has taken her leave."

"Oh, dear, I did not even say good-bye to her."

"That is a pity," said his lordship, sitting down at the table. "Do sit down, Mrs. Hastings. You must finish your breakfast."

"That is so kind of you, my lord," said the housekeeper, taking her seat. "It was so delightful having Miss Morley here," said Mrs. Hastings. "I am so fond of her."

"I am glad to hear it," said his lordship, taking up a piece of toast and buttering it liberally. "After all, she may soon be mistress of Longmeadow." When the housekeeper regarded him in some confusion, he smiled. "I have just asked Sir Arthur for his daughter's hand."

The earl had the great satisfaction of completely dumbfounding Mrs. Hastings. So astonished was she that it was some moments before the usually loquacious housekeeper could express her great joy at such unexpected news.

As the carriage made its way to Highcroft, Georgiana thought about Dunraven. It was clear that the earl thought the situation very amusing. To propose marriage to her! Whatever would he do if she accepted him?

"I suppose you will plead for me to allow you to marry him," said Sir Arthur.

Georgiana looked over at her father, who was seated next to her on the leather carriage seat. Up to now, the baronet had seemed lost in his own thoughts. Georgiana had been glad that he hadn't asked her any questions. "I will understand if you must refuse, Papa," said Georgiana.

"Will you?" said the baronet, rather surprised at the meekness of her reply.

"Indeed, you know what is best."

"Do I? Well, it is the first time you've admitted it, my dear. Wait until your mother hears of this. Dunraven offering for you!"

"I know it must have been a shock."

"Yes, it was that. And, of course, he is quite unsuitable. There is no use to argue with me on that account. He has a reputation as a rakehell and I do not wish to see my daughter married to a man who will only make her miserable." Sir Arthur stroked his chin thoughtfully. "Unless, of course, he has truly mended his ways. While I don't consider that likely, perhaps it is not impossible."

While Georgiana doubted that Dunraven had changed his ways in the least, she could hardly say as much. Turning her head to look out at the passing scenery, she frowned and considered that, since her misguided walk to Longmeadow, everything had become a frightful muddle.

Chapter 10

As expected, when Georgiana and her father arrived at Highcroft, Lady Morley reacted with shock and amazement to learn that her daughter had received a proposal of marriage from Dunraven. While she stated very firmly upon hearing of it that she was very much opposed to the idea, later reflection and discussion with her husband made her reconsider.

When the two of them discussed the situation in her ladyship's sitting room before retiring to bed, Sir Arthur suggested the possibility that the earl might have reformed. The baronet conceded that Dunraven was hardly an ideal suitor. Yet, upon further consideration, Sir Arthur thought they should think on the matter.

After all, pointed out the baronet, Dunraven was a nobleman of high rank. While Lady Morley quickly countered that his rank wasn't as high as Lord Belrose's, she had to admit that an earl was a notable personage indeed.

The baronet also told his wife that Dunraven was a handsome fellow, who looked respectable enough. And, suggested Sir Arthur, although his lordship might be unacceptable at court, one could never know what might happen in the future.

Wealthy lords had been known to redeem themselves from time to time. Perhaps if he were married to a respectable girl like Georgiana, suggested Sir Arthur, Dunraven's past indiscretions might be forgotten.

And, as Sir Arthur noted to his wife, the earl appeared to be a man of fortune. He had purchased Longmeadow outright and everyone in the village commented on the splendor of his horses and carriage. Despite Dunraven's obvious failings, concluded the baronet, it was good to know that he was not a fortune hunter like Lord Thomas Jeffreys.

After prolonged discussion, Lady Morley was leaning in the direction of changing her mind. Of course, she would have to meet the earl and see for herself what sort of man he was.

Unaware that her parents were actually giving serious consideration to the idea of her becoming Dunraven's bride, Georgiana sat in her bedchamber attired in her dressing gown. She thoughtfully studied her reflection in her dressing table mirror while Agnes stood behind her brushing her hair. "I am glad you came to no harm at Longmeadow, miss," said the maid. "I was worried, but I knew Mrs. Hastings was there to see to you."

"Yes, she is a dear woman and very kind."

Finishing her work, Agnes put down the hairbrush. "There you are, miss. Will you be needing anything else?"

"No, Aggie, do go to bed."

The maid made a slight curtsy and left the room, leaving her young mistress to her reflections. As she got up from the dressing table, she frowned. Things had become very confusing, she decided. She tried to think of Thomas, but he seemed to fade into the background with Dunraven coming to fore.

It was hard to stop thinking about last night. If she were in love with Thomas, she asked herself, why did she react so to Dunraven's kiss? Slipping off her dressing gown and then climbing into bed, Georgiana blew out the candle on her night table and stared into the darkness. It was all very disturbing, she thought.

After a short time, the door opened and the light from a candle appeared. "Georgiana!"

"Kitty."

"We really didn't have a chance to talk," said Georgiana's younger sister, coming toward her. Placing the candle on the table, she sat down on the bed. "Mama and Papa were always about. Indeed, we hadn't a moment alone. I was simply dying to find out what happened at Longmeadow. Now you must tell me everything!"

"What a goose you are, Kitty. There is nothing more to tell."

"I should think there is," said Kitty. "You go off yesterday having only met Lord Dunraven once before in your entire life and you return this morning with a proposal of marriage. It seems to me as if something must have happened."

Fearing that she was blushing, Georgiana was glad that the light in the room was dim. "Truly, it is not so exciting."

"Not exciting. It must have been exciting! Did he fall in love with you the moment he met you?"

"Indeed not! What a gudgeon you are, Kit. He didn't fall in love with me at all."

"But Papa said he did."

"That is because he told Papa that. He only did it to vex me. You see I had to explain to him all about my scheme." She stopped. "Kitty Morley, it is all your fault. I shan't soon forgive you."

"Forgive me?" cried Kitty.

"Yes, you told Charlotte, didn't you? You told her that Dunraven had taken Longmeadow because of me."

"Oh, I couldn't help it, Georgie. It was such a wonderful, romantic story. And she swore she wouldn't tell a soul."

"Well, she told someone. I don't doubt she told everyone. Dunraven had heard of it."

"Oh, no!" cried Kitty.

"You can imagine my mortification when he told me a friend had told him that I was purportedly quite taken with him."

"Oh, I am furious with Charlotte," said Kitty. "Oh, I am sorry."

"Well, it is done now," said Georgiana. "But you must know that Charlotte is such a tattlemonger."

"I am sorry, Georgie," cried her younger sister.

"Oh, I forgive you, you silly birdwitted creature."

"Oh, I am glad," said Kitty, very much relieved. "But it must have been dreadful. Lord Dunraven heard that you were taken with him."

"Yes, so what could I do but tell him the truth? I explained how I had said that he was in love with me so that Papa and Mama might think Thomas looked good by comparison."

"Oh, Georgie, you didn't tell him that!"

"I couldn't help it," said Georgiana.

"Was he very angry?"

"I daresay he thought it rather funny," said Georgiana.

"But if he doesn't love you, why does he wish to marry you?"

"My dear lackwit, he doesn't really wish to marry me. He knows that my parents would never hear of it."

"And you don't think that they will approve?"

"I most certainly hope not."

"Well, I find this all very disappointing," said Kitty. "I had thought it was fate that brought Lord Dunraven to Longmeadow. It was so romantic. And to think you stayed there all night in that terrible storm! Weren't you afraid?"

"Not very afraid," replied Georgiana.

"I should have been quite terrified," said Kitty. She paused before continuing. "Did he kiss you?"

"What a question!" said Georgiana.

"But did he?"

"I suppose he did kiss me," said Georgiana.

"Oh, I knew it!" cried Kitty. "And he is handsome. Oh, perhaps not quite as handsome as Lord Thomas, but very handsome nonetheless. Do you think he will call tomorrow?"

"I don't know," said Georgiana. "I doubt it. He might have thought it amusing this morning, but by tomorrow I daresay he will have forgotten all about it."

"What nonsense," said Kitty. "I believe you are wrong. I fancy the earl has truly fallen in love with you. Indeed, maybe he fell in love with you in the park. Maybe that *is* why he took Longmeadow."

"Don't be a simpleton. He didn't know who I was in the park."

"Oh, that is true," said Kitty rather disappointed. "But have you fallen in love with him?"

"Do you think I am such a fickle creature as that? You know I am in love with Thomas," said Georgiana as forcefully as she could.

"Yes, I had almost forgotten Thomas," said Kitty. "He would be so heartbroken if you married Lord Dunraven. But if you are truly in love with Thomas, you should marry him. He is so dashing, after all. Of course, he is not an earl. If you married Lord Dunraven, you would be a countess."

"Really, Kitty, if I cared of such things I should marry Lord Belrose. He is a marquess."

"That is true," said Kitty, "but then he is not in the least romantic. Lord Dunraven is so very romantic, isn't he?"

"I don't know," said Georgiana, who was growing impatient with her sister's interrogation. "I am very tired, Kit. It is time for you to go to bed."

"Oh, very well," said Kitty, rising from the bed with some reluctance. "But I do think you might tell me more tomorrow."

The following day Dunraven looked up from his newspaper as the butler entered the morning room. "My lord, there is someone to see you. It is Mr. Buckthorne."

Since he had not expected Buckthorne to return so soon, he was rather surprised. "Well, do show him in, Canfield."

The butler nodded gravely and then departed. A short time later he returned with the visitor. Buckthorne's ruddy face glowed with pleasure at seeing his friend. "Dunraven, my dear fellow, and Macduff." The terrier, who had been sitting at the earl's feet, hurried over to see his master's friend, his tail wagging excitedly. Buckthorne leaned down to scratch him behind his ears. "What a good lad you are," he said.

"Buck, what on earth are you doing here? It is scarcely eleven o'clock. Rather early for you, isn't it?"

"Oh, I rise early in the country," said Buckthorne, scooping Macduff into his arms. "Indeed, I was so eager to return to Longmeadow that I was away at the crack of dawn. You will not believe my good fortune. Do come out and see."

"Good God, I hope you aren't going to tell me you have brought those hounds here."

"Of course, I've brought them here. What else am I to do with them? Macduff is eager to see them, aren't you, my boy?"

"Buck, I warned you that I wanted nothing to do with these hounds of yours."

"You will change your mind when you see them. There are sons of Golden Trumpet among them."

"I don't care a fig whose sons they are," said the earl.

"Come and see them. It's all I ask."

"Oh, very well," said the earl, trying to sound irked. Actually, he was very much amused by his friend. He followed Buckthorne from the room. When they arrived outside, they found a pack of approximately thirty foxhounds milling about under the care of a solemn-faced man on horseback.

Macduff, seeing the horde of canine interlopers, squirmed in Buckthorne's arms and barked ferociously. The foxhounds ignored him. "Calm yourself, Macduff," said Buckthorne. "You must behave like a gentleman."

"Yes, quiet, Macduff," said the earl, looking over the hounds. "There are a good many of them, Buck."

"Oh, yes, aren't they lovely? And that is Jenkins, your new kennel master."

"*My* new kennel master?" said Dunraven.

"M'lord," said the man on horseback, doffing his cap.

"Jenkins is an excellent man. You are very lucky to have him."

"*I* am lucky? I thought these were your hounds, Buck."

"And they are, but I fear you'll have to pay Jenkins's wages. You know I'm a bit short of blunt lately." Buckthorne smiled happily. "What marvelous hunts we'll have." He sighed. "If only it were hunting season."

Dunraven shook his head. "I don't see why I put up with you, Buck."

"Because you are so dashed fond of me," replied Buckthorne with a broad grin. He looked at Jenkins. "Do take the hounds away, Jenkins."

"Aye, sir," said Jenkins, whistling to the dogs as he rode off.

"And now do you think I might have something to eat, Dunraven? I am so frightfully hungry."

"I should toss you and your infernal hounds from my door," said the earl.

"Of course you should, my dear fellow. You have the patience of a saint to put up with me. Now what about a bit of breakfast?"

A slight smile came to Dunraven's face. "Oh, very well, but you are a damned rogue."

"I do not deny it," said Buckthorne, putting Macduff down.

Returning inside, the earl ordered some food for his friend. As they waited in the morning room, Buckthorne talked enthusiastically about the hounds.

"Good God, must you babble on about those accurst dogs? I don't want to hear another word about them and Macduff most certainly detests the subject."

"Oh, as you wish," said Buckthorne. "I shan't say any more in deference to Macduff." He looked down at the little dog. "Don't worry, my lad, you won't mind them in the least once you've grown accustomed to them." Macduff only cocked his head in reply.

A servant appeared to announce that the food was ready and the two friends went off to the dining room, where Buckthorne partook of a hearty breakfast. Dunraven sat drinking a cup of coffee.

"You haven't even told me what you have been doing in my absence," said Buckthorne, taking up a forkful of kippers.

"That is because you have not allowed me to ge a word in," returned his lordship.

"Well, do tell me how you are enjoying Longmeadow. I can see it is making a new man of you. It is the country air, of course. How did you spend these two days since I've been gone? Exploring your new estate, I'll be bound."

The earl nodded. "That and proposing marriage to a girl I met," said his lordship, nonchalantly sipping his coffee.

"What!" cried Buckthorne, nearly choking on his food.

Dunraven laughed. "Yes, I proposed marriage to Miss Georgiana Morley."

Buckthorne stared wide-eyed. "I believe you are serious!"

"Yes, I am quite serious. I happened upon Miss Morley in a thunderstorm. And can you imagine, Buck? I had met her in town shortly before coming here. I didn't know her name, but there she was again appearing on my doorstep. It must have been destined by the gods."

"What the deuce!" cried Buckthorne. "You are gammoning me, Dunraven. This is some sort of joke."

"I am quite serious. Miss Morley was forced to stay at Longmeadow for the night since the bridge was impassable and there was no way for her to return home. We had a most memorable evening, I must say. And in the morning, I made her an offer of marriage."

"I daresay it must have been a memorable night," said Buckthorne. "But you propose marriage? Good God!" He continued to regard the earl in considerable astonishment. "Georgiana Morley? Isn't that the girl who has been saying you are in love with her? And you said you had never met her before."

"I didn't realize who she was. I met her in the park shortly before coming here. But she was saying I was in love with her only because she wanted her father to feel more kindly toward a certain Lord Thomas Jeffreys, whom she fancies herself to be in love with. She assumed Jeffreys would look far better in her father's eyes when compared to a dissolute rake such as myself."

"The devil you say!" said Buckthorne. "This Miss Morley sounds like a troublesome minx."

"I daresay you are right, but I must warn you not to speak so of the future Lady Dunraven."

"The future Lady Dunraven!" cried Buckthorne. "You cannot be serious in thinking of marrying her. Why, you only just met the girl." He seemed to mull over the matter for a moment. "Oh, I see, you think you ought to marry her. But it is a high price to pay for one night's amusement."

"You are very much mistaken, Buck. I have kissed Miss Morley, but that is all."

"Then for the life of me, I can't understand you. My dear fellow, marriage is not to be taken lightly. I am in a position to know."

"I am not taking it lightly," said Dunraven.

"And you are truly serious about marrying this Miss Morley?"

The earl nodded gravely. While he had at first thought it very amusing to shock Georgiana with his offer of marriage, the more he thought about wedding her, the more he liked the idea. She was a very desirable young woman and the idea of finding her in his bed each night seemed quite appealing.

Why shouldn't he marry? Dunraven had asked himself. Indeed, he could become a respectable family man and astonish everyone in society. Of late, he had been so very bored with the sort of life he was living. Yes, marriage would make an interesting change.

"I do believe you have lost your senses, Dunraven," said Buckthorne, now sufficiently recovered from the shock of his friend's announcement to resume eating his breakfast. "What do you know about this girl anyway?"

"Almost nothing. But what does that signify?"

"It signifies a great deal," said Buckthorne. "Indeed, I only wish I had known a good many more things about Mrs. Buckthorne before I married her. I daresay, I would probably still be a bachelor to this day. But you are not talking like yourself. I do hope Longmeadow is not affecting your wits, old man."

"If it is, you have only yourself to blame. You are the one who thought it so wonderful for me to buy this estate."

"I know," said Buckthorne with a worried expression. "I shan't forgive myself if you are saddled with some provincial harpy of a wife."

The earl grinned. "Well, you must meet Miss Morley, Buck. We will call at Highcroft this very afternoon."

"I shall look forward to it," said Buckthorne uncertainly. Dunraven smiled again and took another drink of his coffee.

Chapter 11

While Dunraven discussed his surprising proposal of marriage with his friend, his prospective bride was standing in the stables admiring Demon Dancer. "He is a rare one, isn't he, Shaw?" said Georgiana.

The head groom nodded. "Right you are, miss. I've never seen a finer animal in all my life."

"I do wish my father would allow me to ride him," said Georgiana, stroking the horse's gleaming black neck.

"Well, he's a bit too much horse for a lady, miss," said Shaw. "Not that he'd been too much for you, miss, but the master would not want to take a chance of your getting hurt."

"It is ridiculous," said Georgiana. "I can ride as well as any man."

"No one can deny that, miss," said Shaw. "But Sir Arthur was most firm in saying you weren't to be allowed to ride him."

"I know," said Georgiana, "and I am quite vexed with him."

At that moment Kitty walked into the stables. "There you are, Georgie. I might have known you'd be here. Good day, Shaw."

"Good day, Miss Kitty," said Shaw, tipping his cap to her.

"Georgie, Mama has said we may go to the village. She has said that I may go to the bookstore. Do say you will go."

"Oh, I should like to go," said Georgiana, happy for a diversion.

"Good," replied Kitty. She turned to the head groom. "Her ladyship has given permission for Ronald to drive us in the carriage, Shaw. Will you see that it is brought round at once?"

"Very good, miss," said the head groom, tipping his cap once again before going about his duties.

The two sisters left the stables and returned to the house,

where Georgiana changed into a stylish walking dress and matching pelisse of rose-colored silk. When she came downstairs, she found her mother in the drawing room. "Are you not going to the village, Mama?" she asked.

"Oh, no, my dear. I have too may letters to write. But do not tarry too long. I believe Cousin Elizabeth may call this afternoon."

"We won't stay long, Mama," said Georgiana, retying the ribbons of her bonnet.

"Georgie," said Kitty, coming into the room, "the carriage is ready. Do hurry."

The girls took their leave of Lady Morley and left the house. A footman assisted them into the carriage and they were soon off.

It was a short ride to the village and they soon arrived there. The carriage pulled up in front of the bookstore where it deposited the young ladies.

While both sisters loved books, Kitty was the greatest reader. She could scarcely wait to enter the shop. The bookseller, a usually dour individual named Hodges, brightened at the sight of the young ladies. "Miss Morley and Miss Kitty," he said. "I am so happy to see you. I do hope you enjoyed your stay in London."

"Good day, Mr. Hodges," said Kitty. "Oh, yes, London was quite splendid. But I am very glad to be back in the country. I do hope you have some exciting new books in."

"Oh, yes, there are a good many." He picked up one and handed it to her. "A very promising new author, I must say."

Kitty opened the book to the title page. "*Sense and Sensibility?* It isn't a very exciting title, Mr. Hodges."

"I believe you will like it."

Kitty regarded the book a bit skeptically. "Well, I do trust your judgment, Mr. Hodges," she said finally. "I shall take it. Perhaps you might recommend another as well. There wouldn't be a novel about pirates, would there?"

The bookseller suppressed a smile. "I shall see if I can find one."

While Hodges was engaged with Kitty, Georgiana studied the books, picking one up and then another. Finding a volume of poetry, she opened it with interest.

There was a small bell hung on the door to the bookshop,

which jingled when someone entered. At the sound of this bell, Georgiana looked up from her book.

Recognizing the new customer as Lord Thomas Jeffreys, Georgiana nearly dropped her book. "Lord Thomas!" she cried.

"Miss Morley." Taking his tall beaver hat from his head, Thomas approached her, a broad smile on his handsome countenance. He was resplendent in his coat of wine-colored superfine with his snowy white neckcloth and gleaming Hessian boots. While he would have attracted notice even in London, here in provincial Richton, he appeared like a peacock among drab gray geese. He took her hand and bowed solemnly. "May I say, Miss Morley, that you look even more beautiful than when I last saw you?"

"Oh, Thomas," said Georgiana, speaking in a low voice, "I did not know you would be in Richton."

"And are you happy to see me?" he said, his voice almost a whisper.

"Yes, of course."

"And I am so happy to see you, my dear Georgiana," he said. "I am staying with my uncle at Pelham Manor. Of course, since your father and my uncle detest one another, I daresay it will hardly be possible for us to call upon one another while I'm here. But even so, there will be opportunities for us to meet. Have you spoken of me to your father?"

"No, I have not. I fear he hasn't changed his opinion of you, Thomas." She looked down for a moment. "There is something I must tell you. I have received another proposal of marriage."

"What?" cried Thomas. "Not from Belrose?"

Georgiana shook her head. "You will think this very odd and I do think it is not to be taken seriously, but the Earl of Dunraven has made an offer for me."

"Good God! The Earl of Dunraven!" cried Thomas in a voice so loud that both Kitty and Hodges turned to look at him.

"You know that by the oddest coincidence he had taken Longmeadow. Well, he asked for my hand. I don't believe he means it."

"This is incredible," said Thomas, stunned at the news. "I pray you aren't going to tell me you have accepted him."

"Oh, no, indeed not."

"This is very queer indeed," said Thomas. "I cannot imagine that your father would allow you to marry one of the most notorious men in all of England."

"That is what is so very strange. I believe Papa is warming to the idea."

"What!" cried Thomas.

Georgiana nodded. "One would never have believed it, but, for all his dreadful reputation, he is an earl."

"Good God," said Thomas. "Your father would marry you to a man like that?"

"Of course, Papa would never force me to marry against my will. But he wouldn't agree to your and my marriage either. It is a dreadful muddle, isn't it?"

"It is indeed," said Thomas, squeezing her hand. "But we will find a solution. I do love you so much, my darling. If need be, I shall spirit you away and marry you without your father's consent."

"Oh, Thomas," said Georgiana, "you know my father. He would cut me off without a penny."

"What do I care for that?" said Thomas, hoping he sounded convincing.

Georgiana regarded him admiringly. It was very clear that he loved her, she thought. And he cared nothing for her fortune. She was sure of that.

"Lord Thomas," said Kitty, coming over to them. She had allowed her sister as much time as possible to speak with her beloved suitor, but Kitty was growing increasingly uncomfortable with Hodges's interest in her sister and Thomas.

"Miss Kitty," replied Thomas, nodding to her.

"Lord Thomas is staying at Pelham Manor," said Georgiana.

"Indeed?" said Kitty.

"I daresay we will see him from time to time."

"I do hope so, Miss Morley," said Thomas.

"I have selected my books," said Kitty. "Mr. Hodges has some very good ones, Lord Thomas. I know he will be happy to assist you."

"Indeed," said Thomas indifferently. He did not read books and his entrance into the bookshop had resulted from the fortunate coincidence that he had been in Richton and had seen the young ladies go by in their carriage.

"Do you wish to buy something, Georgiana? We must be returning to Highcroft. Mama said we mustn't tarry."

"Yes, of course," said Georgiana. "No, I shan't be buying anything."

"Then I have my books," she said, holding two volumes up to her sister. "We really must go, Georgie."

"Very well. We must take our leave, Lord Thomas."

"I shall escort you to your carriage," he said, offering his arm to Georgiana.

After he had handed them up into the awaiting vehicle, he regarded Georgiana with a very soulful look. As they drove off, he stood there watching her like the devoted suitor he purported to be.

"Oh, Georgie," said Kitty as they turned the corner and Thomas vanished from sight, "Papa will be furious when he learns that Lord Thomas has come to stay at Pelham Manor. Did you know he was coming?"

"I did not," said Georgiana emphatically.

"I suppose you are very happy about it."

"Of course, I am," replied Georgiana.

"But, Georgie, I think it far better for you to marry Lord Dunraven."

"What a strange thing to say," said Georgiana. "Better for me to marry Lord Dunraven?"

"Why, yes. Fate has brought you together and you will reform him."

"I daresay he needs reforming," said Georgiana, "but I expect that is beyond my abilities."

"Nonsense," said Kitty. "Don't you remember the baron in *Shadowford Abbey*? How he was reformed by Lady Julia? His black heart was changed by her pure and unselfish love. Oh, I did love that book."

"I believe you take these books far too seriously," said Georgiana severely. "It is quite ridiculous to think that I would marry the earl. As I told you, he offered for me only because it amused him to do so."

"Well, I can scarcely wait to meet him. Then I shall tell Charlotte all about him."

"Kitty, I warn you. Cease gossiping about me with Charlotte or I shall be quite furious with you."

"But what am I to talk about if I can't talk about you?" said Kitty. Seeing her sister's expression, she hastened to add, "Oh, I shan't say anything to Charlotte. I swear by my honor."

"I shall hold you to that. And it would be best if you didn't tell Mama that we met Thomas in the shop."

"But we should tell her," said Kitty. "After all, it won't be a secret for long that he is at Pelham Manor. And Mr. Hodges will doubtless tell everyone that he saw you talking with him."

"Hodges is not a man to gossip."

"But Mrs. Hodges is. And he certainly will tell her. It will be all over Richton in a trice. I do advise you to mention it to Mama before she hears of it from someone else."

"Perhaps you are right," said Georgiana. "I confess you are not always such a goose, Kit."

This remark pleased the younger of the Morley sisters, who smiled brightly. As they continued on, the conversation shifted to the new books Kitty had just purchased. A short time later they arrived at Highcroft.

After devesting themselves of their pelisses and bonnets, Georgiana and Kitty joined their mother in the drawing room. "There you are, my dears," said Lady Morley. "Did you enjoy your ride to the village?"

"Oh, yes," said Kitty. "I bought two books. I can scarcely wait to start them. Mr. Hodges was so very glad to see us."

Georgiana sat down beside her mother on the sofa. "You will never guess whom we met in Richton. Lord Thomas Jeffreys."

"Oh, dear," said her ladyship. "You cannot mean he has come from town."

"Yes, he has, Mama," said Kitty. "He is staying at Pelham Manor."

"Your father will be very vexed to hear it."

"I do hope you are not upset at the news," said Georgiana.

"Well, I don't like it overmuch," said Lady Morley. "It seems that your suitors are very unacceptable, Georgiana. First there is Lord Thomas and then Lord Dunraven. At least Dunraven has a fortune. But how could one announce that her daughter was going to mary such an infamous person as Dunraven? No, I feel it is best for you forget them both. Why don't you consider some of those nice young men you met in town? What of Belrose for example?"

"Oh, Mama, you know that I do not wish to marry him."

"I know that, Georgiana, but Belrose is such a solid young man."

"Do you mean to say stout, Mama?" said Kitty with a mischievous grin.

"I do not mean stout," said Lady Morley. "Well, perhaps he is a trifle stout, but what does that signify? He would make Georgiana a good husband."

"I would much prefer that we discuss something else," said Georgiana. "Is it not time for luncheon?"

"Why, yes, it is," said her ladyship. "Your father will be here shortly. Let us say nothing about Lord Thomas. I don't wish your father to have indigestion."

Georgiana could only frown at this remark. She found it prudent to make no further comment about Thomas. When the baronet appeared a few minutes later, they went to the dining room to enjoy a delicious luncheon.

Chapter 12

In the afternoon Charlotte Fanshawe and her mother arrived at Highcroft. Sir Arthur, who hadn't been able to escape in time, received them with his wife and daughters. The visitors had scarcely sat down in the drawing room before Elizabeth reported the interesting news that Lord Thomas Jeffreys had come to stay at Pelham Manor.

"What?" said Sir Arthur, frowning at his wife's cousin.

"Yes, it is rather a surprise," said Elizabeth. "I know how you dislike the young man, Sir Arthur."

"And with good reason," said the baronet. "He is nothing but a fortune hunter. It was a dashed bad business him coming to town. I took considerable expense to give Georgiana a London Season so that she would meet other gentlemen and forget about Jeffreys. And what does the young popinjay do but come to London and contrive to put himself in her way at every opportunity. I am not very pleased to hear that he has come here."

"He is certainly a persistent young man," said Elizabeth.

"I do think we should change the subject, Cousin," said Lady Morley. "Nothing will put Arthur in a worse humor than talking of Thomas Jeffreys."

"I am only too happy to speak of something else," said Elizabeth. "Indeed, so many interesting things are happening in our little community. For example, the Earl of Dunraven taking Longmeadow." In saying this, Elizabeth directed a meaningful look at Georgiana, who felt herself reddening.

"Arthur met the earl yesterday," said Lady Morley, omitting the fact that Georgiana had also had that honor.

"Did you?" cried Mrs. Fanshawe, turning to the baronet. "Did he call at Highcroft?"

"No, I called upon him," said Sir Arthur.

Mrs. Fanshawe regarded this as very fascinating information. "Do tell us what he is like."

"One cannot say on such a brief acquaintance," said the baronet. "He was civil enough."

"Do you believe he means to stay?" said Elizabeth.

"I cannot say," returned the baronet, not wishing to discuss Dunraven with his wife's cousin. After all, Elizabeth Fanshawe was one of the worst gossips in the county. He certainly didn't want it put about that the earl had made an offer for Georgiana.

Although Elizabeth made a considerable effort to get Sir Arthur to say more about Dunraven, the baronet was maddeningly reticent on the subject. She finally gave up, switching to a number of other topics before taking her leave.

When the visitors had gone, Sir Arthur brought up the subject of Thomas once again. Rising from his chair, he took on a stern expression before launching into a diatribe against him. Georgiana sat quietly during her father's monologue. Scarcely listening, she found herself thinking about Thomas. Seeing him had been quite wonderful, and yet . . . it had not seemed quite the same since the last time they had met in London.

Fortunately, a diversion appeared when the butler entered the room. He stood rather hesitantly at the door while the baronet continued to speak. Noting that his wife and daughters were looking in the direction of the door, he turned to see the butler.

"Dash it, Griggs. What do you want?"

"I do beg your pardon, sir, but two gentlemen are here. Lord Dunraven and Mr. Buckthorne."

Kitty could not contain her delight. "Lord Dunraven!" she cried. "I have so wanted to see him again."

Georgiana frowned. She was not at all sure how she felt about the earl. While she was happy that her father had ceased haranguing them, she didn't know if she was ready to see Dunraven again.

Sir Arthur looked over at his wife. "Here is your opportunity to meet the man, Isabelle."

"Oh, dear," said her ladyship. "Are you certain we should receive him, Arthur?"

"And why not? He has offered for our daughter and by God,

when I think of Thomas Jeffreys, Dunraven looks good in comparison."

The irony of this remark was not lost on Georgiana, who sighed.

"Show the gentlemen in, Griggs," said Sir Arthur. The butler nodded and returned a short time later.

Dunraven strode into the room followed by a large, red-faced gentleman. Sir Arthur made a slight bow. "Dunraven," he said.

"Sir Arthur," returned the earl. "May I present my friend, Mr. George Buckthorne?"

"How do you do, sir?" said the baronet, nodding to Buckthorne. "Allow me to present my family. My wife . . ." Lady Morley nodded graciously in the direction of the visitors. "My eldest daughter, Georgiana, and my youngest, Kitty."

The earl allowed his gaze to fall upon Georgiana. She was attired in a frock of pale blue muslin with a paisley shawl about her shoulders. Her blond hair had been pulled into a knot atop her head with curls framing her face. Dunraven found himself thinking that she looked exceptionally pretty.

"I am charmed to meet you all," said Buckthorne, bowing to the ladies.

"Do sit down, gentlemen," said the baronet, his foul temper vanishing. The earl and Buckthorne were only too happy to do so, his lordship taking a place beside Georgiana on the sofa.

Georgiana, who found his lordship's close proximity a bit unnerving, glanced over at him. He smiled at her and she looked away. "How do you like Longmeadow, my lord?" asked Lady Morley.

"I like it very well, ma'am," he replied.

"I am glad," said Lady Morley. "I must say we were all very surprised to hear that it had been sold. The Bainbridges had been at Longmeadow for generations. It is a fine estate. Such lovely views."

"Indeed so," said Buckthorne. "His lordship is dashed fond of the views. And I daresay the hunting is very fine."

"Mr. Buckthorne is terribly fond of hunting," said the earl. "He has just bought a pack of hounds to prove it."

"Have you?" said Sir Arthur, very much interested.

"Indeed, I have, sir, and splendid beasts they are," said

Buckthorne. "Several were sired by Golden Trumpet. He was one of Rantor's most famous sons."

This information appeared to impress Georgiana's father, who addressed further inquiries regarding the new foxhounds that Buckthorne was only too happy to discuss. The earl, who had no desire to spend his afternoon talking about the parentage of dogs, interrupted his friend. "I beg you, Buck, cease discussing those blasted hounds. I daresay the ladies care nothing about who begat whom of your precious dogs."

"Perhaps you are right," said Buckthorne rather disappointed. "Sir Arthur and I will discuss it further at some future time."

"I should enjoy that," said the baronet, who was exceedingly fond of foxhunting. He turned to the earl. "You mean to have hunts, Dunraven?"

"Buckthorne means to have them," said his lordship. "I am indifferent to the sport. Indeed, I am too fond of my neck to wish to break it vaulting over fences in pursuit of a fox. But Buckthorne has cajoled me into keeping his wretched hounds so I daresay we will have hunts."

"Then you plan to stay at Longmeadow, Lord Dunraven?" said Lady Morley.

"Oh, yes," said his lordship, looking over at Georgiana. "I have no wish to return to town. I am enjoying my stay in the country."

Lady Morley smiled pleasantly at Dunraven. Although she had been horrified at the prospect of the Earl of Dunraven as a son-in-law, she was beginning to reconsider. He was very different than what she had expected. Certainly his physical appearance wasn't that of a dissipated rake. Perhaps he had a slight arrogance of bearing, noted her ladyship, but that was to be expected in an earl, after all. "I, too, enjoy the country," said Lady Morley. "Of course, I enjoy town as well, and I did regret that we had to cut our stay in London short. But now that we are back at Highcroft, I am glad of it. I did miss my gardens."

"I caught a glimpse of your gardens as we drove up, ma'am," said Buckthorne. "Very beautiful."

"Oh, yes," said her ladyship. "Perhaps you gentlemen would enjoy seeing them."

While Buckthorne had little interest in flowers, he preferred the out-of-doors to sitting in the drawing room. He, therefore, pronounced it a very good idea. "Yes, I would, ma'am."

Georgiana, who was happy to think that she might escape from her place beside the earl, rose to her feet. "What a good idea, Mama. The flowers look best at this time of the afternoon."

Everyone got up from their chairs and made their way outside. Once there, Sir Arthur commandeered Buckthorne and the two of them began talking about foxhounds again. The ladies and Dunraven were left to view the brilliantly colored floral displays. Highcroft's gardens were quite spectacular and renowned in the area. Throughout the spring and summer, visitors often appeared requesting to see them.

As they walked along the garden paths, Lady Morley pointed out one flower and then another, telling the earl all about them. Georgiana watched the earl as he listened to her mother. She suspected that he was very bored, although he showed no sign of it.

After a time, Lady Morley seemed to recollect that she had given no instructions for tea. "Oh, I do hope you and Mr. Buckthorne will stay for tea. You will stay for tea, won't you, my lord?"

"I should like that very much," returned the earl.

"Then do excuse me for a moment," said Lady Morley. "I must order tea. The girls will show you the lily pond. I am sure his lordship will want to see your water lilies, Georgiana."

This remark caused the earl to express his great eagerness to do so, causing Georgiana to cast a disapproving look at him. Georgiana was not very happy at her mother's abrupt departure, for she had no wish to be alone with Dunraven. Of course, Kitty was there as well, so it was not as bad as it might have been. Yet Kitty soon hurried on ahead of them, leaving her sister with the earl.

Dunraven proffered his arm, which Georgiana ignored. "How could you do it?" she said.

"How could I do what?" said the earl.

"Tell my father that you wished to marry me? I know that you think it is so amusing, but I see nothing in the least funny about it."

"Then you believe that I am joking?" said the earl. "I assure you I am perfectly serious. I wish to marry you. Indeed, I am quite determined to do so."

"That is quite absurd," said Georgiana, rather disconcerted by the seriousness of his tone and the intent way his brown eyes were fastened on her face.

"Absurd? My dear Georgiana," he said, surprising her with this use of her Christian name, "it is no more absurd than most ideas of marriage."

"You couldn't actually wish to marry me," said Georgiana. "You scarcely know me."

"I could and I do," he said. Reaching out, he took her arm and tucked it into his own. "I'm not the sort of man to leave a thing undone. I started something with that kiss at Longmeadow. We'll complete it on our wedding night."

Turning very red, Georgiana tried to pull her arm free, but Dunraven held it fast. "How could you think I'd marry you? My parents would never allow it."

"Don't be so sure of that. And don't pretend that you don't want to marry me."

Georgiana regarded him indignantly. "I am not pretending, my lord. I don't want to marry you."

Dunraven smiled for a brief moment before pulling Georgiana into his arms. "What nonsense," he said.

"Are you mad," cried Georgiana. "My father will see you."

"And what of it?" said the earl. "He knows we're to be wed." Before she could say another word, he kissed her.

Astonished, she pushed him away. "You *are* mad!" she cried.

Dunraven laughed. "Mad for you, my love. Come, let us have no more girlish protests. Tell your father you will have me or nobody. He'll give his consent."

Georgiana's blue eyes flashed angrily. "I shan't marry you. And don't imagine that I don't know that you are not in the least serious about marrying me. If I were to go to my father and say I wished to marry you, you would be horrified. It would serve you right if I did so."

To her annoyance, he eyed her with an amused look. "If you choose to believe that, you may do so. But I should like nothing better than for you to tell your father you wish to marry me. The sooner the banns are posted, the sooner we'll be wed."

Georgiana stood there glaring at him, unsure of what to do next. Could he be serious? Did he really want to marry her? And even if he did, why would she consent to marry such a man?

"What is the matter?" Kitty's voice caused them both to turn to look at her.

"Nothing is the matter," said Georgiana.

"I reached the lily pond and I turned around and you weren't there. You are very slow."

"Your sister and I were admiring those . . ." he said, gesturing toward some tall flowers.

"The foxgloves?" said Kitty. "Oh, they are lovely, aren't they? But do come and see the lilies."

"No, I think his lordship has seen enough of the garden," said Georgiana. "I am sure he would much rather see Papa's new horse." Turning, she walked off, hurrying down the garden path. Coming past a boxwood hedge, she saw her father and Buckthorne still engaged in discussion.

"Papa!" she called.

"Yes, my dear?"

"I told Lord Dunraven that you would show him Demon Dancer. He was so very eager to see him."

"Oh, would he?" said the baronet, looking toward the garden to see the earl approaching with Kitty.

"Demon Dancer?" said Buckthorne.

"My new hunter. I suspect you are a good judge of horseflesh, Mr. Buckthorne."

"I do admit I can spot a right one as well as the next man," said Buckthorne. By this time, Dunraven and Kitty had joined the others. Georgiana tried hard to avoid his gaze. "Dunraven, Sir Arthur would like us to see his new horse."

"Yes, I should like you to see him," said the baronet, eager to show off his most prized possession.

Saying that she and Kitty should join her mother, Georgiana took her leave of the gentlemen. As they went into the house, Kitty walked beside her. "Georgie, you must tell me what happened. I looked back and you weren't following me."

"The way you rushed off, Kitty Morley, I believe you wished for me to be alone with Lord Dunraven."

"Of course, I did," said Kitty.

"I should box your ears," said Georgiana.

Kitty only laughed. "It is so clear that the earl is in love with you. And I don't think he is so very wicked."

"He is wicked enough, I assure you," replied Georgiana. "And I cannot see how you are so birdwitted as to believe he could be in love with me."

Kitty ignored this comment. "Tell me what you discussed. Did he kiss you again?"

"Kitty!"

"He did!" cried Kitty triumphantly. "I can see that he did. He must be very much in love with you."

"Must I remind you again that I am in love with Thomas?"

"I know you *were* in love with him."

"And I am so inconstant that I love Thomas one day and then Dunraven the next?"

"Well, maybe you didn't really love Lord Thomas. Yes, that must be it."

The conversation was cut short by the appearance of Lady Morley. Hearing that the gentlemen had gone to see Demon Dancer, she rolled her eyes heavenward. "Who knows how long they will be? When you father begins to talk about horses, he will be all day. And I have ordered tea. It will be ready shortly. Well, come, my dears, we may as well wait in the drawing room."

Georgiana nodded and followed her mother and sister down the hallway.

Chapter 13

Dunraven and Buckthorne stayed rather late at Highcroft. Since the visiting gentlemen had been so impressed with Sir Arthur's new horse, they had spent a long time admiring Demon Dancer. To the baronet's delight, the earl and Buckthorne had proclaimed the black horse one of the most splendid they had ever seen.

When the gentlemen had finally been persuaded to come in, they lingered over their tea and cakes. Conversation continued to center on Demon Dancer, a fact that pleased Sir Arthur as much as it had frustrated his wife. By the time his guests had taken their leave, the baronet had begun to believe that both Buckthorne and Dunraven were the most amiable and agreeable of companions.

That evening after returning to Longmeadow, the earl and Buckthorne sat down to dinner. Despite the lavish refreshments that had been served at Highcroft, Buckthorne was famished. Pronouncing each course that was set before him excellent, he ate heartily.

"You are damned lucky to have such a good cook," said Buckthorne as one of the footmen placed the next course on the table in front of him.

"Yes," said the earl absently.

"Yes, yes, this is excellent," proclaimed Buckthorne after sampling the roast pheasant. "I have had such wonderful food since leaving town. And I so enjoyed tea at Highcroft this afternoon. I daresay I never had such lemon cake in all my life. I shall have to get that recipe."

Dunraven, who was in an excellent humor, regarded his friend with an indulgent smile. Not sharing Buckthorne's obsession with food, he had given little thought to the lemon cake. He had been more interested in watching Georgiana Morley.

Buckthorne continued. "And what a dashed bit of blood and bone Morley has added to his stable. I shouldn't doubt that his Demon Dancer is one of the finest horses in the kingdom. If I had your blunt, old fellow, I would buy that stallion at once."

"You couldn't believe Morley would sell him, do you?" said the earl. "He would sooner sell his daughters."

This comment provoked a hearty laugh from Buckthorne. "His daughters are damned pretty girls," he said. "I confess I had thought you were gammoning me when you first said you wished to marry Miss Morley, but I am convinced you mean to do it. And while my own experience of the married state has been decidedly less than blissful, I have a feeling that you will do far better." He lifted his glass toward his lordship. "My heartiest congratulations!"

"Thank you, Buck," said the earl. "Although you are a bit premature. Miss Morley pretends to have an aversion to me."

"Pretends?"

"It is mere pretense, I'm sure of that. However, the lady doesn't quite know her mind. She still fancies herself in love with some cub named Thomas Jeffreys."

"I don't know him," said Buckthorne. "I shall have to ask my wife about him. She knows everyone, of course." He sighed. "I suppose I'll soon be seeing Mrs. Buckthorne."

"What do you mean?"

"Oh, didn't I tell you? I must return to town tomorrow."

"Tomorrow?"

"Oh, I don't want to go, but there are some things I must attend to. I shan't be gone long."

"I do hope you intend to take those hounds of yours with you."

Buckthorne laughed. "My dear Dunraven, hounds belong in the country. Indeed, I am told they love Longmeadow already."

"Well, Macduff dislikes them."

Buckthorne cast a glance at the terrier, who was seated on the floor beside his master's chair. "Nonsense, Macduff enjoys having other dogs about, don't you, old man? No, indeed, Macduff would be shattered if the hounds left him."

"He would be ecstatic," said the earl.

"You are very much mistaken," said Buckthorne with a wide grin. He returned to his dinner for a moment. "You should accompany me back to town. We could visit Mrs. Trotter's."

"I am done with Mrs. Trotter's," said Dunraven.

"What!" cried Buckthorne. "You can't mean that. Indeed, there are no prettier girls to be found in the kingdom. Indeed, I told you of that bit of fluff I met when I was last there. She was a saucy wench named Marie. Now there's a lass who knows how to please a gentleman."

"You've told me about her more than once, Buck," said the earl with a bored look.

"I am beginning to worry about you," said Buckthorne. "Not wanting to go to Mrs. Trotter's is uncommon odd. Indeed, no place provides a better supper in all of London."

Dunraven smiled slightly. "Well, you enjoy yourself in town, Buck. But do not stay too long or I shall sell your accurst hounds."

"Don't even joke about such a thing!" cried Buckthorne.

The earl laughed and continued to eat his dinner.

The Morleys were joined for dinner that evening by Lady Morley's cousin Elizabeth and her family. Elizabeth Fanshawe's husband was a somber-looking gentleman who said very little. His silence was more than made up for by the loquacity of his wife and daughter, Charlotte.

Georgiana was not very happy to find that the Earl of Dunraven was discussed incessantly at table. Her mother had lost no time in informing the Fanshawe's of Dunraven's proposal of marriage, a piece of news they found quite remarkable.

When they were then informed that Dunraven had called at Highcroft, Elizabeth wished to know every detail of the visit. Lady Morley and Kitty were more than happy to oblige her.

Georgiana remained quiet most of the time, allowing her mother and sister to chatter on. After dinner, the ladies retired to the drawing room, leaving Sir Arthur and Mr. Fanshawe to their port.

Once the ladies were seated, Elizabeth smiled at Georgiana. "I must say you have caused such excitement in the county, your bringing Dunraven to Longmeadow."

"Truly, Cousin Elizabeth," replied Georgiana, "I cannot say for certain that I brought him here."

"My dear girl, it is perfectly obvious that his affection for you caused him to buy Longmeadow."

"It is so romantic," said Charlotte with a sigh.

"It is indeed," said Kitty, glancing at her sister with a mischievous look.

"It is such a pity that the earl's reputation is not what one might wish," said Elizabeth.

Lady Morley nodded. "I do agree, Cousin. While I have been somewhat relieved upon meeting him, I will say that I am still very much bothered at the idea of Georgiana marrying such a man."

Elizabeth looked at Georgiana. "Yes, my dear, I know you are so very fond of the earl, but you must allow yourself to be guided by your parents. If they don't wish you to marry Dunraven, you must accept it."

"I feel I could accept it," said Georgiana. Noting that everyone was regarding her with great interest, she added, "I know that my parents have my best interests at heart."

"How very sensible of you to say so," said Elizabeth.

"Do you think it would be quite bad for Georgiana to marry him?" said Lady Morley.

Elizabeth hesitated. While she was more than happy to be called upon to express her opinion on this question, she thought the subject unsuitable for her daughter and Kitty. "Perhaps Charlotte might play something for us on the pianoforte."

"Oh, Mama," said Charlotte, "I am rather out of practice."

"Oh, nonsense. You and Kitty used to play that duet. We would love to hear it."

"That is a good idea," said Lady Morley.

Kitty and Charlotte reluctantly rose to go to the piano, where they spent a considerable time rummaging through the music in search of their duet.

Thinking the younger girls now safely out of earshot, Lady Morley broached the subject again. "Elizabeth, do you believe that Georgiana would be ostracized in society if she married Dunraven?"

"That is a very good question," replied her cousin. "I fear that I shouldn't be surprised. You see, I just had a letter from my dear friend, Lady Wickstead. I had written her about Dunraven buying Longmeadow and being fond of Georgiana.

"It is Lady Wickstead's opinion that marrying the earl would be quite disastrous for anyone wishing to succeed in the first circles. She wrote that the Prince Regent was so furious with Dunraven for that business with Lady Coningsby that he will never forgive him. And how can one be accepted in society if the Prince himself so disapproves?"

"Did you hear that, Georgiana?" said her mother. "It may be a very bad idea for you to think of marrying him."

By this time Kitty and Charlotte had found the music and had sat down on the piano bench. They began to play. The music distracted Elizabeth and Lady Morley for a time as they watched the young ladies with maternal pride.

Georgiana was happy for the diversion. Yet, as she listened to her sister and Charlotte, she could think of nothing but Dunraven. She thought of him in the garden with her that afternoon. He was quite insufferable, she told herself, and yet . . . Georgiana found herself remembering how he had kissed her there. He had certainly behaved in a most ungentlemanly fashion, and yet the memory of the kiss kindled rather unsettling feelings within her.

When Kitty and Charlotte finished their duet, they were heartily applauded by their uncritical audience. Lady Morley insisted that they play again. The request caused the two girls to consult for a long time about what they could play and whether Charlotte should sing and Kitty play or the other way around.

By the time Sir Arthur and Mr. Fanshawe joined the ladies, it had been determined that Kitty would sing first while Charlotte accompanied her, and then Charlotte would have a chance to serenade the company. Sir Arthur, who had little regard for his youngest daughter's talents, was rather disturbed to find that his wife and her cousin had apparently settled on an evening of music. He could only take a seat beside his wife on the sofa and listen politely as Kitty began.

After her first song, Kitty once again had to take a good deal of time discussing the next selection with Charlotte. This afforded Lady Morley a chance to make a comment to her husband. "Elizabeth has told me that her friend Lady Wickstead wrote saying that Dunraven will never be accepted in society. The Prince Regent is quite set against him."

"Indeed?" said the baronet. "Well, I don't believe that signifies in the least."

"Doesn't signify?" said her ladyship. "Whatever can you mean, Arthur?"

"Why, I never cared a fig for London society myself. Why should Georgiana care for that if she is fond of her husband? Indeed, I must say I've given much thought to this matter of Dunraven. After talking to him this afternoon, I've come to the conclusion that he isn't such a bad fellow. No, indeed, I'm sure his reputation is much exaggerated.

"And he is dashed good with horses. Demon Dancer took to him immediately. And Dunraven took scarcely one look at Dancer before declaring that he recognized Jupiter's bloodline in him. Now that shows a dashed good eye for horses." Sir Arthur turned to his daughter. "I believe the earl is genuinely fond of you, Georgiana. And I must say that when I compare him to Thomas Jeffreys, he begins to look very good indeed."

Once again Georgiana was forced to think how ironic it was that her father thought Thomas made Dunraven appear to advantage.

"I saw Lord Thomas this afternoon," said Elizabeth. "He is such a handsome young man, but I must say there is something about him one does not like. There is a certain disingenuousness about him."

"Yes," said Sir Arthur. "He's naught but a fortune hunter. Thank God, Georgiana has found another beau she prefers. Why, I was at wit's end when she thought herself in love with Jeffreys."

"I do fear you will be very vexed with me, Sir Arthur," said Elizabeth as Charlotte began to sing.

"What do you mean?" returned the baronet.

"I have sent an invitation to our ball to the Pelhams and I also invited young Thomas," whispered Elizabeth. "Mr. Fanshawe insisted I invite them. We can scarcely not invite them after all."

While this admission displeased Sir Arthur, Georgiana brightened. She would see Thomas at the Fanshawes' ball. Her spirits greatly improved, Georgiana turned her attention to Kitty and Charlotte.

Chapter 14

L ord Thomas Jeffreys turned to direct a furious look at the manservant standing beside him. "Idiot!" he cried, tossing a long piece of snowy white linen at the man. "That neckcloth is quite hideously wrinkled! Get me another!"

"I am sorry, m'lord," said the servant, hurrying to the bureau to fetch another.

Thomas cast a critical eye on the new neckcloth that was handed to him. "It will have to do," he muttered. "You are all terribly lax in this household, Wheeler. 'Tis a wonder my uncle doesn't sack the lot of you. Now get out. I don't need you."

The servant hurried from the room, eager to leave Lord Thomas. He and all the servants in Sir Francis Pelham's employ disliked their employer's nephew. Indeed, since the young man had arrived at Pelham Manor, complaints about him had filled the servants' hall.

Had he known of his unpopularity among his uncle's staff, Thomas wouldn't have cared in the least. Servants scarcely existed in his world. They were only there to be used without thought, like pieces of furniture.

Wrapping the long piece of linen carefully around his stiff collar, Thomas stared intently into the mirror. Tying cravats was a very serious matter requiring great concentration. He was proud of his skill as he tied the material into a complicated knot. "There," he said aloud. "Well done."

Taking up his coat, he put it on. As he did so, he rather wished he had not dismissed Wheeler so hastily, since getting into the tight-fitting garment was far easier with the aid of a servant. Still, he managed well enough and now that he had finished dressing, he gazed at his reflection in the mirror, well pleased at what he saw.

After scrutinizing his appearance for a time, he turned rather reluctantly away from the mirror. As he walked out of his room, he found himself thinking that his efforts were wasted in this provincial place. He had always detested the country and he had never liked his uncle's estate Pelham Manor. There were so few interesting people about and his uncle and aunt were so dreadfully boring. Indeed, he would never have left London if it weren't for the necessity of seeing Georgiana again.

Thomas entered his uncle's drawing room with the indolent gait adopted by young gentlemen of fashion. Finding his aunt seated at her embroidery, he came toward her and made a slight bow. "Good afternoon, Aunt."

"Good afternoon, Thomas," said Lady Pelham, continuing to place tiny stitches into her ornate needlework. "Do sit down, my dear boy. I am so eager for company."

Thomas suppressed a sigh. Life was so dull at Pelham Manor. He wondered how his aunt could bear it. Of course, she was a very dull woman herself, he decided, so perhaps she didn't notice. He sat down in an armchair beside Lady Pelham. "Where is my uncle?"

"He has gone to see one of his tenants about a sow," replied his aunt matter-of-factly.

"I see," said Thomas. How very typical, he thought. His uncle spent an uncommon amount of time with livestock.

"I hope you are not finding your visit tedious," said Lady Pelham.

"Indeed not," said Thomas.

"I shouldn't be surprised if you did, for we lead such a quiet life here. But I did receive a note from Mrs. Fanshawe that will please you. We are invited to their ball Thursday next."

Thomas perked up a bit at this news. It seemed there was so little society in the Richton area. Finally, there was to be a ball. And certainly Georgiana would be there. "Would Miss Morley be in attendance?" he said.

Lady Pelham smiled. "I'm sure she would be there. Mrs. Fanshawe is Lady Morley's cousin, you know. Indeed, everyone in the area will come. The Fanshawes have the finest balls." His aunt adopted a serious look. "I do hope you won't be disappointed about Miss Morley. It is being spread about that she will marry Lord Dunraven."

"That is preposterous," said Thomas. "The fellow is notorious."

"He is a man of fortune and an earl," said Lady Pelham. "One can forgive a rich man a good deal. And there is the fact that Sir Arthur so dislikes your uncle. I don't believe they have spoken in more than thirty years."

"That is an unfortunate state of affairs to be sure," returned Thomas, frowning. Things were not turning out very well at all. As each day went by, it seemed more and more likely that Georgiana would slip through his fingers.

"Oh, you received two letters," said Lady Pelham. "They are there on the table."

Thomas rose from the chair to take up the letters. He recognized one of his brothers' hands on one of them. Noting the scent of perfume on the other one, he knew immediately that it was from Claire. Thomas frowned. He had specifically told his mistress that she must not write him at Pelham Manor. And it was just like her to douse it with perfume.

"One appears to be from a lady," said Lady Pelham, eying her nephew with interest. "You may open your letters. I don't mind in the least."

"Oh, I shall read them later," said Thomas tossing them back down on the table and returning to his seat. After an hour of conversation, he was able to take his leave of his aunt. Picking up the letters, he returned to his room. There he broke the seal on Claire's letter and read the short note. "Milord Tom," it began. "I couldn't bear another night away from you so I have come to Suffolk. You mustn't be angry. I have taken a room at the Boar's Head in Hillborough. Come to me tonight. Your faithful Claire."

While somewhat irked that Claire had come from London, Thomas was not really displeased. After all, Hillborough was far enough away that he might visit her without anyone knowing about it. The idea of enjoying Claire's generous favors once again was very appealing. His spirits lifted by this turn of events, a smile appeared on his face as he picked up his brother's letter and opened it.

Georgiana had spent most of the morning in her sitting room writing letters to London friends, unaware that a grave crisis had been brewing in the stables. Demon Dancer had appeared fine in the morning although a bit off his feed. Later in the day, the prized stallion had taken ill and Sir Arthur had been summoned from the house.

When Georgiana learned of Demon Dancer's condition, she hurried to the stables. To her horror, she found the black horse barely able to stand, his breathing labored and his eyes listless. "Oh, Papa, what is wrong with him?"

"I wish to God I knew," said the baronet, eyeing his beloved horse with a worried look. "We have sent for Mr. Brown."

Georgiana nodded. Mr. Brown was renowned in the county for his knowledge of horses. "He'll know what to do," she said.

Shaw, the head groom, stood beside the horse, stroking Demon Dancer's neck. While he had worked with horses for years, Shaw felt helpless. He knew what the animal meant to his employer and his daughter and he was terribly fond of the creature himself. If Demon Dancer didn't recover . . . No, Shaw wouldn't even allow himself to think that.

After what seemed a very long time, one of the servants appeared with devastating news. Mr. Brown had gone to visit his daughter in Cornwall. The baronet regarded Shaw with a stricken look. "Damnation!" he cried. "What are we to do now?"

"I don't know, sir," said Shaw, quite dismayed that Mr. Brown was not coming to their rescue.

After a long discussion of various courses of action, the men seemed uncertain what to do. Very upset, Georgiana went back to the house to inform her mother and Kitty of the seriousness of the situation. As she approached the door, she saw a carriage coming up the gravel drive.

Recognizing the vehicle as Dunraven's, she wasn't sure whether she was happy or irritated to see him. However, since her father had proclaimed him very knowledgeable about horses, the thought occurred to her that he might be of assistance with Demon Dancer.

Dunraven's driver pulled the horses up at the door and the earl jumped down from the carriage. "Georgiana, is something wrong?"

"Indeed, yes," said Georgiana. "It is Demon Dancer. He is very sick."

Dunraven's face clouded. "Sick? Take me to him. I may be able to help."

Georgiana took heart. She didn't think Dunraven the sort of man who would suggest he could help if he couldn't. "I do hope you might know what is wrong with him, my lord," she said. "He was taken ill so suddenly. He was perfectly fine yesterday. We are so worried."

"Sometimes things seem far worse than they are," replied the earl, walking beside Georgiana. When they arrived at the stables, they hurried inside.

"Papa," said Georgiana, "Lord Dunraven is here."

"Dunraven?" said the baronet, turning from Demon Dancer to see his daughter and the earl. "Good. Perhaps you will know what to do."

His lordship came up beside the horse and studied him in silence. Speaking calmly to the animal, Dunraven examined him carefully. The others stood watching, hopeful expressions on their faces, for there was something about the earl's manner that inspired confidence.

"I have seen this before," Dunraven said finally. "It is serious, but he is strong, and I believe it will be treated in time. There is much work to do."

This pronouncement infused optimism into what had seemed a hopeless situation. Sir Arthur was only too happy to allow Dunraven to take over. His lordship began to give orders and the stablemen hurried to do his bidding.

Georgiana stood watching, her feelings for Dunraven confused as always. She could not help but be impressed by the calm, commanding way he had taken charge of the situation. That he knew and loved horses so much was also a great commendation in her eyes.

Demon Dancer's treatment continued throughout the day. Despite Lady Morley's pleas that her husband and daughter come to the house for food, they refused to leave the stable.

As the day wore on, the horse showed no improvement. He lay down on the floor of his stall, appearing to grow weaker. Georgiana sat on the floor, stroking his head and murmuring encouragement.

When it grew dark, Lady Morley came to the stable to entreat her husband and daughter to come into the house. "It is very late. You haven't had dinner."

"No, I will stay," said the baronet who, despite his fatigue, didn't wish to leave Demon Dancer.

"And so will I," said Georgiana.

"You most certainly will not!" cried her ladyship. "You will come in at once."

"Do go in, Georgiana," said Dunraven. "You are exhausted. As are you, too, sir. Shaw and I will stay with him through the night."

"What?" said Lady Morley. "You will spend the night in the stables? Indeed, my lord, that will not do. You'll catch your death."

"I assure you I'll do no such thing," said the earl. "Now do go in."

The baronet and Georgiana protested again, but finally realized that Dunraven was right. They were exhausted and there was no reason for them to stay. "Very well, Dunraven," said Sir Arthur. "But you must tell me if there is a change. Do not hesitate to wake me, no matter what the time. And thank you, Dunraven. I am heartily grateful."

The earl nodded to Sir Arthur. He then looked at Georgiana. Their eyes met for a moment. Then Georgiana looked away in some embarrassment. "Good night, my lord," she said, and then accompanied her mother and father back to the house.

Even though she was very tired, it was hard for Georgiana to fall asleep. She could not help worrying about Demon Dancer and thinking of the earl spending the night in the stables beside the sick horse. It was some time before Georgiana fell into a fitful sleep.

Awakening at dawn, she hurried out of bed and dressed. Then, leaving her room, she hastened to the stables. Fearing the worst, Georgiana's eyes grew wide in astonishment and relief as she caught sight of the horse. Demon Dancer was on his feet! He was standing there very calmly, eating hay. Standing beside him was Dunraven, patting his neck and looking very pleased.

"Oh, Dunraven!" cried Georgiana. "He is well!"

Turning toward her, the earl nodded. "He passed the crisis two hours ago. I believe he'll be fine."

Georgiana rushed to the horse's side and pressed her face against Demon Dancer's neck. "Oh, you dear creature. Thank God, you are well again." Turning to Dunraven, Georgiana smiled gratefully at him. He looked quite disheveled. His dark hair looked wild with bits of straw stuck in it and there was a dark shadow on his unshaven face. He stood in his shirt-sleeves. His coat had been discarded some time ago and lay in a heap on the floor. "We are so grateful to you, my lord," she said. "No one knew what to do."

He smiled down at her as she stood before him. "By God, you look beautiful in the morning. Just like a fairy sprite."

"And you look quite dreadful, my lord," said Georgiana. She reached up and pulled a piece of straw from his hair. "I daresay your valet will be very distressed to see you like this."

She reached up to take another bit of straw from his hair, but he caught her hand and brought it to his lips. Georgiana felt a tremor pass through her as he kissed her hand. "Oh, Dunraven," she said weakly.

Needing no further encouragement, the earl enfolded Georgiana into his arms and kissed her lips. While she vaguely felt that she should protest or try to break away, she only returned his kiss with a fervor that matched his own. Suddenly, Demon Dancer snorted, bringing both of them to their senses. Someone was entering the stable.

Pulling away from Dunraven, Georgiana turned to see her father and Shaw enter the stables. "It is true!" cried Sir Arthur, hurrying over to the horse. "The dear fellow is better! I could scarcely believe it when Shaw told me. And here you are, Georgiana. I sent one of the maids to tell you, but you have preceded us."

"Isn't it splendid?" said Georgiana, embracing her father. "Demon Dancer is well again."

"Yes, indeed," replied the baronet, smiling at Dunraven. "And we have his lordship to thank for it. I'll not soon forget your assistance in this, Dunraven."

"You should thank Shaw as well," said the earl. "He's a good man."

The head groom seemed rather embarrassed at Dunraven's remark and assured his employer that it was his lordship who must have the credit. "You must be starving, Dunraven. Come in for some breakfast."

The earl shook his head. He picked up his coat from the floor and put it on. "I fear I'm not fit to be seen and, indeed, I

am in need of sleep more than anything. My carriage is ready
and I shall return to Longmeadow."

Although both Georgiana and her father urged him to stay,
Dunraven could not be persuaded. They saw him to his carriage and waved farewell as he rode off.

When he had gone, the baronet and Georgiana returned to
the house, where they were greeted by Kitty and Lady Morley.
"Is Demon Dancer going to be all right?" said Kitty.

Her father nodded. "One can scarcely believe it. This morning he looks fit as always, and just last night I thought he
would never recover. Dunraven and Shaw stayed with him all
night long, giving him Dunraven's cure at hourly intervals."

"Dunraven's cure?" said Lady Morley.

"Some concoction he had instructed Cook to make," said
the baronet. "Why, the man is quite wonderful. I don't care a
fig for what is said of him. Indeed, should Georgiana wish to
take him for a husband, I should like nothing better."

Georgiana made no reply, but found herself wondering if
perhaps she, too, would like nothing more than being Dunraven's wife.

Chapter 15

It was growing dark by the time Thomas Jeffreys arrived at the Boar's Head Inn. Pulling his horse up in front of the establishment, he jumped down and relinquished the animal to the osler. Thomas was not in the best of moods. It had seemed a very long ride from Pelham Manor. Thomas was not much of a horseman and he would have preferred to have taken his uncle's carriage. However, since that could not have been arranged without an elaborate explanation of where he was going, he had decided to go on horseback.

Entering the inn, Thomas looked around with a disdainful gaze. The room was filled with customers eating and drinking. It was a noisy, boisterous group.

Seeing Thomas enter his establishment, the innkeeper hurried to be of assistance. It was not often that such a well-dressed gentleman of quality appeared there. "And how might I serve you, sir?" he said, wiping his hands on his soiled apron.

"I am to meet a lady," said Thomas, directing a condescending gaze at the man. "Her name is Miss Stevenson."

"Oh, yes, Miss Stevenson. She is here, sir. I'll have one of my girls tell her you're here, sir."

"That won't be necessary. I shall go to her. Tell me where she is."

"I don't know, sir," said the innkeeper. "I don't like gentlemen seeing ladies in their rooms. 'Tis a respectable house I run here, sir."

Frowning, Thomas pulled a coin from his pocket and handed it to the innkeeper. "Now where is the lady?"

The innkeeper eyed the coin for a moment. "Follow me, sir," he said.

After leading Thomas to the door, the innkeeper left.

Thomas knocked once and then entered the room, closing the door behind him. "Claire."

"Oh, Tom!" she cried, leaping to her feet to rush to his embrace. Extricating himself, Thomas sat down on the bed. "Help me with my boots," he commanded.

"Yes, m'lord," replied Claire leaning over to grasp one of his gleaming Hessian boots and pull it off. She tossed it on the floor. "Take care with that," cried Thomas, extending his other foot.

"It didn't come to any harm," said Claire, taking hold of the other tight-fitting boot and pulling it off with some difficulty. She placed it carefully on the floor. "There, is that better?"

"That it is," said Thomas rising from the bed and divesting himself of his coat and waistcoat. "Now come here, my girl."

"Oh, Tom, I have so missed you," said Claire. "You cannot imagine how I suffered there in town all alone with you in the country." Uninterested in conversation, he began to unfasten the back of her dress. "What an impatient man you are," she said as the garment slipped to the floor and Thomas began to undo the laces of her stays. Once they were removed, Claire pulled her shift over her head to stand naked before him.

Thomas's eyes ran up and down her voluptuous figure with admiration as he hastily removed his shirt. Smiling, Claire then watched him fumble with his trouser buttons. "It seems you are eager to see me," she said directing a bold gaze at his groin.

Catching her roughly, he threw her to the bed. "You'll see how eager," he said, falling on top of her and pressing his lips against hers with bruising force.

In the morning Claire lay awake watching Thomas as he slept. Her body ached from their lovemaking, which had been far more brutal than she had been accustomed to from him. Still, she was not upset with him. After all, she loved him very much and if he was selfish and insensitive to her, well, he was a man and a gentleman at that.

He stirred in bed and opened his eyes. "Good morning, my love," said Claire.

"What time is it?" he asked crossly.

"Nearly ten o'clock."

"Damn," he said. "I'll have to leave at once. I've got to return to Pelham Manor."

"Oh, you must stay a while longer," she said, reaching out to caress his shoulder.

"I can't," he said.

"But you'll come back tonight."

"If I can," he replied.

"I do wish you hadn't left town," said Claire. "I am so miserable without you."

"You know very well that I must stay here until I become engaged to Miss Morley."

"You cannot think that I should be happy at the idea of you getting married."

"If I don't marry money, my girl, you'll be even less happy. If I don't find a wife to pay my debts, I'll soon be in a sorry state indeed. Miss Morley has a goodly fortune and she is in love with me."

"But you don't love her, do you?"

"Love her?" said Thomas in a tone implying it was an absurd question. "A gentleman doesn't expect to love his wife."

"But she is pretty."

"Pretty enough," he said, getting up from the bed and starting to dress.

Claire watched him sullenly. "I do wish I was a lady with a fortune."

He smiled. "So do I." Thomas shook his head as he buttoned his shirt. "You know very well I cannot marry as I choose. I don't want to marry Miss Morley. By my way of thinking she's a spoiled creature too accustomed to having her own way. But in any case, I'm far from marrying her. And to make matters worse, she has another suitor, the Earl of Dunraven."

"Dunraven?" said Claire. "Why, I've heard of him. My friend Meg told me she was once very friendly with him. That was years ago, of course. And he wants to marry Miss Morley?"

"So I'm told. I had thought his reputation would prevent her parents from allowing such a match, but now it seems they are warming to the idea. He's damned rich and an earl. But you must tell me about this friend of yours and Dunraven. It won't hurt to have a bit of information to spread around so that details of Dunraven's past get back to the Morleys."

Only too pleased to enlighten Thomas about her friend's affair with the earl, Claire began to tell him all she knew of the matter.

After returning to Longmeadow, Dunraven retired to bed and slept for a long time. By the time he rose, it was too late to call on the Morleys, so he spent his time idly roaming about the estate with Macduff at his side.

In the morning, he retired to the library to devote his attention to plans for repairs and renovation of the house. Having grown unusually fond of Longmeadow, the earl was determined to restore it to its original state, along with necessary modern improvements that would make it more livable. Dunraven had never cared much for his other houses. Even his childhood home, Dunraven Castle, had little appeal for him. But Longmeadow was very different. He felt as if he belonged there and he knew that when he and Georgiana were married, they would live there most of the year.

Seated at his desk in the library, Dunraven studied some of the old drawings of the house. He began to make notes which he would send to his architect in London.

"Excuse me, my lord," said the butler, entering the library.

"Yes, Canfield?" said the earl, looking up.

"The post, my lord," said Canfield, depositing a stack of letters on the earl's desk.

"Thank you, Canfield," said Dunraven, taking up one letter and opening it. It was an invitation to a ball from a Mrs. Fanshawe. The earl tossed it aside. He detested balls. Even before he was disgraced in society, he never attended them.

And, of course, since he had been declared persona non grata by the Prince Regent, he was never invited to balls in London. Dunraven stared at the invitation. How odd that this unknown woman in Richton had invited him. Obviously, she was unaware of his reputation. Or, reflected the earl, perhaps she was aware of it and wished to exhibit such a dangerous animal as himself to her guests. A sardonic smile appeared on his face. Well, he certainly had no desire to attend a ball at the home of someone he had never met.

Dunraven picked up another of his letters, but after a time, took up the invitation again. Perhaps Georgiana would be attending this ball. If she were, it may not be such a bad thing to go. After all, it would give the locals the opportunity to stare at him to their hearts' content. The thought amused the earl. He looked down at Macduff, who was sleeping underneath his desk. "What do you think? Shall I go to the ball?"

Macduff opened his eyes and raised his head for a moment, but then plopped it back down and resumed his nap. Dunraven grinned and began to open one of his other letters.

While Dunraven occupied himself in his library at Longmeadow, Georgiana sat in the drawing room, staring pensively out the window. Since parting from the earl yesterday morning, she had thought of him constantly. As she stared out at the park surrounding Highcroft, she considered her feelings for Dunraven.

"Georgie!" Kitty's voice brought her from her reverie.

"Yes?" said Georgiana turning toward the door to see her sister come into the room.

"Mama has said that we could go to Richton. Do say you will come, for I must go to Mr. Cox's shop to see if he has any ribbon that will do for my bonnet, the one I am redoing."

"You are always redoing some bonnet or another," said Georgiana. "If you had to take up a trade, I daresay you would be a milliner."

"I should indeed," said Kitty. "It would be far better than a cook or a barmaid to be sure."

This remark caused Georgiana to burst into laughter. "What a simpleton you are, Kit. Well, I shall be glad to walk to the village with you. It is a fine day for it."

The girls fetched their bonnets and reticules and were soon off accompanied by their redoubtable maid, Aggie, who, as befitted her position, walked several paces behind them. Kitty talked about her bonnet for a time, but switched the conversation to more serious matters before they had gone very far.

"Georgiana, you must tell me. Have you decided to marry Lord Dunraven?"

Georgiana frowned. "I don't know what to do, Kit."

"And why not? Both Papa and Mama will not object. Papa thinks there is no one like Dunraven, ever since he helped Demon Dancer. And I know you do fancy him. Truly, it is as wonderful as a novel that the earl just happened to buy Long-meadow. Indeed, if that is not fate, I should be greatly amazed. And you will live at Longmeadow and we will see you all the time."

"It is not so simple," said Georgiana.

"Isn't it?" replied Kitty.

"No, it isn't. Perhaps I do have feelings for Dunraven. But what about Thomas? I have feelings for him as well."

"But Papa would never allow you to marry Lord Thomas, Georgiana. Surely you wouldn't think of eloping with him."

"No, of course not."

"Then you must forget about him."

"But what sort of person am I to change my affections so quickly? And Thomas loves me so dearly. It will crush him if I reject him now."

"But if you love Dunraven better, you must tell Lord Thomas," said Kitty. "It is cruel to allow him to believe you still love him."

"But perhaps I do still love him," said Georgiana.

"I do think you should decide if you do," said Kitty, a trifle impatiently.

"It is not so easy," said Georgiana. "When you are older, you will understand."

Since Kitty didn't like to be reminded of her comparative youth, she didn't appreciate her sister's remark. She was about to apprise her sister of this fact when she caught sight of a horseman coming up the road. "Good heavens," said Kitty, "I do believe that is Lord Thomas. And to think we were just talking of him."

Georgiana looked down the road to see a rider approaching them. She saw that Kitty was right. It was Thomas. She watched him silently, acutely aware that the old excitement that had previously greeted his appearance was no longer there.

"He doesn't sit a horse very well, does he?" said Kitty.

Georgiana directed a disapproving look at her sister even though she knew that Kitty was right. Thomas was no horseman.

Thomas, who was returning from his trip to Hillborough, could scarcely believe his good fortune in meeting the Morley sisters. Applying his riding crop to his horse's flanks, he hurried ahead. Coming up to them, he pulled the animal up short and dismounted.

"Miss Morley, how good to see you," he said, tipping his hat politely. "And good day to you, Miss Kitty. I hope you ladies are enjoying this fine weather."

"Yes, we are, Lord Thomas," said Georgiana.

"You are on your way to Richton?"

"Yes," said Georgiana, "Kitty is in need of ribbon to trim her hat. I am happy for any excuse to take a walk on such a day as this."

After a few more exchanges of innocuous remarks about the weather, Thomas decided it was time for bolder action. "I must speak with you alone for a moment, Georgiana. Your sister will excuse us."

Agnes, who had been standing behind them eyeing Thomas with disapproval, cleared her throat. Georgiana turned to her. "Aggie, Lord Thomas must speak with me for a moment. We'll only take a few steps."

"Miss Georgiana," said Agnes sternly, "I don't think that—"

Georgiana interrupted. "Don't be an old stick, Aggie. I shall only be a short distance away. Not out of sight."

"Yes, Aggie," said Kitty, happy that her sister would have an opportunity to tell Thomas that her affections were engaged elsewhere. "There is no harm in that."

Agnes would have protested further, but Kitty winked at her in such a knowing way, that she desisted. As Georgiana and Thomas walked off a few paces with the bay mare following behind, Kitty whispered to Agnes. "Don't worry, Aggie, this is Georgie's chance to tell Lord Thomas that she will marry Lord Dunraven."

"Indeed?" said Agnes. "Then I shan't object. The master will be glad if she does so. He doesn't like that young man."

Nodding, Kitty continued to watch her sister. When Georgiana and Thomas had gone a sufficient distance to be able to talk privately, they stopped and Thomas began. "My dearest Georgiana, I so wished to talk to you. I have been so disturbed by reports that you will marry Dunraven. Tell me you have no intention of doing so."

Georgiana looked down in confusion. "I don't know what to say, Thomas. It is all so very odd. I only just met Lord Dunraven, but I must confess that I have developed an attachment for him."

"An attachment?" cried Thomas. "You have developed an

attachment for such a man? My poor darling, you cannot know what sort of man he is."

"I know that he has not behaved altogether well in the past."

"Not altogether well? That is mild censure indeed for a man who is a notorious rake. And were such behavior only in his past, one might not find him so reprehensible."

"What do you mean?" said Georgiana.

"My dear girl, you cannot think a man such as that doesn't keep a mistress?"

Georgiana regarded him in surprise. Oddly enough, that had not occurred to her. "You don't even know him," she said irritably.

"Everyone knows of him. Meg Aldridge, the actress, was his mistress. And there were many others."

"That doesn't mean he has one now," said Georgiana.

"Indeed?" said Thomas. "I happen to know that he has a mistress in London. And I shouldn't doubt that she is only one of many."

Georgiana could only regard him in astonishment. "How could you say such a thing? It isn't true."

"My dear Georgiana, upon my honor, I would never tell you this if it wasn't true. I love you, Georgiana. I do not wish to see you marry a man such as Dunraven who would cause you nothing but misery."

Georgiana was so taken aback by this speech that she could not reply. Turning away from him, she hurried back to Kitty and Agnes. "Georgiana!" said Thomas following after her.

"I pray you leave me," said Georgiana.

"But Georgiana . . ."

"You had best be off, m'lord," said Agnes, placing her hands on her hips in a belligerent pose.

Thomas hesitated for a moment before mounting his horse and riding off.

"What did he say to upset you?" said Kitty.

"I can't speak of it," said Georgiana.

"My dear miss," cried Agnes, "you must tell us what is amiss."

"No, I don't wish to say anything about it."

"But did you tell Lord Thomas you no longer wish to marry him?" said Kitty.

"I don't know if I wish to marry anyone," said Georgiana

hotly. "And I am going home." Turning, she strode off in the direction they had come. Kitty and Agnes exchanged a glance and then walked off after Georgiana.

Dunraven did not call at Highcroft that afternoon, much to Georgiana's relief. She had no wish to see him so soon after her disturbing conversation with Thomas. They had other callers, however, and Georgiana managed to be pleasant to their guests.

She said little at dinner and afterward refused to tell Kitty what was the matter. After an evening spent playing cards, Georgiana retired to her room, where Agnes assisted her to get ready for bed.

"Aggie," said Georgiana, "I must ask you something."

"Yes, miss?"

"Do all married gentlemen keep mistresses?"

Agnes was quite astonished by the question. "Miss Georgie, I cannot imagine that you would ask such a thing!"

"I don't think Papa has a mistress," she said.

"Indeed, he does not!" said Agnes.

Georgiana turned to look up at her maid. "But how can you be sure?"

"I am sure," said Agnes stoutly. "The very idea that the master . . . Truly, Miss Georgiana, I cannot imagine why you would say such a thing."

"But many gentlemen do have mistresses. And I know that many ladies don't mind. But I should mind terribly."

"As well you should," said Agnes severely.

"Then you don't think a man must have a mistress, in addition to his wife?"

"Indeed not!" cried Agnes. "Why, it is sinful to suggest such a thing. A man should be faithful to his wife as a wife must be faithful to her husband." She regarded Georgiana closely. "Now, miss, why are you asking me these questions?"

"Oh, nothing, Aggie."

"But, my dear lamb, you must tell Aggie." She placed a sympathetic hand on Georgiana's shoulder.

Georgiana managed to recover. It wouldn't do to discuss the matter any further with Agnes. "No, really, Aggie, it is nothing. You may go. Good night, Aggie."

Thus dismissed, Agnes could only bid her young mistress good night and take her leave.

Chapter 16

Gray clouds shrouded the afternoon sun as Dunraven rode his bay mare toward Highcroft. Although overcast and rather cool for that time of year, it was a fine day for riding, and the earl was in particularly good spirits as he continued down the road that led to Georgiana's home. Macduff, who had been allowed to accompany his master, ran happily behind the horse, pausing now and then to investigate an interesting sound or smell.

Turning into the gravel lane that led to the house, the earl noted a lady sitting in front of the house with a sketchbook. Thinking it was Georgiana, he urged his horse ahead. When he drew closer, however, he recognized that the young lady wasn't Georgiana, but her sister.

Kitty looked up as he approached. "Lord Dunraven," she said with a smile.

"Miss Kitty," he said, tipping his hat and then dismounting from the horse. By this time Macduff had joined them. He ran up to Kitty, wagging his short tail.

"What a dear little dog," said Kitty, patting the terrier's head.

"Are you an artist?" said the earl.

The question made Kitty laugh. "Oh, no, I am not in the least talented. But I do enjoy drawing. I am sketching the trees over there." Placing the sketchpad and drawing pencil down, she rose from her chair. "I am so glad you are here, although Papa shall be quite vexed to have missed you. He has gone off riding Demon Dancer. Mama had a headache and is resting, but Georgiana is in the garden. I do hope she will be happy to see you."

Seeing the earl's expression at this remark, Kitty hastily continued. "Oh, I should think she would be, but she has been acting very strangely since you were last here. She has been quite gloomy and she won't tell me what's wrong. I believe it's something Lord Thomas Jeffreys said to her yesterday."

"Jeffreys?" said the earl with a frown.

"Yes, we met him on the way to the village."

"He is here in Suffolk?"

"Yes," said Kitty, noting that this clearly displeased the earl. It was obvious that he was in love with Georgiana. Kitty suppressed a sigh. The earl was so romantic. Georgiana was so lucky to have such a suitor.

One of the servants had come out to see to the earl's horse. "Why don't you join Georgiana in the garden, my lord?" said Kitty. "I fear I must stay here and finish my drawing."

The earl nodded and took his leave of Kitty. Walking around the house, he entered the garden. He saw Georgiana at once. She was attired in a peacock-blue dress and matching spencer, and she wore a broad-brimmed straw hat trimmed with blue ribbons. Dunraven found her stooping beside some flowers, clipping blooms with scissors and depositing them in a basket. Intent upon her work, she was unaware of his approach.

"Georgiana."

She turned to regard him in some surprise. "Lord Dunraven," she said, rising to her feet.

He smiled. She looked very charming standing there with her basket of flowers. Macduff, who had followed his master into the garden, ran up to Georgiana. "Oh, here is Macduff," she said, leaning down to scratch him behind the ears.

"The flowers are beautiful," said Dunraven, "nearly as beautiful as yourself."

"I do not expect such flummery from you, my lord," said Georgiana, looking at him for the first time. As her blue eyes met his brown ones, she felt a now familiar tremor of excitement. She could not deny that she felt an exceedingly strong attraction to him. And yet, she couldn't help thinking about Thomas's words. If he did have a mistress, she couldn't bear it.

"Georgiana," he said, reaching out to take her arm, "I would like to talk to you. Why don't we walk to that lily pond of yours?"

"No, I think not," said Georgiana, pulling her arm away.

"Why don't we sit here?" She motioned to two wrought-iron benches.

"As you wish," he said. She sat down and he took a seat beside her. "What is wrong?"

"Nothing," she said.

"I can see that there is something wrong."

"I assure you are mistaken, my lord," said Georgiana.

Slipping his arm around her waist, he was encouraged that she did not try to remove it. "You know that I want you to be my wife. Say you will marry me."

His closeness made her feel weak. "We scarcely know each other."

His arm tightened around her. "I know that I want you more than I have ever wanted any woman. I know that you are destined to be my wife."

Pulling away, Georgiana rose from the bench, mustering her self-control with great difficulty. "I am not so certain that we are well suited, my lord."

Rising up to stand before her, Dunraven caught her hand. "Not well suited? By God, that night at Longmeadow I thought we were well suited indeed."

Georgiana turned very red. The earl continued. "I am determined to have you for my wife, Georgiana Morley." The earl would have taken her into his arms at that point except for the untimely appearance of Sir Arthur.

"Ah, Dunraven!" cried the baronet, striding toward them. "I just returned and Kitty told me you were here. I was riding Demon Dancer. He really is doing splendidly. You must come and see him."

While his lordship was not very pleased at being interrupted, he nodded to Sir Arthur in a civil manner. "Very well, sir, I should be glad to see Demon Dancer."

"Come, then," said Sir Arthur, taking him by the elbow. "And you, too, Georgiana."

"Oh, I must take the flowers in," said Georgiana. "Do excuse me." With these words, she took up her basket and hurried into the house.

Sir Arthur led the earl to the front of the house, where Demon Dancer stood with one of the grooms. The two men discussed the horse for what seemed a long time before going into the house. "You will have tea, Dunraven?" said the baronet.

"Thank you, yes," replied the earl. He directed a stern look at Macduff, who was standing at his feet. "You stay here, Macduff."

"Why, there is no need of that," said Sir Arthur. "The little fellow may come in if he pleases. I've no objection to a dog about the house. Indeed, he is a fine-looking fellow. I've always been fond of terriers. Why, I had a wonderful little dog in my youth. Her name was Pixie. What a hellion she was. I carried her about in a saddlebag when I went hunting. If the fox went to ground, she'd dig him out."

"I daresay Macduff would not take kindly to being hauled about on a horse," said the earl. "We will leave the hunting to Buckthorne's hounds."

"I should like to see those hounds very much," said Sir Arthur. "And Mr. Buckthorne."

"Buckthorne has gone to town, but he will return shortly. The hounds remain at Longmeadow, and you are most welcome to come and see them at any time."

"I shall do so very soon," said the baronet. "I must say I am looking forward to your hunts. I can tell that Demon Dancer will enjoy a bit of sport." Sir Arthur escorted his guest into the house and to the drawing room, where they found Georgiana and Kitty waiting.

"The earl will stay to tea," said Sir Arthur.

"I have ordered it, Papa," said Georgiana.

"Good," said the baronet, motioning for Dunraven to be seated.

Georgiana was careful to take a seat as far from the earl as possible. "How was Demon Dancer, Papa?"

"Oh, he was wonderful. I've never had such a horse in all my life. And to think that if Dunraven had not been there to help him, we might have lost him."

"Oh, I don't doubt that Shaw would have managed," returned the earl.

"I don't know about that," said the baronet.

Georgiana sat regarding Dunraven with a serious expression. All she could think about was what Thomas had said. Did the earl have a mistress? Did he profess love to her and imagine going to another woman's bed? The idea was simply horrible.

"Will you be going to Mrs. Fanshawe's ball, Lord Dunraven?" said Kitty.

The earl looked first at Georgiana and then her sister. "I expect I will. Especially if Miss Morley will do me the honor of reserving a dance for me."

"Of course, she will," said the baronet, answering for his daughter.

"Oh, I cannot bear that I am not going," said Kitty, turning to her father. "My parents believe I am too young. But I have turned fourteen. Surely that isn't too young."

"It is indeed," said the baronet sternly. "Females spend their first years wishing to be older and the rest wishing to be younger."

"Truly, Papa," said Georgiana, "is that any different from boys and men?"

"I suppose not," admitted Sir Arthur. "Well, I would gladly avoid this ball if I could. But one must humor the ladies."

At this moment the servants entered with the tea things, presenting a distraction. During tea, the conversation was polite, but Dunraven noted that Georgiana seemed distracted. It was rather frustrating not knowing what was the matter. However, no opportunity presented itself to speak with her privately, so the earl left Highcroft and returned to Longmeadow feeling very much dissatisfied.

Shortly before dinner time, Dunraven sat in his library studying Longmeadow estate books when Canfield entered the room. "Mr. Buckthorne has returned from town, my lord."

"Has he? Good," said the earl. "Have him come in."

The servant returned shortly to announce him. Buckthorne strode into the library. He beamed at seeing Dunraven. "My dear friend, how glad I am to be back at Longmeadow." He sat down in an armchair near the earl's desk.

"I didn't expect you back so soon, Buck."

"Why, I never wanted to go at all," said Buckthorne. "And Mrs. Buckthorne was in an exceedingly ill humor the entire time I was there. And her mother! By my oath, Dunraven, I have never known a more disagreeable woman. I cannot live under the same roof with her for long. I completed my business and hurried away as fast as I could. But what are you doing?"

"I am going over the estate records."

"Good God, I cannot imagine anything duller. Yes, indeed, I am worried about you. I come back to find you sitting with some dusty old ledger book. You should have come with me. I could have stayed at your town house. Well, no, I daresay I could not have done so. What if Mrs. Buckthorne had heard of it? But I didn't even go to Mrs. Trotter's. Mrs. Buckthorne had me go to some dull parties. I couldn't escape. It was excruciating to be sure." Buckthorne looked over at the mantel clock. "I do hope I am not too late for dinner, Dunraven."

"No, it will be ready soon," said the earl with a smile.

"Good, I am so hungry," replied Buckthorne. "And how are my hounds?"

"I imagine they are well."

"Imagine? You haven't seen them?"

"I confess I do not spend my time with them. But as I have heard nothing from your man, Jenkins, I suspect your hounds are well enough. And I see from the butcher's bill that they are being well fed."

"Good, one must feed them well, you know."

"Apparently," said Dunraven.

"You'll not regret a thing when we have the finest hunts in all of England." He smiled broadly. "Yes, it is good to be here. Oh, I did ask Mrs. Buckthorne about that Jeffreys. She knew all about him. I knew she would. It seems he is known to be a fortune hunter in pursuit of your Miss Morley. Mrs. Buckthorne told me he is also addicted to gambling. I believe her tone implied that he wasn't the only one so addicted. But indeed, you don't believe I'm a hopeless gamester, do you, Dunraven? I'll wager you don't think so."

Dunraven laughed. "You *are* a hopeless gamester, Buck. But I don't wish to talk about you. Tell me about Jeffreys."

"He isn't very popular," said Buckthorne, "according to Mrs. Buckthorne. Of course, few are popular with her. She dismissed him as a young coxcomb. And then when I went to Whites, I saw James Huffington. I brought up Jeffreys and he told me a very interesting bit of information. Jeffreys's mistress is the actress Claire Stevenson. You remember her, don't you?"

"I don't."

"She was in that play we saw at Drury Lane. That one by that fellow Shakespeare."

"You must narrow it down more than that," said the earl with a smile.

"You know the one where the fellow had the skull. He was some sort of prince."

"*Hamlet*?"

"It well could be. Miss Stevenson played the girl who went mad. Olivia."

"Ophelia," said Dunraven. "Well, I haven't seen *Hamlet* for years."

"Well, perhaps you didn't see it then. But she is a dashed pretty girl. Huffington was quite irritated with Jeffreys. It seems he fancied the girl himself. She was quite taken with Jeffreys, even though he hardly has two pennies to rub together."

"Jeffreys is in Suffolk and he has spoken with Miss Morley," said the earl.

"Has he?" said Buckthorne. "I daresay he is a meddlesome fellow. But what of your proposal of marriage? Has she accepted you?"

Dunraven frowned. "No, she hasn't."

"Well, it has only been a few days after all," said Buckthorne. At that moment, the butler arrived announcing dinner, causing Buckthorne to jump to his feet with such enthusiasm that the earl couldn't help but laugh.

Chapter 17

The days until the Fanshawes' ball passed quickly though unhappily for Georgiana. She remained in a state of confusion over her feelings for Dunraven. The evening after her meeting with him in the garden, she had received a letter from Thomas. Had Sir Arthur known of this correspondence, he would have prevented his daughter from opening it. But Sir Arthur had not been there to look at the post when it had arrived, so Georgiana was able to take the letter to her room and read it.

In a long and forcefully written document, Thomas declared his undying love for her. His words had been so impassioned that Georgiana could not be unmoved. The letter, combined with her doubts about Dunraven, added to her agitation.

Dunraven had called most every afternoon, hoping to have an opportunity to speak to her alone, but he was always frustrated. Upon the rare occasions when he could exchange a private word or two, Georgiana would hardly answer him.

The day of the Fanshawes' ball soon came round. Georgiana, knowing that both Dunraven and Thomas would be in attendance, dreaded it. For the past few nights she had had difficulty sleeping. She had disturbing dreams involving Dunraven and had wakened more than once in a state of feverish excitement.

When it was time to get dressed for the ball, Georgiana sat rather dejectedly in her dressing room while Agnes bustled about, seeing to her clothes. Georgiana wordlessly submitted to her maid's attention. When she was attired in her ballgown, she barely glanced in the mirror.

"Whatever is the matter, miss?" said Agnes finally.

Georgiana sat down to allow Agnes to adjust her coiffure.

"Oh, nothing, Aggie. It is only that I should prefer staying home."

"You prefer staying home? Why, that isn't like you in the least, miss. I never once heard you say you wished to stay home before, especially when you were going to a ball."

Georgiana was spared the necessity of a reply by the appearance of her sister. "You do look beautiful, Georgie!" cried Kitty. "That is my favorite of all your gowns."

"Thank you, Kit," said Georgiana, looking into the mirror. It was a lovely dress, stunning in its simplicity. Fashioned from peach-colored Italian silk, the stylish ballgown featured a high waist, extremely low-cut neckline, and tiny puff sleeves.

Agnes carefully placed some satin roses in her young mistress's hair. "You are wearing your pearls, are you not, miss?" she said.

Georgiana nodded. Fetching the pearls from the jewel case, Agnes fastened them around her neck. "Yes, that does look very pretty, miss."

Kitty sighed. "Georgiana looks like a fairy princess while I cannot even go to the ball. Once again I must stay home like a miserable little girl."

"You are a miserable little girl, Kit," said Georgiana, smiling for the first time.

"You are horrid," said Kitty, laughing in spite of herself.

"Well, don't think I shall enjoy myself. I don't know what I shall do with Dunraven and Thomas both there."

"I should think it splendid to have two dashing suitors," said Kitty. "I should love to have all sorts of men fighting for my hand. But, Georgie, you have been acting so strangely all week. And you will never tell me why you seem upset with Dunraven."

"I am not upset with him."

"But you are. I don't understand it. When he called here, you never seemed glad to see him, although I do think you are in love with him. And I am glad of it, for I do like him."

"Now, Miss Kitty," said Agnes, "your sister is late. She must hurry or her ladyship will be quite vexed."

Georgiana rose from her chair. Agnes handed her gloves and fan, and then Georgiana and Kitty went downstairs to meet their parents. "Oh, Mama!" cried Kitty. "You look beautiful."

"Thank you, my darling," said her ladyship, pleased at her daughter's enthusiasm. She did look very nice in her pale blue satin gown, and she was looking forward to the ball. "But look at you, Georgiana. You are so beautiful. But we are very late, my dears. Elizabeth will be wondering whether we are coming. The carriage is ready and we must be going."

Without further comment, Sir Arthur escorted his wife and daughter out to the waiting carriage, where a footman handed them into vehicle. Kitty waved as the carriage started off. When it was out of sight, she returned to the house, a rather dejected expression on her face.

Some years ago, when Mr. Fanshawe's fortune had increased, he had acquired property and had built a very grand house upon it. The residence was Georgian in design and very elegant, and Elizabeth Fanshawe was terribly proud of it. She was especially pleased that it boasted an uncommonly beautiful ballroom, which was the largest in the area.

That evening, the house was filled with excitement as a line of carriages made their way toward the front door of the Fanshawes' residence. When each vehicle arrived at its destination, it stopped to deposit ladies and gentlemen dressed in their finery.

Once inside, the guests ascended a grand stairway to the ballroom. After being announced they entered the lavish room to be greeted by their host and hostess. There was an atmosphere of gaiety and anticipation among the guests, for this was a great social occasion among the local families.

Sir Francis and Lady Pelham and their nephew Thomas Jeffreys had been among the first guests to arrive. While Thomas would never have committed such a social blunder as to come at such a time, he had had little choice in the matter. A stickler for punctuality, Sir Francis always arrived early. Since Thomas didn't have his own carriage, he had had to be ready at the appointed time. After all, Thomas was well aware that his uncle was quite capable of leaving him behind.

The early arrival time did allow Thomas to see all the members of the company come in. While waiting for Georgiana to appear, he amused himself by standing at the side and viewing each guest with a critical eye.

On the whole, Thomas felt the company far beneath him.

There were far too many ladies wearing unfashionable gowns several seasons old and far too many gentlemen wearing ill-fitting coats that would have provoked laughter in town. He stood there bemoaning the fact that he found himself among such provincial nobodies. Thomas twirled his jewel-encrusted quizzing glass in some impatience and wished that Georgiana would arrive soon.

When the Morleys were finally announced, Thomas was very pleased. He brightened as he watched Georgiana and her parents come in. She was unquestionably the most beautiful woman in the room, he thought. He very much approved of the stylish gown she was wearing, which clearly put most of the other poor dowdy creatures to shame.

Although Thomas knew very well that he would receive a cold reception from Georgiana's parents, he lost no time in making his way over to them. Ignoring Sir Arthur's icy stare, he bowed to Lady Morley and then Georgiana. "Good evening, Lady Morley and Miss Morley. Sir Arthur."

Georgiana smiled at Thomas. He looked very dashing standing there in his fashionable evening clothes. She thought of the letter he had sent in which he had declared his undying love for her. Although she had not been unmoved by the letter, Georgiana was acutely aware that the old excitement that Thomas's presence usually provoked was gone. It was replaced by a certain awkwardness and guilt. What sort of person was she, she asked herself, to so easily supplant one gentleman with another in her affections?

"I do hope you will reserve a dance for me, Miss Morley," said Thomas.

"Yes, of course," said Georgiana.

Sir Arthur, who was not in the least pleased with his daughter's response, took her by the arm. "Come, Georgiana."

She allowed herself to be led off. "Confound it," said the baronet irritably, "why did you agree to dance with that jackanapes?"

"I could hardly refuse," said Georgiana.

"Indeed," said Lady Morley, coming to her defense, "one must be civil."

"Well, you are not to dance more than once with him. I can scarcely imagine his effrontery in coming up to us in such a manner. As if he didn't know what I think of him."

"Now, now, Arthur," said Lady Morley, "you mustn't upset yourself."

"We should not have come. Look, there is Pelham over there. I don't like being in the same room with him. And to have to see that nephew of his is quite intolerable."

At that moment they were joined by a lady and gentleman of their acquaintance and the baronet was diverted from his ill humor. Georgiana looked over at Thomas, who had walked to the other side of the room where he stood staring at her. She looked away. If she no longer loved Thomas, she should certainly tell him, she reflected. But thinking that he would be devastated at this admission, she found it difficult to contemplate.

Others approached them and Georgiana became encircled by a group of her parents' friends and acquaintances. All of them were in excellent spirits and soon Georgiana was involved in conversation.

It was some time later before Dunraven appeared at the ball. Since the dancing had already started, the sound of the orchestra prevented a good many people from hearing his name announced. Those who did, however, were very interested in seeing the earl.

Since his arrival at Longmeadow, Dunraven had been much discussed. Few had met him. Indeed, most of the local gentry had been rather uncertain if they should call at Longmeadow. The topic had been debated at most of the country houses of the area with little resolution.

Because Dunraven had remained a rather mysterious and intimidating figure, the news that he had been invited to the Fanshawes' ball had caused a good deal of excitement. Although a good many respectable matrons had expressed reservations about attending a ball with such a disreputable person, no one had refused the invitation. Indeed, the prospect of seeing the earl in the flesh had certainly helped to make the ball extremely well attended.

"It is the Earl of Dunraven," said Elizabeth Fanshawe, who was standing by her husband. She had not yet made Dunraven's acquaintance and was very eager to do so. By fortunate circumstance Lady Morley was nearby. "Isabelle," called

Elizabeth, "there is Lord Dunraven. Do come and introduce us."

As Dunraven walked into the room, he was aware that people were staring at him. He was too accustomed to that to care much about it. He glanced about, looking for Georgiana. He finally caught sight of her among the dancers. There she was taking part in a spirited round dance with a stocky, middle-aged partner.

"Lord Dunraven," said Lady Morley coming up to him with her cousin Elizabeth and Mr. Fanshawe in tow.

"Lady Morley," said his lordship bowing slightly.

"Allow me to present your hostess, Mrs. Fanshawe and Mr. Fanshawe," said her ladyship.

"Mrs. Fanshawe," said the earl. He nodded to her husband. Elizabeth extended her hand. Taking it, Dunraven bowed politely. "Thank you for inviting me."

"Oh, I was only too happy to do so, my lord," said Elizabeth, very excited about finally meeting the infamous earl.

Sir Arthur, who had been talking with a group of gentlemen, looked over to see his wife and the Fanshawes with Dunraven. He quickly excused himself to join them.

"Dunraven!" cried Sir Arthur. "I am so glad you've come. You must meet everyone. I shall be happy to introduce you."

The earl allowed himself to be led around the ballroom, meeting the company. While he normally would have had little patience with such social niceties, he exhibited unusual forbearance. Dunraven was exceedingly civil to all he met, creating a most favorable impression.

One person that Sir Arthur was careful to avoid in making his introductions was Thomas Jeffreys. That young man stood rather aloof from the others. Having heard the earl's name being announced, he had been curious to finally see what his rival looked like.

While he had expected to find fault with Dunraven's looks, Thomas grudgingly admitted to himself that the earl was presentable enough. Although there was nothing of the dandy in Dunraven's appearance, he dressed with an understated elegance that defied criticism.

Thomas watched as the earl was greeted by the Morleys and Fanshawes. He followed his progress about the room as he was introduced to some of the other guests. Thomas frowned to see that Dunraven was being received with such enthusiasm. It appeared that everyone was pleased to meet him.

Annoyed, Thomas set off to talk to some of the others. He was desirous of reminding the ladies and gentlemen in attendance of the Earl of Dunraven's scandalous reputation. Relishing the task, he headed for a group of the Fanshawes' guests.

An extremely popular young lady, Georgiana had committed herself to a good many dances before the music had started. Georgiana loved dancing, and since there were many gentlemen eager to be her partner, her spirits soon improved considerably.

Georgiana had not heard the earl announced. She had, of course, been thinking a good deal about him. Still, her dancing had so occupied her that she had little time to wonder where he was and when he would appear.

At the conclusion of one dance, Georgiana was met by Mrs. Crawford, a stout gray-haired matron who shooed away the gentlemen waiting to dance with her. "Do allow Miss Morley a moment to catch her breath," she said. "Indeed, I should think you would enjoy sitting for a short while, Miss Morley. Do come with me. I am so eager to speak with you."

Georgiana could hardly refuse without appearing rude, so she followed Mrs. Crawford to a row of chairs where they both sat down. Since Mrs. Crawford was a domineering lady altogether too fond of gossip, she had never been a favorite with Georgiana.

"You look so beautiful in your gown, Miss Morley."

"You are too kind, ma'am," replied Georgiana.

"I am so glad to have this opportunity to speak with you. Everyone is talking about Lord Dunraven. I was so glad to finally see what he looks like. He is a very handsome man."

"Is he here?" said Georgiana, looking around the room.

"Why, yes, there he is standing with Mr. Turnball."

Looking in the direction Mrs. Crawford was indicating, Georgiana caught sight of the earl. He looked very distinguished in his black evening clothes and seeing him caused her pulse to quicken.

"I do hope to meet him," continued Mrs. Crawford. "One doesn't often have the opportunity to make the acquaintance of a nobleman of his rank in our little village. Of course, my husband wouldn't be pleased at my speaking to him, considering Lord Dunraven's reputation. But I am told that he has been received at Highcroft. Your parents have obviously judged him acceptable." Her voice changed to a whisper. "I have heard that you are fond of him, Miss Morley."

Georgiana was at a loss for a reply. Noting her discomfiture, Mrs. Crawford only laughed. "I see it is true. And look! Lord Dunraven is glancing in our direction. Now he is coming this way! You must introduce me, Miss Morley."

The earl strode purposefully toward them. He was soon standing before Georgiana and her bothersome companion. "Miss Morley," he said bowing gravely to her.

"Lord Dunraven," said Georgiana, trying hard to maintain a pose of cool indifference. She glanced over at Mrs. Crawford. "Ma'am, allow me to present Lord Dunraven. My lord, this is Mrs. Crawford."

The earl directed a polite nod toward Mrs. Crawford, who appeared very thrilled at meeting the scandalous earl. "Oh, my lord," she cried, "this is a very great pleasure meeting you. I do hope you are enjoying your stay in our little community. I do think Longmeadow a charming place. I am sure you find it so. I suppose that you—"

At this point Dunraven cut her short. "I am enjoying Longmeadow, madam," he said. "You are good to inquire." Then, turning to Georgiana, he continued. "Miss Morley, I believe you have promised me a dance. Will you do me the honor of the next one?"

Nodding, Georgiana took his proffered arm and allowed the earl to lead her away. She was experiencing conflicting emotions as she walked alongside him. As usual, his closeness was provoking a feeling of intense excitement within her, but this was tempered by some resentment. If he had a mistress and was only pretending to care for her, it would be too much to bear.

Sensing something was wrong, the earl looked down at her. "What is the matter, Georgiana?"

"Nothing," she replied, not meeting his gaze.

They continued wordlessly until they arrived beside the other dancers. The orchestra began to play the opening strains of a waltz. After bowing formally to her, the earl took Georgiana's hand in his and placed his other hand on her waist. They began to dance.

Being in Dunraven's arms caused Georgiana to feel strangely lightheaded. His closeness brought back the memory of the night at Longmeadow. Remembering his passionate kiss caused Georgiana to blush.

The earl was experiencing not dissimilar feelings as he whirled about the room. He was very much aware of the scent of her perfume and the fact that her low-cut gown provided an enticing display of her charms. If only they were alone at Longmeadow, he thought.

"Have you given any thought to the date for our wedding?" said Dunraven, smiling down at her.

Georgiana looked up into his brown eyes. "You must stop saying such things."

"Why? Good God, Georgiana, a man cannot be expected to wait forever. And when you look so damned beautiful, I don't believe I can wait at all. It seems barbarously cruel for a man to hold you in his arms and then be expected to go home alone to his bed."

Georgiana frowned. "If that *is* what you do," she said in a low voice.

"What did you say?" said his lordship, regarding her in surprise.

"Nothing," said Georgiana.

"Indeed, you did say something. I believe it was 'If that is what you do.' Whatever do you mean, Georgiana?"

"Nothing," she said, frowning at him.

The earl stopped abruptly. "Now what did you mean?"

"Please," said Georgiana, "we cannot stop dancing. Everyone is looking at us."

"As if I would give a fig for that," said his lordship. Grasping her by the arm, he led her away from the dancers. When they arrived at a less crowded part of the ballroom, Dunraven stopped. "Now explain what you meant."

Georgiana looked down for a moment. Then meeting his gaze once again, she nodded. "Very well, my lord. I shall tell you. I did say 'If that is what you do,' because I was told that you have a mistress in town."

"What the deuce!" cried the earl. Several other ladies and gentlemen looked in their direction. "Who told you that?"

"That does not signify," said Georgiana.

"Indeed, it does," said Dunraven. "Tell me who told you this."

"Then it isn't true?" said Georgiana hopefully.

"By God, it isn't," returned the earl. "You know very well I have not led a blameless life. Far from it. And I have had mistresses. I'll not deny it. But there is no one now and hasn't been for some time. I want no woman to share my bed but you, Georgiana Morley."

"Then it was a lie," said Georgiana, a great wave of relief sweeping over her.

A glimmer of enlightenment came to Dunraven's face. "I believe I can guess who told you this. It was that fellow Jeffreys, wasn't it? Yes, I can see by your face it was. He is eager to slander me, to turn you against me."

"Oh, Dunraven, I am so glad it wasn't true," said Georgiana, resisting with some difficulty the urge to throw herself into his arms. "I did not want a husband who could not be faithful, who would make a fool of me." She regarded him earnestly. "I was so miserable thinking of it."

"You little goose," said the earl, smiling at her. "Then you do love me?"

"Oh, I do," said Georgiana.

Dunraven needed no further encouragement. Grasping Georgiana by the hand, he led her quickly toward the closest doorway, which led out into a corridor. Once outside the ballroom, he pulled Georgiana into his arms and embraced her fiercely. Then finding her lips with his own, he kissed her passionately. After holding her mouth prisoner for a very long time, his lips roamed down her neck and then to the tops of her breasts, where they lingered.

"God in Heaven!" cried a masculine voice. "Have you no shame, sir!"

Dunraven spun around to see a well-dressed young man standing before them. "Dammit," said the earl, his face reddening with anger. "You are not wanted here, sir."

"I can see that," said Thomas Jeffreys, swinging his quizzing glass. "Did you intend to ravish the lady here in the hallway? It seems that is audacious even for you."

Georgiana, who had by now regained her composure,

placed her arm on the earl's. "Come, my lord, we should re-join the guests."

"Yes, I think that would be wise," said Thomas, adopting the languid pose he favored in London drawing rooms. He smiled at Dunraven. "I don't believe we have been introduced, Dunraven. I am Lord Thomas Jeffreys."

"Jeffreys?" said the earl, frowning at him.

Thomas made an ironical bow. "Your servant, sir," he said.

While Dunraven liked to think that the hotheaded days of his youth had long since passed, at that moment he felt his temper rising. He walked toward Thomas, with Georgiana clinging to his arm. "You have been spreading lies about me to this lady," he said, glowering darkly.

Although Thomas didn't like the look in Dunraven's eye, he stood his ground bravely, hoping to impress Georgiana. "I cannot imagine what you mean."

"You know damned well what I mean," said Dunraven.

Georgiana glanced from Thomas to the earl. Seeing his angry expression, she pressed her hand against his arm. "My lord, we should return to the ballroom." She frowned at Thomas. "I know that you weren't telling the truth, Thomas."

"About the earl and his mistress?" said Thomas. "Why, you cannot believe he would admit the truth to you. Of course, he would deny it."

"You damned villain," said the earl, losing his temper completely and rushing up to Thomas. Grasping him roughly by the lapels of his coat, Dunraven scowled. "You're a scoundrel, sir."

For all his apparent bravado, Thomas was not without misgivings about rousing the earl's anger. "Do unhand me, Dunraven," he said, his face reddening.

The earl released him roughly, causing Thomas to stumble backward and nearly lose his footing. "Now get out of my sight," Dunraven said.

Thomas retreated toward the entrance to the ballroom. He paused to smooth the front of his coat. "If you think I shall leave a man like you alone with Miss Morley, you are very much mistaken. Georgiana, return to the ballroom at once. You do not know your danger. This man is entirely unprincipled."

"Dunraven, please!" cried Georgiana, frightened by the enraged look that now appeared on the earl's face.

Thomas took a few steps backward until he stood in the doorway. "I shall summon Sir Arthur. He'll not be happy to hear of the liberties you have taken with Miss Morley. To lead a young innocent girl away from the watchful eyes of the company to have your way with her. Why, it is the height of debauchery! You appall me, Dunraven."

The earl could bear this no longer. Pulling free of Georgiana's restraining arm, he lunged toward Thomas, who retreated hastily into the ballroom. Blinded by anger, Dunraven ignored Georgiana's pleas. He caught up with Thomas inside the room. "You dare to speak to me in such a manner!" he said in a voice so loud that a number of ladies and gentlemen turned to stare.

"I shall speak to you in any manner I wish!" said Thomas, whose courage was faltering a bit as the enraged earl stepped toward him.

"You'll regret your insolent lies," muttered Dunraven.

"I suppose you'll call me out, hoping to shoot me in a duel? This is your custom, I believe."

These words caused the color to drain from Dunraven's face. Then losing all self-control, he directed a punch to Thomas's midsection, causing that gentleman to bend over gasping. "I shall kill you with my bare hands!" shouted the earl, directing another blow to Thomas and causing him to fall to the floor.

"Dunraven!" cried a horrified Georgiana, who had hurried up beside him. She grasped his arm. "Do stop! For my sake!"

By this time a good many of the guests had turned their attention upon the unfortunate scene. They had gasped in horror as Dunraven had hit Thomas. Among them had been Sir Arthur, who now rushed forward.

"Are you mad, Dunraven!" cried the baronet. "Stop it! What has come over you!"

The earl looked first at Sir Arthur and then at Thomas, who was still on the floor moaning and cursing. It took a moment for Dunraven to come to his senses. "I am sorry," he said.

"By God, I should hope so," said Sir Arthur. "I suggest you leave here, Dunraven, before more harm is done. Your behavior is indefensible."

"Yes, do go," said Georgiana, pressing his arm.

"Georgiana, come here," commanded Sir Arthur. Releasing the earl's arm with some reluctance, she went to her father.

"Go, sir!" said Sir Arthur.

The earl could only cast a pained look at Georgiana before retreating from the room. While Sir Arthur and another gentleman hurried to assist Thomas up from the floor, the ballroom buzzed with talk of the astonishing scene that had just transpired.

Georgiana sat forlornly in the carriage as it made its way from the ball. They had left soon after the unfortunate incident. Thomas, who had recovered from his punishment, had been eager to tell Sir Arthur of how he had discovered the earl taking shocking advantage of Georgiana.

Sir Arthur, who sat opposite his wife and daughter in the darkened vehicle, folded his arms across his chest. It was some time before he spoke. "I can see that I was wrong to believe Dunraven was not so bad as he had been painted. What he did tonight was totally inexcusable."

"But he was sorely provoked," said Georgiana.

"Sorely provoked? Good God, a gentleman does not start a brawl in a ballroom with ladies present, no matter what the provocation. And I know that young Jeffreys isn't so innocent. You know how I detest the young cub. Still, that doesn't excuse Dunraven." He shook his head. "I don't think he is the sort of man you should marry. A man with a temper like that can't be trusted. No, I should worry about you too much."

"You cannot think that he would harm me?" said Georgiana.

"One never knows," returned the baronet.

"Georgiana," said Lady Morley, "your father is right. Lord Dunraven is too hotheaded. To resort to fisticuffs at a ball is too much to be borne."

"And that he took Georgiana from the ballroom," said Sir Arthur.

"Papa, I love him. We are to marry."

"That doesn't excuse such behavior," said the baronet. "Indeed, I wonder if you have any sense at all. And I shall have to think very carefully about whether to allow you to marry such a man. It seems I have been lulled into thinking him a fine enough fellow simply because he is dashed good with horses."

"But Papa," said Georgiana, "he did lose his temper. It was wrong of him to strike Thomas. I know that, but Thomas made him so angry. And it was Thomas who told me Dunraven had a mistress and it was a lie."

"I don't want you talking about such things," said Sir Arthur. He turned to his wife. "Do you know about this?"

Lady Morley nodded unhappily. "Everyone was talking about Lord Dunraven at the ball. Elizabeth told me that she heard he does have a mistress. And with his reputation, it isn't surprising."

"Thomas has been spreading calumnies about him," said Georgiana. "He tried to turn me against him."

"Well, I think it best we speak no more about it," said Sir Arthur. "I have no wish to distress your mother any more."

Georgiana made no reply. As the carriage continued on, she reflected that once again, things had become a dreadful muddle.

Chapter 18

By the time Dunraven returned to Longmeadow, he had cooled down considerably, but he was still in a state of some agitation. He found Buckthorne in the drawing room, drinking port and looking over some sort of book. Sleeping at his feet was Macduff. When the earl entered, the terrier woke up and hurried to greet his master.

"Good old Macduff," said the earl, reaching down to scoop up the dog.

"Good God!" said Buckthorne. "What are you doing home so early?"

"I do wish you had gone with me, Buck," said his lordship, placing Macduff on the sofa. Taking the decanter from the table, he poured himself a glass of wine.

"My dear fellow, you know how I detest such affairs."

"Well, had you gone, I might not have got into this mess." Dunraven sat down on the sofa beside Macduff.

"What can you mean?" said Buckthorne. "What happened?"

The earl shrugged. "I completely lost my temper. I knocked this Jeffreys fellow to the floor."

"What the devil!" cried Buckthorne. "At a ball?"

The earl nodded grimly.

"And were you drunk?"

Dunraven shook his head. "I was completely sober."

"Well, this is quite extraordinary," said Buckthorne. "Do tell me what happened."

The earl took a sip of his wine. "Right before this happened I was the happiest man in the world."

"Then Miss Morley said she would marry you?"

"Not precisely, but it seemed that she would. You see, I took her into the hallway and kissed her."

"You rogue, Dunraven," said Buckthorne, smiling at him. "But then what happened?"

"Jeffreys came upon us. The blackguard had told Georgiana that I had a mistress. It seems he wished to prejudice her against me."

"That would prejudice a woman," said Buckthorne. "You recall how Mrs. Buckthorne reacted when she found out about that ballet dancer. Indeed, she is quite unreasonable. A man has to be dashed discreet to keep peace in one's own house. You'll find that when you marry."

An indulgent smile crossed the earl's lips. "I think you had best stay away from dancers, Buck. They cause you grief in the end."

"That is so true," said Buckthorne. "I believe actresses and opera singers are far better. But do tell me more of how you pummeled this Jeffreys."

"There is little to tell. He made me so angry that I couldn't think. He mentioned the duel."

"Oh, dear," said Buckthorne.

"So I completely lost my head and hit him. Twice. Unfortunately, this occurred in the ballroom with a good many witnesses."

"Good God!" exclaimed Buckthorne.

"I was an idiot," said the earl. "Georgiana probably thinks me a madman. I would give a great deal to undo what I have done this night."

"That is always the worst of it," said Buckthorne sympathetically. "One can't undo it no matter how one wishes to. Damned bad luck, old friend. But I shouldn't be glum. I don't believe this will prevent Miss Morley from wishing to marry you. Why, a girl likes some fight in her man."

This remark caused the earl to raise his eyebrows slightly at his friend. Noting the book in Buckthorne's lap, he commented, "Good heavens, Buck, don't tell me you are reading a book."

"And what is so odd about that?" returned Buckthorne. He help up the volume. "The hounds' stud book."

A smile came to Dunraven's face and he took another drink of wine.

Shortly after arriving home, Georgiana took her leave of her parents and retreated to her bedchamber. She was soon joined by Agnes, who had been knitting in the servants' hall when she was informed that the Morleys had returned.

"Miss Georgiana," said Agnes, "you are home very early. Wasn't the ball to your liking?"

Turning around so that her maid could unbutton her gown, Georgiana sighed. "Something quite dreadful happened, Aggie."

"What was it!" cried a youthful feminine voice. Georgiana turned her head to see her sister enter the room.

"Kitty," said Georgiana, "you should be asleep."

"Why, it is still quite early," said Kitty, who was attired in her dressing gown and cap. "I could scarcely believe it when I heard your door open. But do tell me what happened."

"I fear it was quite horrible," said Georgiana, as Agnes assisted her out of her gown. "Lord Dunraven struck Thomas."

Both Agnes and Kitty regarded Georgiana in astonishment. "Struck him?" cried Kitty.

Georgiana nodded. "He completely lost his temper. You see I told Lord Dunraven that Thomas had told me that he had a mistress."

"He told you that?" cried Kitty. "Now I know why you were so vexed after you talked to Lord Thomas that day."

"Really, Miss Georgiana, this isn't a topic for young ladies to discuss."

"Don't be an old stick, Aggie," said Georgiana. "I am soon to be a married woman after all. Or at least I think I am to be."

"But does Lord Dunraven have a mistress?" said Kitty.

"No, he does not," said Georgiana emphatically. "Thomas only said it to make me dislike him."

"The master never liked Lord Thomas," said Agnes. "Now you see what sort of man he is, miss."

Georgiana nodded. "I can scarcely believe I fancied myself in love with him. But I was such a green girl then."

Agnes raised her eyebrows, but said nothing at this remark.

"I think it is so romantic that two men were fighting over you, Georgie," said Kitty.

"They weren't fighting over me," replied Georgiana.

"Why, of course they were," said Kitty.

"Well, perhaps they were, but I do wish Dunraven had not lost his temper. It was a shocking scandal. A good many people were watching. Papa saw everything."

"Oh, dear!" said Kitty. "You are involved in a scandal, Georgie." She grinned. "But it is so exciting. Oh, I cannot wait until I am involved in a scandal of my own."

"Miss Kitty!" cried Agnes. "You had best go to your room."

"Oh, very well," said Kitty. "But I do expect to hear more tomorrow." And with that she was gone, leaving Georgiana to finish getting ready for bed.

Chapter 19

In the morning, Dunraven rose early and went downstairs with Macduff at his heels. He had not slept very well since thoughts of Georgiana prevented sleep. He was greeted by Mrs. Hastings, who smiled pleasantly. "Good morning, my lord. And there is wee Macduff." The terrier wagged his tail. "It will be a very fine day, my lord," continued the housekeeper.

Although Dunraven was not in the best of moods, he replied in a civil tone, "I am glad to hear it."

"We have had some lovely weather, haven't we, my lord?" said Mrs. Hastings. "Mr. Buckthorne was just commenting to me about it."

"You cannot mean Mr. Buckthorne is up and about at such an hour?"

"Indeed so, my lord. He went to the library."

"Then I shall go to him," replied Dunraven, surprised to hear that Buckthorne had risen so early. His friend was not usually an early riser. When the earl entered the library, he was surprised to find Buckthorne sitting at the desk, busily writing.

"Writing letters, Buck?" said his lordship. "You are industrious."

"Why does that surprise you?" said Buckthorne, a smile appearing on his ruddy face.

"I don't doubt that Mrs. Buckthorne will be pleased to hear from you."

"Mrs. Buckthorne? What an idea. I am writing to Matthew Osgood. He owns a very good dog. I was thinking of him last night and wondering if Osgood might part with him. We need some new blood in the pack."

"Good God! Not another hound! Isn't there enough racket with those you already have?"

"Nonsense," returned Buckthorne, "they are quiet as mice. And we have need of Jasper's bloodline. Osgood's dog is one of Jasper's sons, you know."

"I don't know anything of the kind," said the earl. "Now I am going to breakfast. You may join me, but you speak of hounds at your peril."

"What an unreasonable fellow you are, Dunraven," said Buckthorne, putting down his pen and rising from the chair. Eager for his morning meal, he was only too happy to oblige his friend.

Once seated at the table with a plate of food before him, Buckthorne smiled brightly. "Your cook never disappoints me." With these words he ate heartily, scarcely saying another word. Dunraven was glad for the silence. As he ate his food, the earl found himself thinking about Georgiana.

After a time, Buckthorne spoke. "Will we call at Highcroft today?"

The earl, who was seated across the wide mahogany table, nodded. "Yes, I am eager to see Georgiana. And I must convince her father that I am not such a villain."

"Oh, that shouldn't be so hard. You're not a villain after all. Indeed, you're a dashed good fellow. And what of the little incident last night? It will soon be forgotten."

"What an optimist you are," said the earl.

"I suppose I am," said Buckthorne, taking a piece of bread and coating it with jam. At that moment, there was a commotion outside the dining room.

"I will see him!" cried a childish voice.

"What is going on?" said the earl, looking up from the table and gazing at the door. Suddenly the door opened and a small figure darted into the room. Dunraven regarded the intruder in surprise. It was a boy of perhaps nine years of age. Dark-haired and slender, the youngster was dressed in ill-fitting and well-worn clothes.

"I beg your pardon, my lord," cried Canfield, running after the boy into the dining room and catching hold of his arm.

"What is the matter, Canfield?"

The butler frowned. "This boy came to the door. To the front door, I might add, my lord. He said he wished to see your lordship. When I asked his business, he said it was a personal matter. I told him to be off and the next thing I knew he entered the house from another door and was roaming the halls trying to find you.

"I shall see that he doesn't disturb you, my lord. Now come on, lad."

"But I must see the earl!" cried the boy, trying to extricate himself from Canfield's firm grip.

"Good heavens," said Buckthorne, "what a loud young fellow he is."

"Release him, Canfield," said Dunraven. "I shall hear what he has to say."

"But my lord—"

"It will do no harm to listen to him," said the earl.

Canfield released the boy, who hurried up to Dunraven. "Thank you, m'lord," he said.

"Now speak. Tell me why you wish to see me."

The boy looked at Canfield. "I cannot say it with him here, my lord."

"Very well. Leave us, Canfield."

"If you are certain, my lord."

"I am, Canfield," replied the earl.

The butler nodded and retreated, closing the door behind him.

Dunraven regarded the boy expectantly. "Yes?"

"You are the Earl of Dunraven?"

"Yes, and this is Mr. Buckthorne. And now that you have the advantage of us, I hope you will tell us your name."

"My name is Jeremy . . . Jeremy Aldridge." The boy paused as if expecting some reaction from the earl.

"Yes, Master Aldridge?"

" 'Tis a private matter, my lord," said the boy, looking toward Buckthorne. "It don't concern this gentleman."

"Mr. Buckthorne is my dearest friend. I have no secrets from him. You may speak freely."

"If you say so, m'lord," said the boy. His face took on a serious expression. "My mother's name is Meg Aldridge."

"Meg Aldridge, the actress?" said Buckthorne.

The boy nodded. "Yes." He regarded the earl solemnly.

"Go on," said Dunraven, eyeing the boy with new interest.

"My mother is in America now, m'lord. And she don't know about me coming here. You see, I found some things she wrote about the time when I was born. And I learned something, something that surprised me. You see, m'lord, I found that you are my father. That's why I come to see you."

Buckthorne's mouth dropped open at this surprising announcement, but Dunraven only frowned slightly and appeared thoughtful.

Apparently relieved that the earl was not going to rise up from his chair and drive him out of the room, Jeremy continued. "I know it is a surprise to you. I mean you can imagine what it was to find my father was a lord and all. And so when I discovered it, I thought I should find you."

"And how did you discover this surprising information?" said Dunraven.

Jeremy pulled a paper from inside his coat. "This letter here. I found it in a book what was my mother's."

"Let me see it," said the earl.

"I don't know," said Jeremy, holding the paper tightly against his chest. " 'Tis all the proof I have. Your lordship might toss it into the fire for all I know."

"Why, you insolent puppy," said Buckthorne. He turned to the earl. "I'd have him horsewhipped and sent on his way, Dunraven."

"Now, now, Buck, don't get your back up," said the earl mildly. "Come, lad, give me the letter. I'll give no credence to your claim without some evidence."

The boy hesitated before reluctantly handing the paper to Dunraven. "I'll be wanting it back."

Ignoring him, the earl perused the letter. It was a very short missive written in his hand and addressed simply "Meg." A date placed it some eleven years ago. Hardly a passionate love letter, it said, "I shall take you to supper after the play. I eagerly await seeing you again. D."

The earl passed the missive to Buckthorne, who read it quickly. "Why, this is nothing at all."

"But his lordship did write it, didn't you, m'lord?"

"I cannot deny it," said the earl.

"I didn't know who 'D.' was at first," said Jeremy, "but a woman what knew my mother from the stage remembered about her and his lordship. She said D. was 'Dunraven.' And this was written scarce nine months to a day before I was born."

Buckthorne returned the well-worn paper to Jeremy. "This

proves nothing except that his lordship might have known your mother." He turned to Dunraven. "As I recall, the lady shared her favors with a good many others at that time."

"That's a lie!" cried Jeremy indignantly. "Gentleman or no, you'll not say such things about my mother."

"Yes, do not upset our guest, Buckthorne," said the earl. "Well, we will look into this matter at some length. But you must be hungry. Perhaps you will join us for breakfast. Do sit down. Buck, would you be so kind as to ring for a servant?"

Buckthorne regarded the earl as if he had lost his senses. Yet, he did as he was asked. When Canfield answered the summons, the butler was quite astonished to find the young ragamuffin seated upon one of the dining room chairs.

"Canfield, would you bring some food for Master Aldridge?" said Dunraven. "And after he eats, he'll need a bath. And perhaps you could speak with Mrs. Hastings about finding some clothes for him. Do have her come to fetch the boy."

While Canfield found this quite extraordinary, he only nodded and murmured, "Very good, my lord," in a deferential manner.

Jeremy could hardly believe his good fortune as the servant set a plate of food in front of him. He ate ravenously.

"Good God," said Buckthorne, "my hounds take more time with their food."

Macduff, who had been sitting near the earl's chair, got up and went over to the boy and stared at him. "What a good little dog," said Jeremy, who was very fond of animals. "Might I give him a bit of food, m'lord?"

"Only a little," said the earl.

Jeremy took a piece of meat from his plate and fed it to the dog. "What is his name, m'lord?"

"Macduff," replied Dunraven.

" 'Lay on, Macduff,' " said Jeremy in a theatrical voice, " 'and damned be him who first cries, Hold enough!' "

"What's that?" said Buckthorne, regarding the youth strangely.

"*Macbeth,*" replied the earl.

"*Macbeth?*" said Buckthorne, eyeing him with a blank look.

"The play," said Dunraven. "Good, heavens, Buck, you must know it."

"I don't like plays overmuch," said his friend.

"Don't like plays?" said Jeremy, regarding him in astonishment.

"I like some plays, of course, but others have too many dashed words," replied Buckthorne. "Certainly, I'm not averse to going to the theater when the girls are pretty enough."

"Don't mind Mr. Buckthorne," said the earl, addressing Jeremy. "He is a sporting gentleman with little taste for literature. But it appears you're an actor?"

"Aye, m'lord," said Jeremy. "I've trod the boards some in my time. What with my mother, 'tis in my blood."

"You don't appear to be a very successful actor," said Buckthorne.

"I should be when I'm older," said Jeremy.

"I shouldn't doubt it," muttered Buckthorne.

Jeremy returned to his food, finishing it quickly. In a short time the housekeeper appeared. "This is Master Jeremy Aldridge," said the earl. "Do see to him. Now go with Mrs. Hastings, and do what she says."

Jeremy obediently rose from his chair. "Thank you for the food, m'lord," he said. The earl replied with a nod and the boy went off with the housekeeper. Macduff followed after them, pausing at the doorway to look back at his master.

"Go on then," said the earl and the terrier scurried off. "Macduff seems to have taken a fancy to the boy."

"It seems you have as well, feeding him like that."

"I would feed a hungry cat," replied the earl.

"And never be rid of it," said Buckthorne. "Truly, Dunraven, I advise you to send this boy on his way. You will have nothing but trouble if you don't."

"But he could be my son."

"Could be. That is very different than is. I daresay a good many others could be his father as well. As I recall, your ardor cooled for the lady when you found her in flagrante delicto with that Frenchman. What was his name? The Comte du . . . something."

"I don't remember."

"Well, it does not signify. In any case, I advise you to be rid of this boy. Can you imagine what Miss Morley would think if she hears about him? Good God, no lady wishes to find one of her future husband's by-blows about."

Dunraven nodded absently. He couldn't deny the wisdom of Buckthorne's words. Yet he was not a man to abrogate responsibility. If he became convinced that the boy was his son, he would not shirk his obligation to support him.

"Well, I find the whole thing suspect," said Buckthorne. "If Meg Aldridge thought you the father of her child, she would have asked you for money years ago. And, for that matter, are we certain that she even had a child?"

"What a suspicious fellow you are, Buck," said the earl with a smile. "But don't worry, I shall have inquiries made in town. We'll get to the bottom of this."

"Good," said Buckthorne, happy to see that his friend was speaking in a sensible fashion. The two gentlemen rose from the table and made their way out of the dining room.

After accompanying her father on a morning ride, Georgiana returned to the house. Sir Arthur stayed behind in the stables discussing Demon Dancer with Shaw. A fast gallop on his prized steed had improved the baronet's mood, a fact not lost upon Georgiana, who was glad that her father didn't say a word about Dunraven.

After changing from her riding habit into a striped muslin morning dress, Georgiana joined her mother in the drawing room. Lady Morley, who was seated on the sofa with her embroidery, looked up as her daughter entered. "Oh, you are returned, my dear. Did you have a good ride?"

"Quite splendid."

"But where is your father?"

"I imagine he is still in the stables. I left him there with Shaw. Has Kitty already gone to visit Charlotte?"

Lady Morley nodded. "She was so eager to see her. I don't see the harm in her going for a short time. Agnes accompanied her and I sent them in the carriage. I didn't want them walking when it looks as if it will rain at any moment."

"That was wise, Mama. It does look like rain." Georgiana sat down in an elegant armchair upholstered in Italian silk.

"Pardon me, my lady." The butler entered the drawing room. "Mrs. Fanshawe's man Peterson has brought a letter for you."

"Indeed?" returned Lady Morley. The servant approached and extended a silver salver toward her. Lady Morley took the letter from it and hastily broke the seal. "How very odd for Elizabeth to send me a letter by messenger. And the morning after her ball. I cannot imagine that she would be about so early writing letters. Why, one would have expected her to be quite exhausted. I do hope she is not upset about what happened last evening." Her ladyship's voice trailed off as she began to read. "Oh, dear."

"What is it, Mama? Is something the matter?"

Her ladyship did not reply, but continued to read the letter. Finally she frowned at Georgiana. "Oh, dear," she repeated.

"Mama, you must tell me what is wrong. Is she ill? Or perhaps Charlotte or Mr. Fanshawe?"

"No, it is nothing like that." She hesitated before continuing. "In truth, Georgiana I can scarcely know what else is going to be said about Lord Dunraven."

"It is about Dunraven?"

Lady Morley nodded. "First she writes a little about the ball, saying how embarrassed she was about the incident with Dunraven and Thomas Jeffreys. Poor Elizabeth. That was quite dreadful. And then, when she went to retire, her maid informed her of this. Of course, it is only servants' gossip. I cannot imagine why she should repeat it."

"Mama!" cried Georgiana, quite exasperated at being kept in suspense. "You must tell me what Cousin Elizabeth says in her letter."

"Yes, of course, my dear," said Lady Morley. "But I do pray you will not be too upset."

"Mama, you must tell me at once."

"Very well, a young boy has appeared in Richton. He has come from London and he was on his way to Longmeadow. It is being said that he is Lord Dunraven's love child, the result of a liaison between the earl and an actress."

"Oh, Mama!" cried Georgiana.

"I knew you'd be upset."

"I'm only upset that such nonsense is being spoken about. I'm sure it is utterly false. Indeed, it is doubtless a ridiculous rumor spread by Thomas Jeffreys."

"Perhaps you are right, Georgiana. But true or no, the story is being bandied about." She sighed. "I know you are fond of Dunraven, but I do wish you had formed an attachment for someone else. Someone like Lord Belrose, whose reputation is quite spotless. And he was so fond of you. Oh, I know you don't wish me to mention his name, but I cannot help it. Indeed, if you would agree to consider Belrose, I don't doubt that I can persuade your father to allow us to return to town."

"Mama, I could never marry Lord Belrose. I wish to marry Lord Dunraven."

"I am aware of that," said her ladyship.

"And, Mama, you mustn't tell Papa about this absurd rumor Cousin Elizabeth is spreading."

"Very well. In truth, I can see little point in telling him. I shouldn't like him to have a fit of apoplexy. After last night, he has quite turned against Dunraven. No, I shan't tell your father."

"Tell me what?"

Both ladies turned their heads at the sound of a masculine voice. They had been so intent on their conversation that they had not heard Sir Arthur enter the room. Georgiana regarded him with a startled look.

"Oh, there you are, Arthur," said her ladyship. "Georgiana tells me you had a pleasant ride."

"Tell me what?" repeated the baronet, ignoring his wife's remark.

"Nothing, my dear," said Lady Morley.

"It is something. I can tell by your expressions. You are hiding something from me. I demand to know what it is. I distinctly heard you say that you would not tell me something, Isabelle. You were never good at keeping secrets. You may as well tell me."

"Really, Papa," said Georgiana, "it was nothing."

"I shall determine that," said the baronet.

Lady Morley looked over at her daughter. "I fear we must tell him, Georgiana. He will hear of it anyway."

"But, Mama!" said Georgiana, directing an imploring look at her mother.

"Keep still, Georgiana," commanded Sir Arthur. "Isabelle, I am waiting."

Unaccustomed to defying her husband, Lady Morley could only comply. "Very well, Arthur. I received a letter from Elizabeth. She said that a boy arrived in the village. He was going to Longmeadow and it seems that he is purported to be . . ." At this point, she faltered.

"Go on," said the baronet in a stern voice.

"Lord Dunraven's illegitimate child."

"Good God!" said the baronet. "Is there no end to the scandals connected with this man? And to think that I had actually thought that I would accept him as a son-in-law. Why, if you were to marry him, none of us could go anywhere without persons whispering about us."

"Papa, I am sure that this tale is nothing but a rumor devised by Thomas Jeffreys to further discredit Lord Dunraven. I am sure that there is no truth in it."

"You are blinded by your feelings for the man," said the baronet. "You know very little of the world, Georgiana. No, indeed, I am glad I regained my senses where Dunraven is concerned."

"But what if it is a lie?" said Georgiana. "One shouldn't believe every rumor one hears, especially when Dunraven is so often slandered."

"My dear, the man is notorious," said the baronet. "One day you will be glad that I stopped you from becoming his wife."

"I shall never be glad of that," cried Georgiana, rising from her chair and hurrying from the drawing room.

Arriving in her bedroom, she fell onto the bed and began to cry. It was some time before she regained her composure. However, she managed to do so, and when she joined her parents for luncheon, she appeared calm and collected. Thankfully, both her parents said nothing more about Dunraven and the meal proceeded with as little unpleasantness as possible.

That afternoon, an unhappy Georgiana sat with her parents in the drawing room. The baronet read the newspaper while Lady Morley concentrated once again on her embroidery. The butler came in to announce visitors. "My lady," he said, "Lord Dunraven and Mr. Buckthorne are here."

"Good heavens," said Sir Arthur, turning to his wife. "He cannot believe that we would admit him after what happened last night." He looked back at the butler. "Do tell his lordship that we are not receiving, Griggs."

"But, Papa," said Georgiana, "can't we see him? I'm sure Lord Dunraven feels so very wretched about last night. And if you are thinking of that absurd story of the boy—"

"I don't know that it is absurd," said Sir Arthur. "And even if it were completely untrue, his behavior at the ball was enough to cause every door in the county to be shut in his face. No, I shan't admit him at Highcroft. You must accept that."

"But, Papa . . ." said Georgiana.

The baronet ignored her. "Griggs, do as I said."

"Very good, sir," said the servant, hastening to carry out his instructions.

"But I wish to see him," said Georgiana.

"I forbid it," said the baronet in his sternest voice. "I will hear no more about it."

Georgiana made no reply, for she knew very well that it was senseless to argue with her father. Indeed, experience had told her that saying anything further would only harden him against Dunraven. Sir Arthur was a strong-willed man, unlikely to be swayed by tears or entreaties. Georgiana could only hope that her father would be more reasonable later on.

Yet the next week passed without any evidence that the baronet would relent. The earl continued to call at Highcroft each afternoon, but Sir Arthur had given firm orders that he should not be admitted. Although it was exasperating for Georgiana to know that Dunraven was being turned away, she was powerless to do anything about it.

While she tried to busy herself with other things, Georgiana found herself totally occupied with thoughts of Dunraven. That she had not been permitted to see or speak with him seemed impossible to bear.

Then one bleak and cheerless afternoon, Georgiana sat alone in her sitting room. She wished Kitty might have kept her company, but her sister was now busy with her studies.

To Kitty's great disappointment, a new governess had been found for her. A serious, businesslike woman, the new governess had begun her duties that morning. Kitty, who had little inclination for studies, hadn't been very happy to find herself shut up in the schoolroom learning French verbs and geography.

Without her sister's companionship, Georgiana was bored. She tried to read a novel, but found it hard to concentrate. Putting down the book, she rose from the chair and went to the window.

If only she could see Dunraven again, thought Georgiana as she stared out at the expanse of green grass and trees outside.

It was dreadful that her father was being so horribly stubborn in refusing to receive him.

Georgiana sighed, wondering how long it would be before Dunraven ceased coming. Indeed, she was surprised at his persistence. Continuing to stare out the window, she caught sight of her father. Mounted on Demon Dancer, the baronet was setting off on another ride. Georgiana frowned, wishing he had asked her to join him. She would have enjoyed getting out. Of late, she had felt trapped in the house like some fairy-tale princess in a tower.

Folding her arms in front of her, Georgiana watched her father ride off. She lost sight of him when he turned onto the tree-lined village road.

Georgiana's fair countenance grew thoughtful. Her father was probably going to Richton, and he would, in all likelihood, be gone for some time. Lady Morley was resting in her room and had asked not to be disturbed. There was nothing to prevent her from taking a walk, and it wouldn't be unusual to walk in the direction of Longmeadow. After all, there were some very fine views along the way.

A smile crossed her face. Yes, she would go to Longmeadow. Georgiana was well aware that her father would be furious if he found that she had gone there, but if she hurried, she would be back well before Sir Arthur returned home.

Rushing to her dressing room, she selected a pelisse and bonnet. She then made her way carefully downstairs, taking care to avoid Agnes and the other servants. Slipping out one of the rear doors, she walked quickly across the park and through a grove of trees to the road that lead to Longmeadow.

It was a rather overcast day, cool, but pleasant for walking. Georgiana's spirits rose as she made her way toward Dunraven's estate. Turning into a lane, Longmeadow came into view.

Walking briskly toward the house, Georgiana smiled. She would soon see Dunraven, she thought happily. The idea that he might not be at home occurred to her, but she brushed it aside. Of course, he would be there, she told herself resolutely.

Approaching the house, Georgiana caught sight of Macduff, who rushed toward her barking. "Macduff," she said, stooping to pat his head.

"Macduff," said a voice, "mind your manners. You musn't bother the lady."

Georgiana looked up to see a boy. Dressed in a plain coat and knee breeches, the youngster doffed his hat politely, revealing a head of curly black hair. He was a handsome young man, thought Georgiana, realizing that this must be the boy purported to be Dunraven's son. She searched his face for a resemblance to the earl. Perhaps there was a similarity about the eyes, she thought, unhappy to think that the youth could indeed be Dunraven's illegitimate child.

"And what is your name?" said Georgiana.

"Jeremy, miss. Jeremy Aldridge."

"I am Miss Morley."

Jeremy bowed. He had judged from her fine clothes that Miss Morley was a great lady. She was also a very pretty one. "Are you here to see his lordship, miss?"

Georgiana nodded. "Is he at home?"

"Aye, miss, that he is. He's with Mr. Buckthorne. Do come in, miss. I'll tell his lordship you're here."

"That is very good of you, Jeremy," said Georgiana. As they walked toward the door, she glanced over at him. "Are you staying with the earl?"

Jeremy nodded. "Yes, miss."

"I imagine you're enjoying your visit at Longmeadow. It is a lovely home."

"Indeed, I am, miss," said Jeremy. "Macduff and me have been having a right old time, haven't we, my lad?" Macduff cocked his head in reply. "I didn't think I'd like the country. I've lived in London all my life, you see. But for the stage, I shouldn't mind if I never went back to town."

"The stage?" said Georgiana.

"Oh, I'm an actor," said the boy matter-of-factly. "I'll be famous one day. I'll play for the Prince himself, just like Mr. Kean."

"That would be splendid, I'm sure," said Georgiana.

Jeremy opened the massive front door and escorted Georgiana inside. They were met by Canfield. "Miss Morley!" said the butler, very much surprised to see the young lady. He was not at all happy to see that Jeremy was with her.

"Good afternoon, Canfield," said Georgiana. "Would you inform his lordship that I wish to see him?"

"At once, Miss Morley," said Canfield. "Will you wait in here?" He ushered her into a small parlor. Noting that Jeremy seemed intent on remaining with the young lady, he frowned. "You may be on your way, Master Jeremy," he said.

"But I wish to stay with Miss Morley," said Jeremy.

"Now, you are not to bother the lady," said Canfield sternly.

"Oh, he isn't bothering me," said Georgiana. "Not in the least. Do tell his lordship I am here. I fear I am rather in a hurry, Canfield."

"Very well, miss," said the butler, bowing slightly and then retreating from the room.

"He don't like me," said Jeremy in a low voice.

"Oh, I'm sure you are mistaken," said Georgiana.

"No, indeed, 'tis true, miss. He don't like me in the least. But all the others have been kind. And his lordship, he's been very good to me. He's a fine gentleman for all what's said of him."

This remark made Georgiana raise her eyebrows slightly, but before she could get Jeremy to elaborate, Dunraven entered the room. "Georgiana! When Canfield said you had come, I could scarcely believe it."

"Dunraven!" Georgiana's face lit up at seeing him once again. She would have rushed into his arms if it hadn't been for Jeremy's presence.

"Do come to the drawing room. I shall order tea."

"Oh, I can't stay long, my lord. No, I must return to Highcroft at once. It is only that I wanted to see you, if only for a moment."

Jeremy watched this exchange with keen interest. A perceptive young man, it was immediately clear that the earl was exceedingly fond of Miss Morley and that the young lady reciprocated his feelings. "Macduff and I'll be off then, m'lord," said Jeremy.

The earl smiled. "That's a good lad," he said.

Jeremy grinned. "Come on, Macduff. We'll find a rabbit or two." The word "rabbit" seemed to interest the terrier, who eagerly followed the boy from the room.

"What are you doing here, Georgiana?" said the earl. "Did you come alone?"

She nodded. "I so wanted to see you, and no one saw me

leave. My father will never know where I've gone. Oh, Dunraven, I thought I should die if I didn't see you again."

"My darling," said the earl, who couldn't resist taking her into his arms and kissing her with an ardor that made her tremble. "Georgiana, come with me today. We'll leave here and be married."

"You mean elope?" said Georgiana, regarding him with wide eyes.

"Yes, why not?"

"But my dearest Dunraven, my father would never forgive me. I know him. I would be disowned and I could never show my face at Highcroft. No, I couldn't bear that."

The earl took her hands in his. "Then what are we to do? I can't wait much longer, Georgiana. I am not a patient man. Indeed, I can scarcely resist carrying you upstairs at this very moment and making you mine entirely."

Blushing, Georgiana looked down. "You mustn't say such things." She pulled her hands away. "I must go. I must be back at Highcroft before I'm missed."

"But you've only just arrived."

"I know, but I truly must go."

"Very well, I'll send for my carriage."

"No, I shall walk," said Georgiana, smiling up at him.

"And I'll walk with you, at least for a little while."

Georgiana nodded and took his arm. They went out of the house and started down the lane. Jeremy, who was tossing a stick for Macduff to catch, paused to wave to them. "It seems your young guest is enjoying himself," said Georgiana.

The earl's face grew serious. He stopped and regarded her solemnly. "Georgiana," he said, "I must explain about the boy."

She pressed his arm. "I know about him. Or I know what is being said. I thought it was another malicious lie, but seeing him here, I'm not so sure. Is he your son, Dunraven?"

He shook his head. "I don't know. It is possible."

She looked away. "Did you love his mother?"

"Love her? My darling, I've never loved anyone until you."

"Not even Lady Coningsby?"

"No," he said. "Oh, perhaps I fancied myself in love. I was not yet turned twenty and I was an unthinking idiot. Later, I realized that we were two selfish people using each other." He shook his head. "She wasn't faithful to me for long. Scarcely six months after we came to Italy, I discovered her with an Italian count. My temper got the best of me. I called him out.

"I have done many stupid, reckless things in my life, Georgiana, but that was one of the most regrettable. Thank God, he recovered. To think that I almost killed a man over that vain, faithless woman, whom I had come to despise."

"Oh, Dunraven," said Georgiana, looking up at him.

"No, I don't believe I ever knew what love was until I met you, my darling little minx."

This admission delighted Georgiana, who would have liked to have thrown her arms about his neck, but restrained herself. "I do love you so much, Dunraven," she said.

The earl, however, could no longer prevent himself from enfolding Georgiana into his embrace and placing a tender kiss on her lips. "But aren't you upset about Jeremy?"

"I don't know," replied Georgiana, pressing herself against him. "I cannot say I am pleased at the idea, but if he is your son, I cannot dislike him. Indeed, he is very charming."

"Which may indicate he isn't my son at all," said the earl, with a slight smile.

She smiled up at him in return. "What will you do with him?"

"What would you have me do?"

Georgiana grew serious. "If he is your son, you must acknowledge him and provide for him. It is the right thing to do. And I shan't mind. Truly. I have said that I shall not reproach you for your past. It is the present and future that concern me."

"I don't deserve you," said Dunraven. "But I shall be a good husband, Georgiana. Upon all I hold dear, I swear it. My dearest wish is that you will be my wife."

"I will be yours, my dearest Dunraven," said Georgiana, her blue eyes meeting his brown ones. The earl responded by once again placing his lips on hers and kissing her hungrily. She felt very weak as his mouth covered hers.

The sound of hoofbeats brought them both to their senses. Fortunately, trees partially blocked the view from the road and they were fairly sure that the horseman hadn't seen them. While the man was a stranger to Dunraven, Georgiana recognized him as the Reverend Mr. Bentwick. When he was gone, Georgiana pulled away. "My dearest love, it will not do for you to go any further. We might be seen. I must return to Highcroft, but I shall come again."

"Tomorrow?"

"If I can."

Dunraven kissed her once again, releasing her finally with great reluctance. Georgiana hurried away, leaving the earl to watch her retreating form.

Chapter 20

Dunraven and Buckthorne called at Highcroft on the following afternoon, but, as they expected, they weren't admitted. Georgiana stood at the window, watching them ride off, a sorrowful look on her face. Yet she said no words of reproach to her father, knowing well that to do so would do no good.

Although he would never have revealed it to his wife or daughters, the baronet was growing increasingly impressed by the earl's resolve. Indeed, if he persisted for much longer, Sir Arthur knew that he might give in and receive him. Of course, that didn't mean he would ever consider him for a husband for his daughter, the baronet assured himself.

With each passing day, the baronet's anger about Dunraven had eroded a little. After all, every time he rode his beloved Demon Dancer, he couldn't help but remember that Dunraven had saved his prized horse. And Sir Arthur was also pleased that Georgiana seemed reconciled to accept his authority. She didn't whine and try to cajole him as she had done when she first fancied herself in love with Thomas Jeffreys. Indeed, it appeared that Georgiana had gained a good deal of maturity since returning to Highcroft, a fact much appreciated by the baronet.

Although Georgiana would have liked to have repeated her visit to Longmeadow, she had no opportunity to do so. Sir Arthur stayed at home, and when other callers arrived, he was more than happy to receive them.

Later that afternoon, both Georgiana and her mother were very surprised when the butlers announced that Lord Thomas Jeffreys was there. "Another of your unwelcome suitors, Georgiana," said the baronet. "And although I detest the young man, I shan't disappoint him. Do show him in, Griggs."

Astonished at her father's response, Georgiana tried hard to hide her annoyance. That the baronet would admit Thomas while turning away Dunraven seemed unbelievable. It seemed that her father was determined to vex her.

Thomas was as surprised as Georgiana to hear that the Morleys would receive him. Entering the drawing room, he bowed first to the ladies, and then nodded politely to his host. "How good of you to see me," he said.

"Sit down, Jeffreys," said the baronet, motioning him to a chair near Georgiana.

Smiling, Thomas sat down. As always he was impeccably dressed. His pea-green coat fit him to perfection and his snowy neckcloth gleamed brilliantly white. Georgiana studied him with an expression of calm indifference. He was a conceited fop, she told herself. How could she have ever been so foolish as to think she was in love with him?

The conversation was desultory and Thomas was careful not to overstay his welcome. After a quarter of an hour, he took his leave.

While Georgiana thought his visit a tiresome interlude, Thomas considered it a triumph. Leaving the house, he climbed into his curricle and drove off, smiling. The fact that he had been admitted at all seemed remarkable, and while Sir Arthur had not been overly friendly, the baronet had been civil enough. Since Georgiana's father usually treated him with undisguised disdain, Thomas had reason to feel very pleased.

He drove from Highcroft directly to the village of Hillborough. There he made his way to the Boar's Head Inn and into the arms of Claire Stevenson.

"You are in a happy mood, Tom," said Claire, once she had disengaged herself from his embrace.

"Indeed, I am," he said. "I have just come from Highcroft where I was admitted. Sir Arthur was quite civil to me."

"Oh," said Claire, "that is good."

"Yes, it is," said Thomas. "Perhaps Sir Arthur finally sees that I am a better match for his daughter than Dunraven. By God, I don't doubt that our plan is working."

"I shouldn't wonder," said Claire. "What with everyone talking about that bastard of his."

Thomas grinned as he sat down on the bed. "Fetch me some ale, wench," he said, good-naturedly. Claire was only too

happy to comply with this request, hurrying from the room to
return a short time later with a flagon of the inn's powerful
brew. Thomas took a long drink, and then placing the tankard
down on the table next to the bed, he motioned for Claire to
come to him. When she did so, he pushed her against the bed
and kissed her.

"Tom, I got a letter from Jeremy."

"Did you?" said Thomas. "What did he say? It is going
well, isn't it?"

" 'Tis very short. The lad ain't much for writing. But he
says Lord Dunraven hasn't a notion that Jeremy ain't what he
claims to be. His lordship's treating him very well."

"Good," said Thomas, sitting up. "I find it very amusing
thinking of your brother at Longmeadow posing as Dunraven's whelp. You were a clever girl to think of it."

"Well, when I thought of Meg Aldridge and Dunraven, it
come to mind how my mum was expecting Jeremy at that
time. If Meg had had a baby with him, he'd be the same age as
my brother. And I knew Jeremy would do well. He's a clever
lad."

"That he is. Nearly as clever as his sister," said Thomas,
kissing her again. Very pleased by the compliment, Claire happily returned his kiss.

Jeremy walked into the entry hall at Longmeadow with
Macduff at his heels. "There you are, Jeremy." The boy turned
to see Mrs. Hastings smiling warmly at him.

The housekeeper had taken a liking to the youngster. Having not heard the gossip about him, she had no idea why her
employer had taken him in. She assumed it was an act of
Christian charity, which as a religious woman, the housekeeper applauded.

Mrs. Hastings regarded Jeremy as a handsome, good-
natured boy who was a pleasure to have around. Since it had
been a very long time since children had inhabited Longmeadow, Mrs. Hastings was very happy to hear Jeremy's exu-
berant shouts as he played with Macduff.

She noted that the earl seemed to be fond of the boy. And
even Mr. Buckthorne, who had appeared to dislike him at first,
had been won over. Just the previous evening, Mrs. Hastings

had come into the drawing room to find Mr. Buckthorne teach-ing Jeremy how to play chess.

"Yes, Mrs. Hastings?" said Jeremy.

"Your new clothes are here."

"New clothes, ma'am?"

"Yes, those his lordship ordered from the village. Jane is seeing to them in your room."

"I must go and thank his lordship," said Jeremy.

"That would be a good idea. He is in the library."

"I'll go to him now, unless you think I might be disturbing him."

"Oh, I don't believe so. You go ahead, my dear."

Jeremy smiled at Mrs. Hastings and started off for the li-brary. As he walked through the hallway, he looked pensive. He had lived at Longmeadow for more than a week now, and he was beginning to feel increasingly uncomfortable with the role he was playing.

And now he would be receiving some more new clothes. Je-remy felt a twinge of guilt, which he tried to dispel by reassur-ing himself that the earl had plenty of money and what were a few new clothes to him?

Still, Jeremy didn't like deceiving Dunraven. Indeed, he was growing fond of the nobleman who, although a somewhat for-midable personage, had treated him with unfailing kindness and consideration.

Indeed, everyone at Longmeadow, with the sole exception of Canfield, had been very good to him. His days there had been so extraordinarily pleasant. Having grown up in crushing poverty, Jeremy was unaccustomed to good food, a clean bed, and kind words.

The past few nights, he had lain awake in his room wishing that he might have actually been the earl's son. And now that he had met Miss Morley, he felt even worse about his dishon-esty.

After all, his sister had explained the scheme. His presence at Longmeadow would be an embarrassment to the earl, who wished to marry Miss Morley. The lady's family wouldn't like the idea of a bastard son hanging around. Jeremy understood that well enough.

But now, after seeing Georgiana and the earl, he felt bad about being part of a plot to destroy their happiness. Young as he was, Jeremy was a romantic at heart and he could tell that Dunraven loved Miss Morley.

Jeremy paused at the door to the library, but it was partially open and Macduff ran inside. He followed with some reluctance. Dunraven was seated at the massive cherry desk before a wall of books, more books than Jeremy even knew existed.

"So there you are, Macduff," said the earl. He looked at Jeremy. "Jeremy."

"M'lord," said Jeremy, coming forward.

Dunraven looked down at the small terrier, who was wagging his tail furiously. "I thought you'd abandoned me for your new master."

"He hasn't forgot who his rightful master is, m'lord," said Jeremy. "He's only being kind to me." The boy smiled. "I wanted to thank your lordship for the new clothes. Mrs. Hastings said there were some arrived. 'Twas very good of you, m'lord."

"It is little enough," returned the earl. He motioned toward a chair near the desk. "Do sit down, Jeremy."

"Thank you, m'lord," said the boy, taking a seat.

"Have you given thought to what you might like to do? For example, would you wish to go to school?"

"To school?" said Jeremy.

Dunraven nodded. "With a proper education, you might make something of yourself. You could have a career in law perhaps."

"Oh, I don't think so, m'lord. I'm an actor. I should make my career on the stage."

"That's hardly a proper career for a gentleman," said the earl.

"But I ain't a gentleman," said Jeremy.

"If you are my son, you are a gentleman," said the earl. "While I haven't always been a credit to it, mine is an old and distinguished name."

"I never thought of that," said Jeremy, "of being a gentleman, I mean. Imagine that? Me a gentleman? I don't know, m'lord, I'd be happier as an actor."

"Then why did you come to me? A boy doesn't appear claiming to be a man's son without expecting something."

"Money, you mean, m'lord? Well, a bloke would be a fool not to want that if he be as poor as me. But I won't ask anything of you, m'lord. No, 'tis enough to find you. And I am sincerely grateful for your lordship's kindness. I'll never forget it."

Dunraven smiled. He was very fond of the boy, a realization that surprised him. "Why don't you go find Buckthorne? He was looking for you earlier. There are new puppies in his kennel."

"Puppies?" said Jeremy, very much interested.

"More blasted hounds," said the earl.

"I should like to see them," said Jeremy, getting up from the chair. "Macduff had best stay with you, m'lord. He doesn't like the hounds, you know."

"I know that well enough," returned the earl with a smile.

"Then I'll be off," said Jeremy, making an awkward little bow before taking his leave. Macduff appeared content to stay at the earl's feet.

"So you know where he's going, do you?" said Dunraven. He smiled once again and then returned to his work.

Chapter 21

"Oh, Georgie!" cried Kitty, hurrying into her sister's sitting room. "I have escaped."

Georgiana, who was engaged in studying dresses in a fashion magazine, looked up. "Escaped?"

"From Miss Benson. Actually, she said that I might have some time to take a walk while she prepares the next lesson. I am to return to the schoolroom in a short time." Sitting down in a chair, Kitty sighed. "You cannot know how dreadful it is, Georgie."

"My dear Kitty, I have had my share of lessons."

"But not with Miss Benson. She is so stern. I have never seen her smile. And she knows all kinds of odd things, ancient history and German and botany. Indeed, it may be very well for her to know about such dull subjects, but I cannot imagine why she thinks I should wish to learn about them."

"Poor Kitty," said Georgiana. "Surely it cannot be so bad. I thought Miss Benson an agreeable woman."

"You aren't the one listening to her go on and on about the Punic Wars."

Georgiana laughed. "Well, I don't know what you are to do, Kit. Papa wishes you to be an educated young lady. You must endure it somehow." She held up the magazine. "Do you like this dress?"

Kitty seemed to forget about Miss Benson for a moment. Taking up the magazine, she studied the picture. "Yes, very much."

"I should like to have one just like it in lavender silk."

"Oh, that would be lovely." She smiled at her sister. "That would be a splendid wedding dress."

Georgiana frowned. "Perhaps it would, but I doubt that I shall ever be married with Papa being so horribly unreasonable."

Kitty nodded sympathetically. "Poor Georgiana," she said. "I do wish Papa would change his mind. But you know that everyone in the village keeps saying dreadful things about Dunraven."

"It is all nonsense. One shouldn't listen to gossip."

"Not listen to gossip?" said Kitty, in a tone that suggested that the idea was odd indeed. "Well, perhaps one shouldn't listen to it, but one can't really help it. There is so much talk about that boy who is living at Longmeadow. Do you believe he is the earl's child?"

"I don't care if he is," said Georgiana.

"You don't care?" said Kitty. "Why, I should care very much if I were in love with Lord Dunraven. To have such a boy about would be quite dreadful. Indeed, it is very shocking. And it is said he is a very shabby, common sort of boy."

"That is nonsense. He is a very well-mannered, handsome boy."

"You have seen him?" said Kitty, eyeing her sister in considerable surprise.

Georgiana nodded. "You must swear that you won't tell a soul, Kit. I am in deadly earnest. Tell no one, especially Charlotte."

"I swear," said Kitty eagerly.

"Then I shall tell you. I went to Longmeadow the day before yesterday."

"Oh, Georgiana!"

"No one knew. I walked there when Papa went to the village. Oh, Kitty, I had to see Dunraven! You cannot know what it is to be apart from the man you love."

"But Georgiana, if Papa were to find out, he would be furious."

"He won't find out," replied Georgiana. "I only stayed a few minutes, but I did see Dunraven."

"And the boy?"

Georgiana nodded. "I saw him as well. He is a very nice young man. I thought him charming."

"But what did Dunraven say? Is he the boy's father?"

"He cannot be sure of that."

"Oh, Georgiana."

"But what does it signify if he is Dunraven's son? One cannot change what is in the past. I still love him, Kit, and I wish to marry him."

"But, Georgie, how could you marry him when Papa is so against it?"

"I could elope."

"Georgie!"

"Oh, I don't wish to do it, but what else can I do? If Papa won't relent, I must consider it. How can I bear to live without Dunraven as my husband?"

While Kitty had no wish to encourage her sister to run off with the earl, Georgiana's plight appealed to her romantic nature. "What is to be done?" she said.

"I don't know," replied Georgiana. "I do wish I could see Dunraven again. It is odious of Papa to refuse to admit him. Poor Dunraven has come so many times and he is turned away like some itinerant tradesman selling pots and pans. Perhaps I could go to Longmeadow again this afternoon."

"Oh, Georgiana, I cannot think that is a good idea. Perhaps you might try speaking with Mama. She might persuade Papa to receive Dunraven next time he comes."

"She can never persuade him to do anything when he is so determined," said Georgiana glumly.

"But I have an idea." Kitty smiled. "I believe the earl has come to Highcroft each afternoon at approximately the same time. I daresay he may come again today. You might go to the garden. Then, if you walk through the grove beyond the lily pond, you will have a good view of the road to Longmeadow. Then you might, perchance, see Lord Dunraven on his way here."

"What a good idea," said Georgiana. "I do believe it would work. You are clever, Kit."

"Miss Benson doesn't think so," returned the younger Morley sister, who now rose from her chair. "I must go. I told Miss Benson that I would take a short walk and I do want to do so."

"Then I'll join you," said Georgiana, her good humor quite restored at the prospect of seeing Dunraven that day. Getting up, she followed her sister from the room.

In the afternoon, Georgiana announced that she would cut some flowers in the garden. Attired in a plain muslin dress and apron, a wide-brimmed straw hat, and carrying a basket, she set off.

As she walked along one of the garden paths, Georgiana waved to the head gardener, who was supervising two assistants digging up a bush. "Good afternoon, Roberts," she said, stopping to direct one of her brilliant smiles in his direction.

"Good afternoon, miss," replied the head gardener, a small, wiry man of perhaps sixty years of age. Roberts had worked at Highcroft all of his adult life. Like many of the servants, he was devoted to Georgiana. "Will you be needing any help, Miss Georgiana?"

Georgiana shook her head. "Thank you, Roberts, but I have only come for some flowers. Doesn't everything look lovely? You must be very proud."

"Aye, miss, that I am," said Roberts, directing a fond look at his young mistress. "Do tell me if there is aught you need."

"Indeed, I shall," said Georgiana, smiling once more before continuing on her way to the cutting garden located some distance away from the house. Arriving there, she stooped to clip some blooms and place them into her basket. After a short time, she looked around. Satisfied that no one was watching her, Georgiana left the cutting garden, and walked past the lily ponds. Going through a grove of trees, she stood on a slight hill, surveying the road.

If she were fortunate, she told herself, she would see Dunraven riding to Highcroft. Of course, she had no way of knowing that he would even be doing so. Perhaps he would remain at Longmeadow, hoping that she would make her way there once again.

Georgiana stood there for what seemed a very long time, staring at the road. Then finally she saw a horseman astride a fine bay horse. Knowing at once that it was Dunraven, she hurried forward, waving her hand.

Catching sight of her, Dunraven could hardly believe his good fortune. Veering off the road, he urged his bay mare up the hill toward her. Once he had reached her, the earl jumped off the horse and enfolded Georgiana in his arms with such exuberance that he lifted her completely off the ground.

"Dunraven! I am so glad you came," cried Georgiana, joyfully trying to kiss him. When her wide-brimmed straw hat interfered, Georgiana laughed before snatching it from her head and then raising her lips to meet his. "Kitty gave me the idea to meet you here."

"Then I am grateful to your sister," said Dunraven, holding her tight and kissing her again and again. His kisses grew increasingly demanding and Georgiana responded with an ardor that delighted him. "God, how I want you," he murmured, filled with nearly overpowering desire for her.

Georgiana's senses reeled. She was aware of nothing but Dunraven and his fervent kisses. The two of them sank down upon the grass, where the earl, quite overcome with passion, continued to kiss and caress her.

"Georgiana!" A thunderous shout brought them both to their senses.

Startled, Georgiana turned to see Sir Arthur, his face purple with rage. He had come on foot from the grove of trees. Rushing forward, the baronet pulled his daughter from the earl's grasp. "Papa!" she cried, horrified at her father's look of outrage.

"Get up from there!" cried the baronet, reaching down and grabbing her arm. She was pulled roughly to her feet. "I'll hear not one word from you, my girl!" he shouted.

Turning to the earl, who had sprung quickly up from the ground, Sir Arthur raised a fist in a threatening gesture. "Your behavior is infamous, sir," he cried. "First you force your attentions on Georgiana at the ball and now here. I see that Thomas Jeffreys was right about you. You go too far, Dunraven."

"I am in love with Georgiana," said Dunraven in a calm voice. "You know I wish to marry her."

"And you know I will not have it," said Sir Arthur, shaking his fist. "It is clear you have no scruples. God in heaven! You are to leave here at once. You are never to set foot on my property again. I never want to see you."

"You are being unreasonable, sir," said Dunraven.

"Unreasonable? By my honor, is it unreasonable to wish to keep my daughter from an unprincipled rogue like you? Leave here at once."

The earl hesitated, not wishing to further anger the man he hoped would be his father-in-law. Dunraven stood regarding Sir Arthur in some frustration. "Very well, Sir Arthur, I shall go." He mounted his horse. "Do not think you will stop me from marrying Georgiana. There is nothing on this earth that will prevent me from having her for my wife." These words were spoken in a tone of such calm assurance that the baronet was rather taken aback. The earl then rode off down the hill and started back in the direction of Longmeadow.

"Papa," said Georgiana, "you know I love Dunraven."

"I don't wish to hear another word from you, miss. This business with Dunraven has gone far enough. I'll never allow you to marry such a man."

"I will never marry anyone else," said Georgiana resolutely.

"That is enough, I say," said the baronet. "Now go back to the house. You will stay in your room until you are sent for. Now go!"

Knowing it was useless to protest, Georgiana walked back to the house. Once in her room, she flung herself onto her bed and burst into tears.

Chapter 22

When the earl arrived back at Longmeadow, he left his horse with a groom and then entered the house. He was in a decidedly foul temper after his unfortunate encounter with Sir Arthur. Indeed, this latest incident appeared to be the last straw. He was not a mild-tempered man and he was growing increasingly frustrated.

Entering the drawing room, he rang for a servant. "Yes, my lord?" said the butler, who had answered the summons.

"Bring me some wine, Canfield," said his lordship.

Noting that his master did not appear in the best of moods, the butler hurried to do as he was bid.

When he had a glass of wine, the earl sat down upon the sofa and stared glumly at the fireplace. He would elope with Georgiana, he told himself. They would go off and be married. Perhaps they would live on the continent, possibly Italy or Spain.

Considering this possibility, the earl brightened. Yes, that was the answer. After all, he was growing tired of England. And if he was considered to be an unprincipled scoundrel anyway, why shouldn't he behave like one?

Dunraven sipped his wine thoughtfully. He wished Buckthorne were still there at Longmeadow so that he could discuss the matter, but his friend had set off for town that morning. Family and business obligations would keep Buckthorne away for a fortnight, a fact that greatly displeased the earl. After all, it was Buckthorne who usually kept Dunraven from becoming blue-deviled.

"M'lord?"

Dunraven turned from the fire to see Jeremy. Macduff, who had entered the room with the boy, hurried to his master's side. "There you are, Macduff," said the earl, reaching down to scratch the terrier behind his ears. "What mischief have you been doing?"

"Oh, Macduff has been very good, m'lord," said Jeremy, coming closer until he stood before Dunraven's chair. "We took a walk. 'Twas a fine day for it."

"Is it a fine day?" said Dunraven. "I hadn't noticed."

"But it is, m'lord," said Jeremy. Noting that the earl did not appear to be in a very good mood, he stood there hesitantly.

"What is it, Jeremy?" said Dunraven, not unkindly.

"Well, m'lord, I wished to ask you something. You see, when Macduff and I came back, we went to the stables and Mr. Wheeler showed us a new pony what had come from the village this very morning. He told me to ask your lordship about it."

"A pony?" said the earl.

"Aye, m'lord, a fine pony. She's gray with spots and her name is Daffodil."

"Well, that is very peculiar," said the earl, adopting a perplexed expression. "I don't know who in this household would ride a pony." He paused as if considering the matter. "Unless *you* might wish to do so."

"Me, m'lord?" said Jeremy, a broad grin appearing on his face. "I'd like nothing more! Truly, m'lord you are so very kind."

Dunraven smiled. "It was Buckthorne's idea. He couldn't bear to think that you'd never learned to ride. 'How will the lad ever hunt?' he said. Well, I should be glad if you never did, for I have no desire for you to tumble off and break your neck. But a man must know how to sit a horse."

"Oh, Lord Dunraven, 'tis more than I ever imagined. That I should have a pony to ride!"

"Well, let us go and see this Daffodil," said the earl, rising from his chair.

Jeremy was only too happy to do so. He eagerly accompanied Dunraven from the room, with Macduff following behind them.

That evening Georgiana refused to come down to dinner. She sat in her bedroom feeling miserable and wondering what she should do. The more she considered her unfortunate situation, the more she concluded that there was only one thing to be done. She must elope with Dunraven. Even though her father would disown her, there was no alternative.

The idea of running off with the earl caused Georgiana to rise from her chair and pace across the room in an agitated fashion. How did one arrange an elopement? she asked herself. It wouldn't be so easy now that all communication with the earl had been cut off.

How would she send word to him? This problem occupied Georgiana for some time. Knowing her father as she did, she was certain that he would have her watched like a hawk. She could scarcely write to the earl, and ask one of the servants to post a letter for her. Indeed, her father had said that she wasn't to even think about writing to him.

After a while, Georgiana decided that she must indeed write to Dunraven. She would contrive to go to the village and post the letter herself. Surely, there would be a way to manage it. Certainly Kitty would help.

Encouraged by the thought, Georgiana went to her sitting room where she took pen and paper and began to write. When she finished the letter, she carefully folded it, sealing it with wax.

Some time later Kitty entered the sitting room. "Oh, Georgie," said her younger sister, eyeing her with a concerned expression. "How are you?"

"I am perfectly wretched, Kit," said Georgiana, who was still seated at her desk.

Kitty sat down in a nearby chair. "Oh, dinner was quite horrid. Papa hardly said a word. Mama tried to act as though nothing was wrong, chatting on about cousin Elizabeth and Charlotte. All I could think of was you sitting in your room, miserable and hungry. But some dinner is being sent up on a tray."

"I am not hungry," said Georgiana.

"But dinner was excellent," said Kitty. "Of course, I was too upset to enjoy it overmuch," she added hastily. "But you must eat something."

"I'm sure Papa will not care if I starve to death."

"Georgiana! Don't speak nonsense."

"It's true," said Georgiana. "He cares nothing for me. he is being completely odious. One would have thought Dunraven some sort of monster by the way he spoke to him."

"He said he found Dunraven kissing you."

"And what of that?" said Georgiana. "We are to be married."

"That isn't what Papa thinks. He says he'll never allow you to marry Dunraven."

"Well, I will marry him," said Georgiana firmly. "I am resolved to do so."

"You cannot still be thinking of an elopement?"

Georgiana nodded. "I am."

"Oh, Georgiana!"

"There is nothing else to be done. I shall elope with Dunraven as soon as it can be arranged."

"But Papa will never forgive you! You know him well enough to realize that."

"I know."

"And I shall never see you again," cried Kitty, bursting into tears.

"Now, now, Kit," said Georgiana, rising from her chair to comfort her sister. "It isn't as bad as that. And one day Papa will forgive me. I'm sure of it."

"But I'm not," said Kitty between her sobs.

Georgiana could only sigh and consider that her younger sister was probably right.

While Georgiana tried to console Kitty, Jeremy lay in his bed feeling terribly guilty. While he normally had no trouble falling asleep in the soft featherbed, that night his mind was troubled.

It had been a marvelous day. Indeed, since coming to Longmeadow, he had had many wonderful days. It was a carefree existence—there with plenty of food, good clothes, and kind servants to look after him.

How different it was from the sort of life he had had in London, working for a pittance in the theater. Although his sister Claire had given him a little money from time to time, he had lived on his own. Often, he had been cold and hungry and afraid.

That he was deceiving the earl had bothered him from the beginning. But now that he was so fond of Dunraven, it was becoming far worse. Jeremy was aware that the earl was beginning to think of him as his son. He frowned in the darkness as he remembered how they had gone to see the pony.

Dunraven had commanded one of the grooms to saddle the diminutive mount and Jeremy had had his first horseback lesson. It had gone exceedingly well and the earl had declared that Jeremy was a natural-born equestrian.

Afterward, he had joined his lordship for dinner and they had had a splendid time talking about horses and all sorts of different subjects. Jeremy had enjoyed himself immensely despite the gnawing feeling that he was wrong in continuing to lie to Dunraven.

Pulling the covers about his neck, Jeremy frowned. What was he to do? If he told the earl the truth, Dunraven would hate him. He would be sent away from Longmeadow. He would never see Macduff or Daffodil or Mr. Buckthorne again. And he would never see Dunraven again. That was perhaps the worst of it, for Jeremy had begun to think of the earl as the father he had never had. A tear began to run slowly down Jeremy's cheek. Wiping it away, he frowned again and soon fell into a troubled sleep.

Chapter 23

The next three days were difficult ones for Georgiana. Due to her father's watchfulness, she hadn't been able to post her letter to Dunraven. Sir Arthur had been so upset about finding the earl with his daughter that he had devoted himself to making sure that there was no communication between them.

Expecting that Georgiana would try to send a message to Dunraven, her father had given strict orders that no servant was to carry a message or post a letter for her. He also forbade her to go to the village, unless accompanied by himself.

Sir Arthur also scrutinized incoming letters to his daughters. When one did arrive from the earl, the baronet sent it back unopened.

Feeling as if she were a prisoner, Georgiana grew increasingly exasperated with her father. Yet, the more she protested, the more resolute he became.

A long discussion with Kitty one night made Georgiana realize that it was foolish to further anger Sir Arthur. Kitty reminded her of a fact that she knew well—no one was more stubborn and determined than their father.

As he had formerly been resolved that she would not marry Thomas Jeffreys, now Sir Arthur was just as unbending in his disapproval of the earl. It seemed that all his previous admiration of Dunraven as a man and horseman had vanished to be replaced by a strong and vigorous dislike of the nobleman.

After thinking a good deal about the situation, Georgiana decided that it was useless to plead with her father. Instead, she would say nothing about Dunraven, hoping in time that Sir Arthur would be more reasonable.

Lady Morley, who hated family disagreements more than anything, had been nearly as miserable as her daughter. She was very glad when on the third day since her daughter's meeting with the earl, Georgiana seemed to perk up and act more like her old self.

The baronet, too, noticed the change and was happy that Georgiana was behaving more sensibly. Feeling more kindly disposed toward his wayward daughter, Sir Arthur took his wife and Georgiana to the village, where he insisted they buy anything they wished at the linen-drapers.

The following morning, the baronet seemed anxious to make amends with Georgiana. Finding her in the drawing room before breakfast, he invited her to go for a ride.

Thinking it prudent to accept this proffered olive branch, Georgiana was only too happy to accept. After hurrying to her dressing room to change into her plum-colored riding habit, she joined her father outside.

The baronet appeared in the best of humors. Georgiana found him near the stables talking to Shaw in an animated fashion. Demon Dancer and Georgiana's mare were saddled and ready. Georgiana patted the black horse's sleek neck. "Well, Papa, are you going to allow me to ride Dancer this morning?"

"No, miss, you'll have to be content with your Hera."

"I was only gammoning you, Papa," said Georgiana with a smile. She went from the black horse to her roan mare and planted a kiss on the animal's soft muzzle. "In truth, I shouldn't like to hurt Hera's feelings by riding another horse. Would you help me, Shaw?"

The head groom hurried to boost his young mistress into the sidesaddle. The baronet mounted Demon Dancer and they rode off. The weather had turned colder and there was a gusty wind coming from the north. Georgiana found the weather exhilarating and she appeared in genuinely good spirits as they started off.

Georgiana's mare was eager to run and when they had trotted some distance, she eased the spirited animal into a canter. The baronet followed suit and the two riders rode quickly along, soon arriving at the road to the village.

Although she had expected her father to travel toward Richton, the baronet turned Demon Dancer in the opposite direction. Georgiana couldn't help but think that they were heading in the general direction of Longmeadow. If only they might see Dunraven, she found herself thinking. Yet, she told herself, what good would that do? Sir Arthur would never allow her to exchange even a polite greeting with him. No, it would be better not to see him, she concluded, as they continued on.

They cantered for some time, and then, at one stretch of road, the baronet allowed Demon Dancer to break into a gallop. Since the big stallion had been eager to run, he sped forward, racing way ahead of Georgiana. Urging her mare into a gallop, Georgiana followed as best she could, but her Hera was no match for Demon Dancer.

Veering off the road into a meadow, the baronet joyfully raced ahead. He had never ridden a finer horse in all his life and he was eager to take a few fences and hedges. The stallion sailed easily over a stream and then jumped over a stone fence.

Now a good distance behind, Georgiana tapped Hera's flank with her riding crop. The mare, who loved to run as much as Demon Dancer, increased her speed, racing quickly across the dew-covered ground in pursuit of the other horse and rider.

An accomplished horsewoman, Georgiana enjoyed jumping. She smiled as Hera took the stream easily and then the stone wall. They continued on, galloping after Demon Dancer and the baronet, who were not far ahead of them.

Sir Arthur, who felt as though he were riding the wind itself, let out a jubilant cry as Demon Dancer increased his speed. He directed the big animal toward a tall hedgerow that bordered a field. It was a rather formidable barrier, one that would daunt a lesser rider, but the baronet had no qualms about taking such a jump.

Georgiana, following behind, was only somewhat less confident, for Hera was a game little hunter who had cleared such obstacles in the past. She smiled as she watched Demon Dancer sail over the hedge. However, her smile quickly turned to dismay. From her vantage point on higher ground she could see the other side of the barrier. While he jumped the hedgerow easily, the big stallion landed on very soft and uneven ground on the other side. Demon Dancer stumbled, causing the baronet to fall.

"Papa!" cried Georgiana, urging Hera forward. Coming to the hedgerow, the mare didn't hesitate, but jumped over the tall growth, coming down on the other side. Georgiana hurriedly pulled the mare to a stop and jumped down from her saddle.

"Papa! Are you hurt?" cried Georgiana, rushing to his side and stooping down beside him. The baronet lay inert upon the ground. "Papa!" cried Georgiana, horrified to see him appearing lifeless.

At first there was no response, but in a few moments Sir Arthur's eyes opened. He stared at her in some confusion. "Georgiana?" he said finally.

"Oh, Papa! I was so worried! Are you badly hurt?"

"Hurt?" said the baronet, still appearing rather befuddled by the fall. He winced suddenly. "My leg."

Looking at his legs, Georgiana had a sickening feeling. Her father's right leg seemed at an odd angle. Sir Arthur reached down and touched it. "God in heaven!" he cried, grimacing with pain.

"Oh, Papa!" cried Georgiana once again.

"Damnation," muttered the baronet. "I fear it's broken. Indeed, I know it is. I could feel the bone, Georgiana. You must fetch help for me."

Georgiana looked around. There was no one in sight. Demon Dancer had run off but, thankfully, Hera was there, grazing contentedly nearby. "I don't like to leave you," she said hesitantly.

The baronet winced in pain. "You'll do no good here. And I cannot move. Go for help. I'll need the surgeon. He must be sent for. Now go quickly, Georgiana."

Nodding, Georgiana rose to her feet. Going to her horse, she mounted. Momentarily confused as to where she was, she paused to get her bearings. Surveying the area, she could see Longmeadow in the distance and the village road. Turning Hera toward the road, she hurried off.

She hadn't gone very far when a rider appeared. Georgiana regarded him in relief. Perhaps it was Dunraven! Yet, as he neared she could see it was a stranger.

Happy to see someone who would come to her assistance, Georgiana rushed toward him. "Sir!" she cried. "I am in need of assistance."

"Do calm yourself, madam," he said. "Do tell me what is wrong."

Georgiana looked at the stranger. Mounted on a gray gelding, he was a young man less than thirty. She noted that he was dressed like a gentleman, although his clothes appeared worn and hardly fashionable. "My father has fallen from his horse." She pointed toward the meadow. "He is there on the other side of the hedgerow. He has broken his leg. I am on my way to the village to fetch the surgeon. But if you would go to Richton and bring Mr. Pitney, I could stay with my father. I should be so grateful to you, sir."

"My dear young lady," said the stranger, "I shall be happy to assist you. But as I have a good deal of experience with broken bones, I may be able to help him at once."

"Are you a physician, sir?"

"No, indeed not, but I have set a good many bones in my time."

Georgiana's relief was enormous. "He is in terrible pain, sir," she said.

"Then we must go at once."

Turning her horse, Georgiana headed into the meadow and toward the hedgerow. Unwilling to risk jumping again, she led the stranger around the barrier to where her father lay.

"Georgiana?" said the baronet, surprised to find her returned.

"Oh, Papa, this gentleman has come to help. He said that he has set broken bones."

"Thank God," said Sir Arthur, who was feeling weak with pain.

The stranger got down from his horse and looked at the baronet's leg. "That does look very bad, sir," he said.

"Do you think you might help?" said Georgiana, bending down beside her father and taking his hand.

When the stranger made no reply, she looked up at him. To her astonishment she saw that he had pulled a pistol from beneath his coat and was now pointing it at them. "I fear I have exaggerated my abilities to set broken bones," he said, smiling. "You see, madam, I am a highwayman by trade. I should be very glad if this gentleman would part with his purse."

"Why, you damned blackguard," said the baronet.

Georgiana stood upright and faced the man, whom she regarded with incredulity. He laughed at her expression. "Oh, I am sorry to have to trick such a pretty girl as yourself." He waved his pistol. "I assure you I am capable of using this. Now get your father's purse and toss it to me. If you do as I ask, I'll not hurt you."

Turning to her father, Georgiana frowned. "Papa, we must do as he says."

The baronet nodded. Pulling a leather pouch from his waist-coat pocket, he handed it to Georgiana, who tossed it to the robber. Feeling its weight, he grinned. "It appears I've got a fat partridge this day. I thank you, sir. And now, I'll have that watch and chain. And that ring you're wearing."

"This ring has been in my family for generations," said Sir Arthur, trying valiantly to withstand the almost unbearable pain in his leg.

"Then 'tis time it saw another owner, by my way of thinking," said the highwayman. "Hand it over."

Georgiana took the watch and ring from her father and gave it to the man. "And now you, miss. You must have a ring or two."

Taking off her gloves, she pulled her rings from her fingers and handed them to him. He smiled happily as he put them in his pocket. Expecting him to mount his horse and leave them, she was surprised when he only stood there.

"We have nothing else," said Georgiana. "You've taken everything."

"I've not taken everything," said the man, staring at Georgiana. "You are a damned pretty wench," he said.

"You stay away from her," said the baronet.

"Be quiet," said the highwayman with a grim look, "or I'll kill you. Now, you're coming with me. There." He motioned to a clump of trees across the field. "That will do nicely. We'll have a bit of privacy."

"I won't go with you," said Georgiana, an indignant look on her face.

"Oh, won't you?" he said. He grabbed her roughly by the arm. "You don't have a choice, my girl."

When she tried to pull away, the man struck her hard on the face. She reeled from the blow, amazed and horrified. The baronet let out an anguished cry as he tried to rise to his feet and come to her rescue. As he moved his leg, the pain went through his body like a knife and he fell back, gasping.

Putting his pistol into his belt, the highwayman took Georgiana's arms and pulled them behind her back, tying them with a length of rope he pulled from his pocket. "Don't think of es-

caping, my love," he said. Then going to the baronet, he pulled
out his pistol again and hit him on the head with the butt of it.

A scream escaped Georgiana as her father slumped over unconscious. "That is enough from you!" he shouted at her. "If
you scream again, I'll kill the old man. I swear it. If you're a
good girl and do what I like, I'll spare you both."

"No, please," said Georgiana, "you have the money. Go,
please."

He smiled a twisted ugly smile as he grabbed her arm once
again and pushed her forward toward the small grove of trees.

Dunraven rode along a path that wound its way from Longmeadow toward the village of Richton. Riding beside him on
the stout gray pony was Jeremy, and following was Macduff.
Although he had only been riding for a few days, Jeremy
seemed an old hand. Dunraven had been very pleased to see
how easily he took to riding. Of course, the earl had found
himself thinking, it's in the blood after all.

Jeremy was enjoying himself immensely. Indeed, he could
think of nothing he would rather do than accompany the earl
on a ride through the beautiful countryside surrounding Longmeadow.

Suddenly Jeremy caught sight of a black horse running toward them. "M'lord," he said, "look, there is a horse. A black
one. He's coming this way."

The earl watched the riderless horse as it galloped toward
them across a meadow. "Demon Dancer?" he said, recognizing the big stallion at once. "By God, it is he." Dunraven directed his bay mare forward toward the black horse. "Whoa,
boy," he called, trying to intercept Demon Dancer.

The horse seemed quite ready to be caught. He stopped
alongside Dunraven's bay, easily allowing the earl to snatch
up his reins. "What happened, m'lord?" said Jeremy. "Where
is the rider?"

Eyeing the empty saddle, Dunraven was filled with an odd
sense of foreboding. "I should like to discover that," said the
earl, "This is Sir Arthur Morley's horse. He may have been
thrown. Perhaps he's hurt. We must go and find him."

With Demon Dancer in tow, they set off, riding from the
path in the direction the stallion had come. They had not gone
far when Dunraven saw a hedgerow some distance away.

There were two horses there and what looked to be a man on the ground. The earl rapped his horse sharply with his riding crop and the mare sped ahead toward the hedgerow.

Even before he saw Georgiana, the earl had a distinct feeling that she was in danger. Catching sight of a man and a woman nearing a grove of trees, he knew somehow that it was Georgiana. Dropping Demon Dancer's reins, he urged his mount forward. He was upon Georgiana and the highwayman in a few moments.

The highwayman, who had been more interested in keeping Georgiana under control, had not heard Dunraven's approach at first. Then, hearing the horse, he looked away from Georgiana to see a horseman galloping toward them. "Damnation," cried the highwayman, shoving Georgiana to the ground and then pulling his pistol from his belt.

Georgiana saw at once that it was Dunraven. She stared in horror as the man leveled his pistol at the earl, waiting to get a clear shot. Georgiana, whose hands were still tied behind her back, struggled to her feet with some difficulty. Dunraven was bearing down upon the highwayman, who pointed the gun at his lordship and prepared to pull the trigger.

Georgiana ran at the man, throwing herself against him, and knocking him off balance before falling to the ground herself. The pistol fired, its sharp retort shattering the pastoral quiet of the bucolic landscape.

The earl, who had by now reached the highwayman, leapt off his horse and onto the robber, knocking him to the ground, and wresting the pistol from his grasp. Dunraven tossed the pistol aside and fell upon the man, who had jumped quickly to his feet. The earl hit him squarely on the jaw, causing the highwayman to fall back, yet somehow retain his footing. Although badly shaken by this assault, the robber was by no means vanquished. Shouting an epithet, he hurled himself toward Dunraven, who deftly stepped aside, allowing the highwayman to fall on his face.

The earl was upon him at once, pulling him to his feet and then landing a series of brutal blows to his head and midsection. Dunraven fought like a man possessed, while a terrified Georgiana lay sprawled on the ground, watching the struggle.

The highwayman's attempts to protect himself proved futile. Dunraven continued to pummel him with blows until finally, wearying, he stopped. The robber fell to the ground, bloody and unconscious. Dunraven hurried to retrieve the pistol.

"Dunraven!" cried Georgiana.

"My darling! Are you all right?" said the earl, pulling Georgiana to her feet and embracing her. "If he harmed you, I swear I shall kill him."

"My hands, Dunraven," said Georgiana, pressing her face against his chest. "He tied them."

The earl hastened to release them, and once freed, Georgiana threw her arms around him and burst into tears. "You're safe, Georgiana," said the earl, hugging her tightly as she sobbed on his shoulder.

Jeremy, who had witnessed what had happened in stunned silence, now jumped off his pony. Picking up the rope that had bound Georgiana's hands, he hurried to the unconscious highwayman. Pulling the man's arms behind him, he bound them tightly. Then unwrapping the linen neckcloth from around his own neck, Jeremy tied the robber's feet together.

"Do take care, Jeremy," cautioned the earl.

"He'll do no harm in that state, m'lord. And he'll not escape from that. I know how to tie a knot."

"My father," said Georgiana. "Oh, Dunraven, he is hurt. He fell from Demon Dancer. And then that man! He said he would help me and then he was a highwayman. He stole my father's purse and his watch, our rings and then . . ." Her voice trailed off.

"Thank God, you are safe," said the earl, continuing to hold her tight. "Come, let us see to your father."

"Yes, of course," said Georgiana, pulling away from Dunraven's embrace and hurrying across the field to her father.

The baronet was barely conscious. The blow to his head had been severe. "Oh, Papa!" cried Georgiana, kneeling down and taking his head in her lap.

The earl felt for a pulse in the baronet's wrist. "His pulse is strong," he said.

"He hit him with the pistol," said Georgiana, gently stroking her father's forehead. "And his leg is broken. Oh, Dunraven, what are we to do?"

Dunraven frowned at the baronet's leg. "It is best not to move him until the surgeon sees to his leg."

"You must go for help, Dunraven," said Georgiana. "Ride Demon Dancer. And do hurry."

Dunraven was reluctant to leave them. He looked over at the inert form of the highwayman. "I don't like to leave you," he said.

"We'll be fine," said Georgiana. "Now go. You must bring Mr. Pitney."

"I'll check him first," said the earl, walking quickly across to the highwayman. After he was satisfied that the man was bound securely enough, Dunraven returned to Georgiana and Jeremy. "The fellow won't cause you any trouble. Jeremy certainly does know how to tie a knot." He smiled at the boy. "Now, you must take care of Miss Morley when I'm gone. I won't be long."

"Aye, m'lord," said the boy. "You don't have to worry. I'll watch that fellow."

"Good lad," he said, tousling Jeremy's dark hair. "I'll be back in a trice, Georgiana." He leaned down to kiss her before retrieving Demon Dancer and jumping up into the saddle.

The earl then set off, riding hard toward the village. It did not take him long to arrive there. Galloping into Richton as if the devil were chasing him, Dunraven attracted a good deal of attention. He pulled Demon Dancer up short in front of the apothecary's shop and leapt agilely from the saddle. "Where am I to find the surgeon?" he demanded of a group of curious onlookers. "Sir Arthur is injured. And I shall need the constable."

This information caused a flurry of activity as one man ran to find Mr. Pitney, and another to fetch the constable. Still another man was sent to obtain a conveyance that would transport the injured man.

The earl urged great haste in these undertakings. Soon he was riding back to Georgiana with an entourage that included the surgeon, Mr. Pitney, and a host of villagers.

Georgiana was very much relieved at Dunraven's return. The baronet had by this time regained consciousness, but he was groggy and in dreadful pain. Mr. Pitney went quickly to work. A serious man of middle years, he was skillful at setting bones. Georgiana couldn't bear to watch as he attended to her father's leg.

Clutching Georgiana's hands, Sir Arthur screamed in agony as the surgeon pushed the bone back into place. Then he fainted. "Don't worry, Miss Morley," said the doctor, fastening a splint on the injured leg. "Sir Arthur is a strong man. The bone will heal, if care is taken. It would be best if he isn't moved more than absolutely necessary. I do wish we were closer to Highcroft. The journey there will do him no good."

"It is much closer to Longmeadow," said the earl. "He must be taken there."

"I would recommend his lordship's suggestion," said Mr. Pitney, addressing Georgiana. "Longmeadow isn't far."

"Yes, yes, of course," said Georgiana.

Some of the men from the village carefully placed Sir Arthur onto a wagon. Georgiana climbed up after him. Another group of men took charge of the prisoner. The earl mounted his bay mare and rushed off to Longmeadow so that the house could hastily be prepared.

By the time the wagon arrived at Longmeadow, the earl's servants were hastily assembling a bed in a sunny parlor on the main floor of the house. Dunraven ordered a table to be brought from the entry hall. Placing the baronet on it, the earl's servants carried him into the house and to the hastily made bed. Mr. Pitney then shooed everyone away so that he could take care of his patient.

Some time later, when things had calmed down, Dunraven, Georgiana, and Jeremy retired to the drawing room. Mr. Pitney and the men from the village had gone off and word had been sent to Highcroft, asking that Lady Morley come at once.

Georgiana sat down on the sofa, exhausted from her experience. "My poor darling," said his lordship, sitting beside her and taking her hand.

"Oh, I am fine, Dunraven," said Georgiana, smiling fondly at him. "Truly, I am."

"Perhaps Miss Morley is hungry," said Jeremy, who, having not had any breakfast, was famished himself.

"Are you?" said the earl.

"I suppose I could eat something," said Georgiana. "Now that Papa is resting, I feel so much better."

"Then why don't we have some breakfast?" said his lordship.

This idea seemed to delight Jeremy and Macduff, who jumped up and started toward the dining room. Smiling, the earl and Georgiana rose from the sofa. Placing a protective arm about her waist, Dunraven escorted her from the room.

Chapter 24

Lady Morley arrived at Longmeadow in the afternoon, accompanied by Agnes and a great deal of luggage. Georgiana greeted her in the earl's drawing room. "Oh, Mama!" she cried, rushing to embrace her. "I am so glad you are here."

"But where is your father? I am so beside myself with worry. I must see him."

"He is asleep," said Georgiana. "Come, take off your bonnet, Mama. We will go to see him at once. But Mr. Pitney said that he needs a good deal of rest. We should not disturb him. But where is Kitty?"

"I thought it best she stay home with Miss Benson. Oh, she begged to come, but I saw no purpose to her being here."

While Georgiana was a bit disappointed that her sister hadn't come, she knew that her mother was right. There was nothing Kitty could do at Longmeadow. It was best that she remain at Highcroft. "I shall write her."

"That is a good idea. I know she is worried. Jackson can take your letter. I am sending him back with the carriage. There is no point in burdening Lord Dunraven with the care of our horses. Now where is your father? I do wish to see him."

She led her mother from the drawing room to the parlor. They quietly entered the room to find Sir Arthur sleeping peacefully. Very much relieved, Lady Morley allowed her daughter to escort her back to the drawing room.

Lady Morley sat down in an armchair. "Oh, Georgiana, he will be well, won't he?"

"Yes, I'm sure he will be, Mama. Mr. Pitney is quite convinced that he will have a complete recovery."

"I thank Providence for that," said her ladyship. "Oh, Georgiana, I was so horrified to hear such dreadful news. But you were not hurt?"

"No, not in the least. I was terribly frightened, of course, but then Dunraven came. Oh, Mama, if you could have but seen him. He was so brave and so fierce. He saved me from that horrid man."

"I am so grateful to him," said Lady Morley. "But where is he?"

"Oh, he was in the library. A man came about some estate matters. I'm sure he'll be here shortly."

"I am eager to thank him," said her ladyship. "It is so kind of him to allow your father to come to Longmeadow."

"It was so much closer than Highcroft," said Georgiana. "Mr. Pitney thought it a good idea."

"I'm sure he knows best," said Lady Morley, "although I must say I'm sure your father would be far happier to find himself at home. Indeed, it is rather awkward having to avail ourselves of Lord Dunraven's hospitality."

Georgiana started to reply, but was stopped by the appearance of Dunraven, who entered the drawing room. After smiling fondly at Georgiana, he turned to her mother. "Good afternoon, Lady Morley."

"Oh, Lord Dunraven," said her ladyship, extending her hand to him. "I am told I owe you an enormous debt. I don't know how we will ever repay it."

The earl took the proffered hand and bowed politely over it. While Dunraven thought to say that Lady Morley could easily repay him by giving him permission to marry Georgiana, he only smiled.

"I am so thankful to you, Lord Dunraven. I am only sorry that we must trouble you. I daresay it will be many days before my husband is fit to travel back to Highcroft."

"It is no trouble, ma'am," he said. "You must stay as long as you wish. I'm sure that Mrs. Hastings will see to your every comfort. And Pitney will be here soon to see Sir Arthur. I'm sure you will be much relieved in speaking with him."

Lady Morley acknowledged that this was so. When the surgeon arrived a short time later, he examined the baronet and pronounced him much improved. Mr. Pitney was very optimistic that he would be completely well in time, but cautioned her ladyship and Georgiana that it would be a very long while before the baronet would be recovered.

The baronet had awakened before Mr. Pitney's visit. Now

far more clearheaded than before, he was not very pleased to find that he was at Longmeadow. Yet, he was quickly persuaded by the surgeon that he must stay there for some time. Mr. Pitney also explained what had happened, how Dunraven had subdued the highwayman and saved Georgiana.

Hearing this story gave Sir Arthur pause. It seemed he was in the earl's debt. Indeed, Dunraven had preserved his daughter's honor and perhaps her life. He would be churlish indeed if he didn't recognize the great service the earl had done for him and Georgiana.

After Mr. Pitney left, Lady Morley and Georgiana entered the room. Her ladyship could scarcely hold back tears as she sat beside her husband. "My dear Arthur, you might have been killed. I do hope you will never ride that black horse again."

"It wasn't Dancer's fault," said the baronet impatiently. " 'Twas mine." He looked over at Georgiana. "How is Demon Dancer?"

"I cannot imagine how you can worry about a horse at such a time," said Lady Morley.

"He is fine, Papa," said Georgiana. "Dunraven found him. That is how he knew something was wrong. And Dunraven rode him to Richton. I hope you won't be vexed that someone else rode your precious darling. I can assure you that Dunraven did him no harm. I daresay he is nearly the rider you are."

"If I were such a fine rider, I wouldn't have tumbled off," said the baronet glumly.

"Nonsense," said Georgiana.

"Well, you must tell Dunraven that he must ride Dancer," said Sir Arthur. "He'll need some exercise. But I don't want you to ride him, mind you, Georgiana."

"I shouldn't dare," said Georgiana with a smile. Then, knowing that the doctor had cautioned them to stay only a short time, Georgiana and her mother took their leave, allowing the baronet to get more rest.

The next three days were difficult for Georgiana, for it was hard being in the same house with Dunraven without having any opportunity to be alone with him. Lady Morley had felt it prudent for her to remain at her daughter's side. Still having grave reservations about Dunraven, she felt it best that Georgiana was constantly chaperoned. She, therefore, stayed close to Georgiana.

Of course, the two ladies were kept busy attending to Sir Arthur. They spent most of their time with him, attempting to cheer him up. A man who had always been in vigorous good health, he did not take well to the role of patient. Georgiana and her mother found that they must constantly distract and amuse him, so that he would remain in good spirits.

The earl was there at the house, of course, and he sat beside Georgiana at meals. So far, however, there had been no opportunity for Georgiana to speak to him alone.

It was worst at night. Lying in her bed, Georgiana was acutely aware that Dunraven was so near. How she longed for him to be there, touching and holding her. She considered going to his room, knocking on his door, and throwing herself into his arms. Instead, she stayed in her room, alone and miserable.

It was likewise difficult for the earl, who found Georgiana's constant proximity wonderful and yet frustrating. To have her beside him throughout the day, to smell her perfume and be close enough to touch her was exceedingly hard for him. He wasn't sure how long he could resist taking her into his arms and carrying her to his bed.

On the third day of Sir Arthur's convalescence, Dunraven felt that it was time to have a word with him. When the ladies had gone for a walk on the grounds, he came to the parlor where the baronet lay. "Sir Arthur?" he said.

"Dunraven?"

"Might I have a word with you? I don't wish to fatigue you."

"No, do come in," said the baronet.

The earl sat down in a chair next to the bed. "How are you feeling, sir? Is your head bothering you?"

"Only a little. Thank God I have such a hard head. My wife never thought it a virtue before, but now she will have to change her mind."

There was a momentary silence. "I wish to talk to you about Georgiana," said the earl. "If it will distress you, I shall come another time."

Sir Arthur frowned. He did not relish this conversation. He knew very well that the earl would renew his request for Georgiana's hand. "No, there is no need for that. We may as well discuss the matter now."

Dunraven nodded. "Very well. I am sure you know what I am going to say. I wish to marry Georgiana. I am hopeful that these circumstances might cause you to reconsider the matter."

"I have considered it, sir," said the baronet. "Indeed, lying here in your house I can scarcely help it. I owe you an enormous debt, Dunraven. I am certainly cognizant of that. Perhaps I owe you my life You have saved Georgiana's honor and, indeed, one cannot know what that villain might have done once he had his way with her. I shall be grateful to you for the rest of my days.

"Yet, you must understand that I am thinking of Georgiana when I withhold my consent. And I still withhold it."

The earl frowned and his lean face took on a cold expression. "You have not changed your mind?"

"No, I have not," said the baronet. "I wouldn't do my duty as her father if I allowed Georgiana to marry you. Your reputation in society hasn't changed, sir. As your wife, my daughter would be the object of gossip. Why, I'm told that that you still allow that boy to live here. Would I wish to see my daughter the mistress of a house where her husband's bastard has a place of honor?"

"Georgiana is fond of Jeremy," said the earl coolly.

"Fond of him? Why, sir, you should never have allowed the two of them to meet. You could at least send the boy away. There would be far less talk."

Dunraven's expression grew icy. "I haven't lived my life worrying about what others say about me, Sir Arthur."

"Well, it is time you did, sir," said the baronet.

The earl stood up. "I shall not send Jeremy away," he said.

"Even if it might influence me to change my mind?"

"Even so," said Dunraven. "I see it is pointless to speak any more about this. Good day, Sir Arthur." With that, the earl turned. Pushing open the door, he walked quickly away.

When he had gone, Jeremy emerged from behind the door. He had been standing there during the conversation and had heard every word. When the earl had flung open the door, Jeremy had jumped to the side, hiding behind it.

While Jeremy had felt increasingly guilty about deceiving the earl, he was now filled with misery. He was preventing

Dunraven from marrying Miss Morley! It was all his fault and he couldn't bear it any longer. After hesitating for a brief moment, he hurried inside the room. "Sir Arthur!" he cried. "I must talk to you."

"What's this?" asked the baronet.

"I am Jeremy, sir," he said, coming forward and standing by the bedside. "I have been pretending to be his lordship's son."

"What the devil?" said Sir Arthur. "Pretending to be his son?"

"Aye, sir. You see, I ain't the earl's son. I wish it could be so, for I should like nothing better. But 'twas just a hoax, sir." The baronet regarded the boy in some astonishment as Jeremy continued. "My name is Jeremy Stevenson. My sister is Lord Thomas Jeffreys's . . ." He stopped. "His mistress. They asked me to pretend to be his lordship's son so that there would be a scandal. So that the earl wouldn't be allowed to marry Miss Morley. Lord Thomas wished to marry her himself."

"Good God!" said the baronet.

" 'Tis the truth," said Jeremy. "I wanted to tell his lordship, but I couldn't bear to have him hate me. He's been so kind to me, sir. Now I must go. I wanted you to know so that you wouldn't think so bad of his lordship."

"And Dunraven knows nothing of this?" said Sir Arthur.

Jeremy shook his head. "Will you tell him, sir? I can't. No, I can't bear to do so. He'll not forgive me. I'm going to leave Longmeadow, sir. I'll not trouble his lordship any more. I should be obliged to you, sir, if you would tell him that I'm ever so sorry." Jeremy's voice faltered with these words, and he hurried from the room.

Fighting back tears, he ran up the great staircase and to his room. Once there, he allowed the tears to flow. How could he have been so wicked, he asked himself. To continue deceiving the earl, who had been so good to him, was unforgivable. He couldn't bear to think of Dunraven hearing the truth. The earl would surely hate him.

Jeremy frowned as he wiped the tears from his cheek and tried to regain his composure. He must leave Longmeadow at once, he told himself. There was a desk in the corner of his room. He went over to it and took up a pen and paper. Since he had had little schooling, he wrote in a childish, shaky hand. "My lord, I am sorry. Goodbye. Jeremy S." He stared at what he had written and added "I shall miss you and Macduff and Daf . . ." Here his pen had faltered for he hadn't known how to spell Daffodil. Finally adding "fy," he put down the pen and left the note on the bed.

He then left the room, intending to go down the back stairway and out of the house. As he walked quietly down the hall, he was met by Macduff. Sensing something was wrong, the terrier followed closely at Jeremy's heels.

"Go away, Macduff," said Jeremy in a soft voice.

Macduff only cocked his head and continued to follow him down the stairs. When he reached one of the back doors, Jeremy knelt down and rubbed the dog's ears. "Good-bye, Macduff," he said, once again fighting back tears. "I'll miss you."

The dog jumped up on him and licked his face. Jeremy pushed him away. "Stay," he commanded, opening the door quickly and leaving the little dog inside. Jeremy then ran across the park and finally vanished into a stand of trees some distance from the house.

Chapter 25

After leaving the baronet, the earl had gone to the drawing room where he had stared out at the expanse of lawn that stretched from the front of the house. He had watched Georgiana walking with her mother, and he had resolved to carry her off at first opportunity.

While he had been mulling over this prospect, one of the footmen had informed him that his solicitor had arrived and was waiting in the library. While hardly in the mood to discuss business matters, the earl had gone to the library and had consulted with the lawyer for nearly an hour.

Shortly after the solicitor had taken his leave, Canfield entered the room. "I beg your pardon, my lord, but Sir Arthur wishes to see your lordship."

"Sir Arthur?" said the earl, rather surprised to hear it. He couldn't imagine why the baronet would wish to see him. Surely, he had said enough at their previous meeting.

"Yes, my lord. He said it was important that he see your lordship."

"Very well, Canfield, I shall go to him." Dunraven left the library and headed to the parlor. Entering the room, he went up to the bed. "You wished to see me?"

The baronet nodded. "Sit down, Dunraven. I have something I must tell you."

"I believe you have told me enough, Sir Arthur. It seems further communication between us is useless."

"Do hear what I have to say," said the baronet. "Sit down."

The earl nodded, reluctantly taking a seat in the chair beside the bed. "Very well. What is it?"

"It is about a very odd conversation I had with that boy, Jeremy."

"Jeremy was here?"

"Yes, he came in just after we spoke together. It seems he had been listening at the door."

"What?" said the earl, very much surprised.

"Yes, he heard our conversation and was upset by it. I was going to tell you immediately, but I was told you were engaged with your solicitor. It is very important news, I assure you."

Dunraven eyed him impatiently. "Do tell me then."

"Yes, I shall do so. The boy told me that he isn't your son, Dunraven. It was a hoax. He wished me to tell you."

"What?" said the earl, regarding the baronet as if he hadn't heard correctly.

"That is what he said," said Sir Arthur. "I daresay this will come as a great relief to you. According to the boy, he was part of a scheme to discredit you. His sister is Thomas Jeffreys's mistress. They had him pose as your son to create a scandal. Jeffreys has wanted to marry Georgiana for a long time. I have always detested him. I cannot believe he would ever think I would approve of him no matter what I thought of you."

Dunraven listened without any betrayal of emotion. Jeremy wasn't his son? For the past week he had been very much convinced that he was.

"I know you must be very glad to find out the truth," continued Sir Arthur. "I will say that the boy was most contrite. He didn't wish to deceive you, Dunraven. I must say that I am very pleased that you will be rid of this boy. His presence here was quite unacceptable."

The earl rose from his chair. "You must excuse me," he said. "I must find Jeremy. And I shall be grateful to you to not say anything about this to Georgiana. I wish to speak with Jeremy first."

"As you wish," said the baronet, "but I don't see why . . ."

Not waiting for him to complete his sentence, Dunraven abruptly left the room. He was very eager to see Jeremy and discover the truth of this. Finding Mrs. Hastings in the entry hall, he asked the housekeeper where Jeremy might be found.

"I cannot say, my lord," said Mrs. Hastings. "Perhaps he is in his room. Or perhaps outside. He loves to roam about. Shall I have someone look for him?"

"No, I shall find him myself," said the earl, going up the stairs and arriving at Jeremy's room. Entering it, he found the room empty. Dunraven started back out the door, but, seeing the paper on the bed, he stopped. Going over to it, he picked it up and read it.

He was soon joined by Macduff, who hurried over to him, wagging his tail and regarding his master with a questioning look. "Your friend has gone, Macduff," said the earl. "But I'll find him. He can't have gone far."

When he left Jeremy's room, the earl asked a maid passing in the hallway if she knew where Miss Morley was. The servant replied that she and Lady Morley were with the baronet. "Tell Miss Morley that I must go out for a time. I shan't be gone for long."

"Very good, m'lord," said the maid, a stout girl who curtseyed respectfully.

"Have you seen Master Jeremy?"

"Why, I did see him some time ago, m'lord. It was more than an hour ago, I should think. I saw him walking across the park behind the house. He seemed in a hurry, m'lord, but young master always be in a hurry."

"Yes, thank you, Jane," said the earl, continuing on. Leaving the house, he went to the stables, where he ordered a horse to be saddled.

Once mounted, Dunraven rode off across the park and through the trees. There was a crossroads a half-mile distant and the earl paused there, unsure which way to turn. Suspecting that Jeremy would take the road toward London, he turned in that direction. Yet, after riding for more than a mile, Dunraven decided that he had taken the wrong turn. He should have come upon Jeremy by now. Indeed, inquiries to persons he met on foot came up with nothing. No one had seen Jeremy.

Turning his horse around, the earl rode back. At the crossroads, he turned the other way and continued on.

While Dunraven was setting off in search of Jeremy, Georgiana was having a surprising conversation with her father. Arriving at his bedside after a pleasant walk with her mother on the grounds of Longmeadow, Georgiana and Lady Morley were encouraged to find Sir Arthur in good spirits.

"You do look better," said Georgiana, kissing her father on the cheek and then taking a seat by the bed.

"Indeed you do, Arthur," said Lady Morley.

"Yes, I am feeling better," said the baronet.

"Is the pain in your leg very bad, Papa?" said Georgiana.

"It is much improved, my dear. Of course, it is a confounded nuisance lying abed like this. But one must endure it. I must tell you that I have been lying here giving a good deal of thought to a certain matter. It affects you, Georgiana."

"Yes, Papa?"

"I believe you will be glad to hear this. You see, my dear, I have decided to withdraw my objection to your marrying Dunraven."

"What!" cried Georgiana, her blue eyes opening wide in surprise. "You can't mean it!"

"But I do," said the baronet. This remark caused Georgiana to rise from her chair and joyfully embrace her father.

"Do take care not to jostle your father!" cried Lady Morley.

Georgiana pulled away. "Oh, I am sorry. I didn't hurt you, did I?"

"No, indeed not."

"Good heavens," said Lady Morley. "I wish to know what has caused this surprising change, Arthur. Do you now think Dunraven a fit husband for Georgiana?"

"I have always liked the man," said the baronet. "For all his reputation. And the more I think on the matter, the more I like the idea of vexing Thomas Jeffreys and that uncle of his. I shall be glad to see Georgiana married, so Jeffreys will finally know that he has no hope at all of wedding her."

"So you care more of vexing Lord Thomas than you do for your daughter's happiness?" said Lady Morley.

"But Mama," cried Georgiana, "I shall be happy. I know it."

"I wish I was so certain of that," said Lady Morley, not altogether convinced about the match. Still, Georgiana was determined to have him and Dunraven was an earl and a man of wealth. And the idea of having her daughter situated so close at Longmeadow was certainly appealing.

"Now, Georgiana," said the baronet, "you must understand that as Dunraven's wife, you may never be accepted into the first circles of society."

"I don't care a fig for that," said Georgiana, reaching out and pressing his hand. "Oh, I am so happy. Did you tell Dunraven this?"

"I haven't had the opportunity."

Georgiana rose to her feet. "Then I must do so at once. Do

excuse me. I must find him." She hurried from her room, leaving Lady Morley to demand further explanation about her husband's change of heart.

Georgiana was greatly disappointed to find that the earl had gone out. The servants were rather vague as to his whereabouts, saying only that he had gone off on horseback and hadn't said when he would return. Thinking that she might find him, Georgiana resolved to go riding herself. She hurried upstairs to change into her riding habit.

Arriving at her room, Georgiana found Agnes tidying her dressing table. "Oh, Aggie," she cried, rushing to embrace the surprised servant. "I have the most wonderful news. My father has said that I may marry Lord Dunraven."

"He did, miss?" said Agnes.

"Yes, he did. Isn't it wonderful?"

Agnes hesitated.

"Aggie!" cried Georgiana. "I love Lord Dunraven and he loves me. We will be happy."

"I do want you to be happy," said Agnes, directing a concerned look at her young mistress.

Georgiana was rather hurt by the maid's response. "I shall be happy, Aggie." Agnes looked down, but made no reply. "Aggie, what is the matter? Oh, I know you have heard all manner of things about Lord Dunraven. He has been the object of gossip for a very long time. But that is in the past."

"Is it, miss?" said Agnes.

Taken aback by this reply, Georgiana frowned. "What do you mean?"

"Nothing, miss," said Agnes, turning to the dressing table and resuming her duties.

"Aggie, what is the matter?" demanded Georgiana, growing rather upset. "Look at me and tell me why you are acting in such a hateful manner."

Turning once again to Georgiana, the maid regarded her with a concerned look. "I know you don't want to be hearing what I'm going to tell you, Miss Georgie. But I should tell you. Aye, 'tis my duty to do so. I recollect that you once were told that his lordship had a mistress."

"Oh, that?" said Georgiana, very much relieved. "It was a lie told by Lord Thomas."

"But I've heard more, miss. And I must tell you for I shouldn't sleep if I let you go to be his bride without knowing the truth."

"What can you mean?"

"Well, miss, there is a woman in Hillborough at the Boar's Head Inn. A woman of easy virtue who has a lord what comes to her."

"What!" cried Georgiana. "You cannot believe it is Dunraven?"

"I fear I do, miss. I was told this woman came from London at the same time his lordship came to Longmeadow. She was an actress, you see. Her name is Claire Stevenson." Agnes shook her head gravely before continuing. "A man visits this woman, miss, a lord. I'm told it is Lord Dunraven."

"It's not true," cried Georgiana indignantly. "How dare you repeat this absurd story to me! Lord Dunraven, indeed! It is an odious lie!" When Agnes only stared sullenly at her, Georgiana lost her temper. "Leave me, Aggie! I don't wish to see you a moment longer." Agnes hastily retreated from the room.

Georgiana was so angry and agitated that she felt like screaming. To think that Agnes would tell her such a thing—that Dunraven had a mistress in Hillborough!

Walking over to the window, she stared out. It was utterly ridiculous. How could Agnes be so willing to believe it? Georgiana frowned. It couldn't be true. Or could it?

The seed of doubt seemed to sprout suddenly in her mind. She tried to dismiss it, but couldn't do so. The earl had had mistresses in the past. Indeed, the presence of the boy, Jeremy, was a reminder of that fact.

Georgiana folded her arms in front of her. If it were true, she could not bear it. "But it isn't true!" She spoke the words aloud. If only Dunraven were there to tell her that Aggie's words were ridiculous, she thought. But he wasn't there. Indeed, he had ridden off, not saying where he was going.

What if he had gone to Hillborough? The idea seemed incredible. She was being absurd. Of course, he hadn't gone there. She paced back across the room. Then, suddenly, she hurried to the wardrobe and pulled her riding habit from it. Flinging it on the bed, she started to undress.

Chapter 26

Jeremy walked along the road toward Hillborough. He had been walking for nearly two hours and was beginning to grow tired. He had decided to find his sister and tell Claire that he would no longer take part in her scheme. Jeremy knew that she would be furious, but he didn't care.

Afterward, he would go back to London and get work with one of the theater companies. He was sure he could do so. Not that it would be easy, of course. In time he would get on well enough and eventually he would be a famous actor.

The thought consoled Jeremy as he continued walking. He was rather hungry. He didn't have any money. Indeed, he had been in such a hurry to leave Longmeadow that he hadn't given that much thought.

There was a tiny village up ahead consisting of only a few houses and a tavern. It looked as though he might be able to rest for a bit there. Encouraged at the idea, he picked up his pace.

He was so intent that he didn't notice the sound of hoofbeats behind him until the horseman was very close. Then, hearing the horse, he stepped off the road and turned to see the approaching rider. He was startled to recognize Dunraven.

"Jeremy!" said the earl, coming up alongside him.

The boy stared wide-eyed, unsure what to do. He never thought the earl would come after him. Perhaps he would bring him before a magistrate. Jeremy considered running, but knew it would do no good. The earl jumped down from his horse. "Thank God, I've found you. Where do you think you're going?"

Jeremy regarded him curiously. Dunraven didn't seem angry. Indeed, he seemed glad to see him. Jeremy looked down at his feet. "I was going to Hillborough."

"Hillborough?"

"To find my sister.

"The sister who had you pretend you were my son?"

Jeremy bit his lip, trying not to cry. He nodded.

"Jeremy, why didn't you come to me?"

"I couldn't face you, m'lord," said the boy in an anguished voice. "How could I after what I did? I'm so sorry for causing you such trouble."

"I don't remember you causing any trouble," said his lordship. "Until now, running off like this. Why, Macduff was heartbroken. You must come back to Longmeadow at once."

The boy regarded him in surprise. "Back to Longmeadow? You can't mean that. I'm not your son. I was only playing a trick on you. You must hate me." He stifled a sob.

"My dear Jeremy, I don't hate you. Good God, I am dashed fond of you. I daresay you had little choice in doing what you did. I will say that I am disappointed."

"Aye, m'lord, disappointed that I am such a worthless fellow."

"No, disappointed that you aren't my son." Dunraven held out his arms to the boy, who threw himself against the earl and burst into tears.

"Come, come, Jeremy," said the earl. "There is a tavern ahead. We'll find something for you to eat. You must be hungry after such a long walk. And then we'll go on to Hillborough. I wish to see that sister of yours before we return to Longmeadow."

Jeremy, still clinging to the earl, was so overcome with emotion that he didn't reply. It was some time before he recovered enough to accompany his lordship to the establishment ahead.

After changing into her riding habit, Georgiana had hurried to the stables where she had demanded her mare be saddled. She then rode off in the direction of Hillborough. Having lived in the area all of her life, Georgiana was quite familiar with the road that led there. In times past, she had visited Hillborough often.

It was nearly ten miles distant, but the road was good and the weather fine. Indeed, Georgiana might have enjoyed the ride if she hadn't had such an unpleasant mission. She didn't know what she would say to this woman, this Claire Stevenson. And what would she do if she found Dunraven there?

Georgiana frowned grimly as she rode on, thinking of Agnes's words and growing more upset with each mile she traveled. After riding for some time, she passed a small village and a tavern. Georgiana took no notice of it. She scarcely looked at the bay horse tied there. She might have recognized Dunraven's mare had she taken more notice of the animal. As it was, she rode on past, hardly turning her head.

In three quarters of an hour, she arrived at Hillborough. It was a picturesque village with well-kept cottages and a village green. Georgiana pulled up her horse in front of the Boar's Head Inn. Jumping down from the sidesaddle, she gave the reins to a waiting servant.

Entering the inn, Georgiana glanced around. The proprietor, seeing a well-dressed and very attractive lady of quality enter his establishment, hurried up to her. "Good afternoon, madam. How may I serve you?"

"I am looking for Claire Stevenson."

"Indeed?" said the innkeeper, regarding her in some surprise.

"Yes, I must see her.

"I fear that isn't possible."

"Why? I'm told she resides here."

"Yes, that is true, but she is indisposed at present."

"Truly, I wish to see her," insisted Georgiana who was resolved not to leave until she had accomplished her goal.

"That is impossible," said the innkeeper, who was starting to reevaluate his opinion of the young lady. If she was acquainted with Claire Stevenson, the proprietor decided that she might not be the demure young lady he had taken her to be.

"It is very important that I see Miss Stevenson," said Georgiana.

"I am sorry, miss, but that ain't possible."

Georgiana frowned, unsure of how to respond. "Very well," she said, "I shall go then." She turned and walked out. She stood outside for a moment, considering the situation.

"Will you be wanting your horse, miss?" said the servant who had taken the mare. He was a gawky country lad about sixteen years old and he stared at Georgiana with unabashed admiration.

"In a moment," said Georgiana, flashing her dazzling smile at him. "Young man, is there a lady here named Miss Stevenson?"

"Yes, miss," said the young man.

Georgiana fished a silver coin from her reticule and tossed it to the servant. "Show me her room."

"But I think she has a visitor at the moment, miss," said the youth.

"Indeed?" said Georgiana, frowning. "But I must see her at once." She handed him another coin. "There must be another way into the inn. Take me to Miss Stevenson."

Pocketing the coins, the servant nodded. "Follow me then, miss." He led her to the back of the inn and into a door. Once inside, he pointed down a corridor. " 'Tis the third door on the right, miss."

"Thank you," said Georgiana. She walked down the hallway, stopping in front of the door. Pausing for a moment, she grasped the doorknob and flung open the door.

What she saw caused her to gasp in astonishment. A man and woman were together in a disheveled bed, both as naked as they had been born. The man turned in surprise. "Good God!"

Georgiana recognized him at once. "Thomas!" she cried before turning and fleeing from the room. She ran down the corridor in the opposite way she had come, entering the public room of the inn and nearly falling into the arms of the Earl of Dunraven.

"Georgiana!" cried his lordship, who had never been more astonished. "What are you doing here?"

"Dunraven! What are *you* doing here?"

"I am here to see Jeremy's sister."

"Jeremy's sister?" Georgiana caught sight of the boy, who was standing behind the earl.

"Good afternoon, Miss Morley," said Jeremy.

"Jeremy," said Georgiana, "your sister is here?"

"Aye, miss. Her name is Claire Stevenson."

"Claire Stevenson!" said Georgiana. "And you wish to see her, Dunraven?"

"Why, yes," said the earl.

"Then I fear you must wait your turn," said Georgiana, pushing past him.

The earl could only exchange a confused look with Jeremy before hurrying after her. He caught up with her outside the inn. "Georgiana!" he cried, grasping her by the arm. "What is going on?"

"You will find your lady occupied," said Georgiana. "Thomas Jeffreys is with her."

"Jeffreys? Good God, you don't mean you found them together?"

"I daresay you will now shoot him in a jealous rage."

"A jealous rage?" The earl's look of astonishment turned to amusement. "By all the gods, you cannot mean you think that I and this Claire Stevenson are . . ."

"Aren't you? Agnes heard that you were."

"Agnes? Well, she is badly misinformed. I came after Jeremy, who had run off." He looked toward the boy, who had remained discreetly behind. "Jeremy isn't my son. I'll tell you that first of all. The boy was playing a part. His sister and Thomas Jeffreys had him do it. Jeremy is Claire Stevenson's brother and Jeffreys is her lover. They hoped to discredit me even further by having a bastard show up at my door. And the plot was effective.

"I am telling you the truth, Georgiana. Jeremy will confirm it. I never met this Claire Stevenson in my life. God, I've lived like a monk since I've met you. You are the only woman I want, you silly little gudgeon."

This strange endearment caused Georgiana to throw herself into the earl's arms and hug him tightly. "I knew Agnes was wrong. I told her so!"

"And that is why you rode ten miles to Hillborough?" said the earl, casting an amused glance down at her.

"Don't be horrid, Dunraven," said Georgiana, looking up at him.

The earl could not resist covering her lips with his own and kissing her soundly. "Georgiana, you must come with me. We won't return to Longmeadow. We'll elope."

"Oh, I should love to elope with you, my dear sweet lord," said Georgiana, suppressing a smile, "but Papa would never forgive me."

"Hang your father," said the earl. "A man can only endure so much. I must marry you."

"And you will," said Georgiana, "but there is no need for us to elope. Papa has said that he won't object to the wedding."

"What?" cried the earl.

"It is true. We have his blessing."

"Well, I'm damned," said his lordship.

She laughed. Then a look of enlightenment came to her face. "Papa knew about Jeremy, didn't he? And Thomas?"

The earl nodded. "Yes, the boy told him everything."

"So that is what changed his mind."

"Whatever it was, I am dashed glad of it," said the earl, pressing her against him and then kissing her hungrily.

The earl hired a chaise to take them back to Longmeadow. He did not have an opportunity to speak to Thomas Jeffreys because that gentleman had dressed hastily and fled out the back door. Jeremy did speak briefly with his sister before climbing into the chaise opposite the earl and Georgiana.

As they started off from Hillborough, Jeremy could hardly believe his good fortune. Not only had the earl forgiven him, but his lordship was taking him back to Longmeadow. And Miss Morley had said he might live with them for as long as he wished.

Jeremy was blissfully happy as he watched the earl and Georgiana. It did his romantic soul good to see two people he cared about so obviously in love.

They had not gone very far before an exhausted Jeremy fell soundly asleep. The earl placed his arm around Georgiana's shoulders. "You really don't mind that Jeremy lives at Longmeadow?"

Georgiana snuggled against him. "No, I don't."

"You know there will still be talk."

"What do I care for that?" said Georgiana, looking up at him with her enormous blue eyes.

He leaned over and kissed her softly. Placing his cloak over them both, he pulled her close. He then stroked her cheek gently for a moment. His hand traveled down her neck and to her breast, where it lingered. She made no protest, but only kissed him again. "Oh, Georgiana, God, how I love you."

"And I love you," said Georgiana, gazing into his eyes.

"Georgiana."

"Yes, Dunraven?"

"I hope you weren't so very upset by what you saw today."

She raised her eyebrows. "What I saw?"

"When you came upon Jeffreys and Jeremy's sister."

"Oh," said Georgiana, blushing. "It was rather a shock." She smiled mischievously at him and whispered in his ear, "I wished it might have been you and I."

"Georgiana!" cried the earl.

She laughed and kissed him with such passion that his lordship hoped a wedding could be arranged very soon.

Epilogue

The wedding at the small church near Richton was a small affair with only a few in attendance. Buckthorne was there, of course, as was Jeremy, who was so very thrilled to see the earl and Miss Morley wed.

Lady Morley had by this time become reconciled to her daughter's marriage. Sitting in the pew beside Kitty and the Fanshawes, she appeared very happy. Sir Arthur was also extremely pleased. His leg was much improved, although he was still being pushed about in a bath chair and it would be some time before he could walk. He had been very glad when he had been finally able to return to Highcroft with his wife and daughter.

After the wedding ceremony, the guests went to Highcroft where they partook of the wedding supper. It was a joyous occasion that was long remembered.

The earl and his new countess were finally able to leave their friends and relations, riding back to Longmeadow in the earl's carriage. They would have Longmeadow to themselves, for both Jeremy and Buckthorne were staying at Highcroft so the newlyweds might have some privacy.

As might be expected, the earl could scarcely wait to get his bride back to his home. Escorting her to the door, Dunraven lifted her easily into his arms and carried her across the threshold. Then, although Georgiana protested that he would surely strain his back, the earl carried her up the stairs and into the bedchamber where he deposited her on the bed.

It was beginning to grow dark and the light from the fireplace and candles cast a warm glow in the room. "Oh, Dunraven," said Georgiana as the earl leaned over her and began to unfasten the buttons of her low-cut bodice.

"My dear, sweet Georgiana," said the earl, kissing her long and lovingly. "How I have ached for you."

"My lord," said Georgiana in a low voice filled with passion, "and I for you."

The earl smiled and, kissing her again, set about finishing the business that he had started with a kiss on Georgiana's first night at Longmeadow.

SIGNET REGENCY ROMANCE

PASSIONATE ENCOUNTERS FROM MARGARET SUMMERVILLE

☐ **FORTUNE'S FOLLY** Miss Pandora Marsh finds it hard to believe her protests of innocence as passion contends with propriety, and desire becomes more and more difficult to deny. (180488—$3.99)

☐ **DOULBE MASQUERADE** Lovely, dark-haired Miss Serena Blake desperately wanted to stop her father from marrying fortune-hunting Arabella Lindsay. Serena would bribe the devastatingly handsome bankrupt libertine, Mr. Macaulay, who could have any woman he wished for. He would turn Arabella's head and steal her heart. Serena's plan was perfect if she could remember that it was Arabella who was to be conquered and not herself. (183878—$3.99)

☐ **THE CRIMSON LADY** Miss Phillippina Grey, better known as Pippa, could not imagine why all of London looked upon the Viscount Allingham as a paragon of perfection. But while enraging the infuriating Allingham was easy, resisting him was hard. Defying his commands meant denying her heart and the growing desire to melt in his arms. (185226—$4.50)

*Prices slightly higher in Canada

Buy them at your local bookstore or use this convenient coupon for ordering.

PENGUIN USA
P.O. Box 999 — Dept. #17109
Bergenfield, New Jersey 07621

Please send me the books I have checked above.
I am enclosing $_____ (please add $2.00 to cover postage and handling). Send check or money order (no cash or C.O.D.'s) or charge by Mastercard or VISA (with a $15.00 minimum). Prices and numbers are subject to change without notice.

Card #_____ Exp. Date _____
Signature_____
Name_____
Address_____
City _____ State _____ Zip Code _____

For faster service when ordering by credit card call 1-800-253-6476

Allow a minimum of 4-6 weeks for delivery. This offer is subject to change without notice.

Ⓞ SIGNET REGENCY ROMANCE

ROMANCES TO CHERISH

☐ **A HEART IN PERIL by Emma Lange.** Miss Christina Godfrey faced the cruellest of choices—give her hand to a man who could never win or wound her heart or give herself to a man who could steal her heart with a kiss ... and then ruthlessly break it.

(181077—$3.99)

☐ **THE JILTING OF BARON PELHAM by June Calvin.** Miss Davida Gresham must choose a suitor among three men: one who will assure lasting safety; one who will offer unleashed sensuality; one who will promise only certain sham. But the question is, which one will light the fire of love in the heart that had to choose for better or for worse?

(183169—$3.99)

☐ **THE FOURTH SEASON by Anne Douglas.** The Earl of Burlingham might be the most scandalous rakehell in the realm, but he was handsome as the devil and seductive as sin. The only question was, did he want Lady Elizabeth Fortescue—best known as Bets— as a wife to love and cherish—or was he pursuing her for far less honorable ends?

(183061—$3.99)

*Prices slightly higher in Canada

Buy them at your local bookstore or use this convenient coupon for ordering.

PENGUIN USA
P.O. Box 999 — Dept. #17109
Bergenfield, New Jersey 07621

Please send me the books I have checked above.
I am enclosing $_____ (please add $2.00 to cover postage and handling). Send check or money order (no cash or C.O.D.'s) or charge by Mastercard or VISA (with a $15.00 minimum). Prices and numbers are subject to change without notice.

Card #_____ Exp. Date _____
Signature_____
Name_____
Address_____
City _____ State _____ Zip Code _____

For faster service when ordering by credit card call **1-800-253-6476**

Allow a minimum of 4-6 weeks for delivery. This offer is subject to change without notice.

Ⓞ **SIGNET REGENCY ROMANCE**

NOVELS OF LOVE AND DESIRE

☐ **THE COUNTERFEIT GENTLEMAN by Charlotte Louise Dolan.** Can Miss Bethia Pepperell win the heart of a maddeningly mocking miscreant who comes from lowly origins and makes his living outside the law? (177428—$3.99)

☐ **AN AMIABLE ARRANGEMENT by Barbara Allister.** Miss Lucy Meredith thought she knew what she was doing when she wed Richard Blount over the opposition of her father and her brother. But she was in need of a husband—Richard was in need of a wife, and their union would solve both their problems—or will it? (179420—$3.99)

☐ **THE RAKE AND THE REDHEAD by Emily Hendrickson.** Beautiful Hyacinthe Dancy finds Blase, Lord Norwood, to be the most infuriatingly arrogant man she has ever met and she vows to stay well clear of this man and his legendary charm.... But when Lord Norwood sets out to destroy an old village, Hyacinthe places herself in Norwood's path, and finds he has the power to ignite more than her temper. (178556—$3.99)

☐ **ELIZABETH'S GIFT by Donna Davidson.** Elizabeth Wydner knew her own mind—and what she knew about her mind was remarkable. For Elizabeth had the power to read the thoughts of others, no matter how they masked them. She saw into the future as well, spotting lurking dangers and hidden snares. Elizabeth felt herself immune to falsehood and safe from surprise—until she met Nathan Lord Hawksley. (180089—$3.99)

*Prices slightly higher in Canada

Buy them at your local bookstore or use this convenient coupon for ordering.

PENGUIN USA
P.O. Box 999 — Dept. #17109
Bergenfield, New Jersey 07621

Please send me the books I have checked above.
I am enclosing $_____ (please add $2.00 to cover postage and handling). Send check or money order (no cash or C.O.D.'s) or charge by Mastercard or VISA (with a $15.00 minimum). Prices and numbers are subject to change without notice.

Card #_____ Exp. Date _____
Signature_____
Name_____
Address_____
City _____ State _____ Zip Code _____

For faster service when ordering by credit card call **1-800-253-6476**

Allow a minimum of 4-6 weeks for delivery. This offer is subject to change without notice.